MW00558919

DEATH'S DAUGHTER

THE BANISHED GODS: BOOK FOUR

L.A. MCGINNIS

Copyright L.A. McGinnis 2019
All rights reserved

Editor: Chris Hall: The Editing Hall
Cover Design: Brynna Curry

All rights reserved. No part of this book may be reproduced, or distributed in any printed or electronic form or by any means, without express permission from the author or publisher. Please do not participate or encourage piracy of copyrighted materials in violation of the author's rights.
Please contact the author for any use in a review.

PUBLISHER'S NOTE:
This is a work of fiction. Names, characters, places and incidents are either the product of the author's imagination or are fictitious, and any resemblance to actual persons, either living or dead, including businesses, companies, events or locales is purely coincidental. This author acknowledges the trademarked status of various products referenced in this work of fiction, which have been used without permission. The use of these trademarks is not authorized, associated with, or sponsored by the trademark owners.

ISBN-13: 978-1-970112-06-1
ISBN-13: 978-1-970112-07-8
Published in the United States of America by
Fools Journey Press, 2019

Please visit my website at www.lamcginnis.com

"I've spent months searching for a way to fill up the space that hopelessness left behind.

Only to discover there isn't enough scotch left in the world."

- Odin

1

THE OUTCAST

Somehow, Hunter always knew she'd end up here.

Even though it was the last place she wanted to be.

She hated Chicago. More so, now that it was burning to the ground. But she didn't have a choice. So here she was, on the doorstep of the last person she ever wanted to see. Leaping down from her vantage point, she landed on broken asphalt before making her way toward the tall, silent Tower on the edge of Lake Michigan.

Twenty minutes later, she arrived in front of the golden sandstone building, working out possible entry points. Barely a month ago, the immortals inside had allowed the dark God of Chaos

to escape their grasp and begin his reign of terror, straight across the northeast. After which, he'd ended up right at her front door.

And she'd watched him decimate her city.

She'd slaughtered her way out of New York. Stolen cars and scavenged ammo and weapons to fight through the hordes of demons and Dark Elves spread across the rust belt, and now she was sporting more injuries than she cared to note. It had taken her a week and every ounce of energy to get here.

But she'd made it.

Frowning, she gazed at The Tower's gothic arches, looking at the stone owl crowning the buildings highest gable. "Wisdom is it?" She allowed herself a wry smile. "What's wisdom gotten us so far in this war?"

No, she thought, *when the world was on fire, and the end drew near, only steel and blood would buy it back.* And for that, she had an immortal god to see. It had been a thousand years and ten lifetimes, but she still remembered every line of his face, the faint scar marking his cheek, his whiskey-flecked eyes, and the set of his stubborn jaw.

After all these years, she doubted he even remembered her name.

Tʏʀ, God of War, rolled his shoulders and felt the dull ache of fatigue. Months had passed since the God of Chaos had blown through a cosmic portal onto earth and begun waging his deadly war.

And they were losing. People. Ground. Blood.

"I fucking hate losing."

The map before him displayed proof of their failures. Their enemy's path of destruction cut a stark, black swath from Chicago all the way to the east coast, a wide slash of evil straight across the northern United States. Fingers of death crept out from that blackness like a cancer, stretching toward Fort Wayne, Lansing, Columbus, Philadelphia. Cities wiped from the map forever.

Proof the dark god's reach grew longer every day.

Modern tech was useless against the Orobus's powers, against the sheer numbers of his otherworldly army. Fuel was growing scarce. Ammo, too. Food would be rationed, starting today. Punching a fist though the concrete wall, Tyr barely felt the impact. The blood dripping from his knuckles, however, was an unwelcome surprise. A testament to the fact he was exhausted and his magic nearly depleted. "Fucking perfect." Distracted, he rubbed it off on his pants.

His eyes darted over the map again, surveying the carnage portrayed by daily updates, where every message sent seemed to tell of one catastrophic failure after another.

He'd best recall Thor, Balder and the rest of the gods from the eastern edge of Pennsylvania, where they'd been maintaining some semblance of a front line. Sending them to attack the Orobus's rear guard had, perchance, slowed him down but hadn't stopped him. Word had come in yesterday—New York city was under siege. Who knew what was next?

Certainly not Odin. Their king had given up. Hiding in the Throne Room, chugging Lagavulin, like the expensive scotch was water, Odin had effectively removed himself from day-to-day operations. Ever since Odin lost his gift of foresight, he'd decided to drink his troubles away. And sure, Tyr would love nothing more than to march in there, yank the bottle out of the pompous bastard's hands, and demand the king get his head back in the game.

Except he'd already tried that. Odin had laughed in his face. Told Tyr he'd seen what was coming. And with a cold, dead look in his eyes—lifted the bottle to his lips again.

Even if things *were* hopeless, they *needed* Odin. Even blind, their king was clever and ruthless; two talents Tyr could use right now. But apparently his blindness, and the tailspin this vulnerability precipitated, wasn't going to be solved overnight. Still...

"Great timing, asshole."

"Tell me about it." Behind him, Mir leaned into the doorway, his face grave, dust covering his Kevlar jacket, something looking suspiciously like dried blood crusting his side.

"Ah, you're back." Tyr measured up the red-haired god, recognized the approaching burnout in those blue eyes. "You look beat to hell. But damn, I'm glad you're here. How are we doing out there?"

"Yeah. Got home a couple hours ago. Checked in on Balder and the others. The lines are holding at the moment, but no telling how much longer. One thing's for sure, I didn't expect to come back to a ghost town."

"Yeah, well, I didn't expect to be living in one." Tyr rubbed the knot on the back of his neck, despising the faint tremor of exhaustion lacing his voice. "Sydney'll be thrilled you're back. I couldn't have run things without her."

Mir's blue eyes flashed. "Of course you couldn't. She's smarter than you. Gods, I've missed her. And once I head upstairs, you probably won't see either of us for a couple of days." Mir rubbed his face, leaving long smears of dirt. "Any sign Odin's decided to sober up and join the ranks of those who give two shits about the world?"

Tyr sliced his head back and forth. "Won't even leave his Throne Room. I'm thinking drastic measures are called for. I've tried once. Maybe you'll have better luck, now that..."

It was hard to say what tipped Tyr off first, that inward tightening in his gut, or the prickling on the back of his neck as if a predator were watching. Whatever the feeling was, when he turned, it did nothing to brace him against the chill in Hunter Wallace's gleaming eyes when they found his own. His breath exploded out of him in disbelief as he gazed, for the first time in centuries, at the woman who had both captured and broken his heart.

Standing right in front of him, head raised defiantly, black hair flowing down her back, her pale skin dusted with the barest hint of freckles, Hunter looked every bit as proud and reckless as the first day he'd seen her. Tyr didn't know how long he'd been staring, but when Mir cleared his throat, he was sure it had been too long.

"What the fuck are you doing here?" Tyr managed, the mere sight of her causing him to flounder for words. Her clothing was bloodied, as were her knives. And the layers of dirt and grime covering her told him the journey here hadn't been easy.

"Trying to figure out how you idiots could be so careless to let that monster get away from you and destroy *my* city." Her voice was still husky, low, and her shrewd gaze didn't miss a thing, taking in the maps, the War Room's general clutter, the disarray of failure.

Mir gave Hunter his own disapproving once-over before spinning away on his heel without a single word, slamming the door behind him just to make his point. Tyr waited until the sound faded away before asking, "*Your* city?"

Her eyes turned into glittering lakes of amber, as she snarled, "That's right. New York City. *My* city."

Hunter might have been born a thousand years ago, but clearly, she'd lost none of her sharp edges. "Eight hundred miles away from *you*, which as it turns out wasn't nearly far enough."

And so it had always been between them. Endless standoffs. Endless silences. Endless, pointless stretches of time. Hundreds of years, in fact, where time slipped by without either of them taking a step forward or a step back.

Tyr leaned his hip against the table in what he hoped was a casual pose and pasted the same look over his face. "Back to my original question. What are you doing here, when the Orobus is in New York? Shouldn't you be defending *your city* with *your team*?" And because Hunter's team was the New York equivalent of their band of elite, immortal warriors, Tyr *didn't* understand why she'd come all this way.

"You truly are a bastard."

"Nope, my bloodline's as blue as the ocean's deep. Can't say the same about you, though."

He had to give her credit. She kept her weapons holstered and her talons sheathed. But those eyes grew darker, and her mouth took on a rigid, intractable set that made him realize his troubles were only beginning.

When she spoke, her voice was soft, and a lesser man might have shuddered. "Once the monster *you* allowed to roam free in our world is shackled and contained, we can debate our dubious, respective ancestries all you want, Tyr. Until then..." She leaned in until she stared deeply into his eyes. "I suggest you work really, really hard and use what little brain power you possess to come up with a means to kill him. And do it fast because you're running out of time."

Here in the flesh, there was a subtlety to the woman that his memories failed to capture, a delicacy to her scent, a burnished gold in the texture of her skin which he'd forgotten, and the sight of her cracked him open like an egg. *Memories*, he thought, *were such deceitful things.*

"I'm here because New York City is gone, Tyr. *Completely* gone." Her lips trembled. So much so that he stopped the smart-ass retort on his tongue and kept quiet while she laid everything out for him.

The Orobus's brutal attack.

The loss of her team.

Her messy, bloody scramble toward Chicago.

When Hunter finished, she blew out a shaky breath before marshalling herself. "Nothing left of the major cities—those are gone. Some smaller towns survived, and I ran across a few rural areas that are relatively unscathed, but it looks as if the creature's armies followed the main highways, picking off the bigger cities one by one."

Tyr offered a shallow nod while his head spun at the revelation NYC was destroyed. "We call him the Orobus. And that's what I gleaned from my reports too. A blueprint to conquest. And we handed it to them."

She didn't disabuse him of his theory.

"The creature's power..." She turned away, and her voice faltered. "Killed everything in his path. Forests turned skeletal, cattle bloated and rotting in the fields, birds fallen from the sky. Wiped out whatever he touched. Hel, the Grim, the Dark Elves...they're just clean up."

"*Hunter.*" He knew exactly where she'd gone to in her head. Hadn't seen her in a thousand years.

But still knew, in a heartbeat, exactly what she was thinking.

Before he figured out what to say next, she'd marshalled herself. And that was Hunter Wallace. Job first, personal shit second. Always.

"The city's gone, Tyr." This time, her mouth didn't tremble. "I stayed long enough to get the rest of my team out, every survivor. Most of them headed north, following the contingency plan." Her eyes turned distant. "You know, the one we never thought we'd have to use?"

"How many made it out?"

"INCLUDING ME? THIRTY-ONE." She didn't have to say anything else. There'd been over a hundred of their kind posted in the New York organization. Immortals. Halflings. And a few like Hunter. Mortals touched by the otherworldly. All of them warriors fighting the Grim. Tasked with keeping Hel's minions under control.

"He's right behind me. Which is the only reason I'm here. To warn you."

For a second, Tyr wasn't sure he heard her right. "You're here to warn us?"

She paused a moment before replying. "To warn *you*. He's already destroyed New York. Now he's coming back, probably to finish off Chicago. I'd say you have two, possibly three days before he arrives. Hel's a day behind him with her horde of Grim."

Her eyes narrowed down to slivers as she measured him up, before shaking her head. "You know, for a long time I've wondered what it'd be like to see you again. But I never expected you to look like this."

His spine popping, Tyr threw his shoulders back. "Like what, exactly?"

"Defeated."

2

THE WARRIOR

When the door slammed open, Tyr raised bleary eyes from the rotations schedule.

"Wanna talk about it?" Freyr leaned his lean, muscular frame against the doorjamb, looking completely otherworldly with his long blonde hair, glowing skin, and halcyon eyes. Middle of a war zone and he still looked supermodel perfect. It was seriously disturbing. "No problem if you don't. Just thought I'd ask."

Tyr turned back to the grid of names in front of him, praying Freyr would just *go away*. Even with Mir back, they were short-handed, and he had a war to run.

"'Cause it seems like there's some deep shit going on between you and the raven-haired beauty." Freyr continued, as if Tyr had time to chitchat right now. "So you can keep being a stoic dickhead until the world ends. Or you can tell me what the fuck is going on."

Rubbing his forehead, Tyr ground out, "She's *my* problem, okay? And between injuries, front line skirmishes, and preparing for an invasion, *not* one I need right now." If he could just concentrate on one disaster at a time, his life would be so much better.

Freyr's eyes danced. "Fine." His body unfurled from the door-frame. As he straightened, his long hair tumbled over his shoulders.

"Maybe I'll go ask her myself." White teeth flashed as he added, "I'll bet I can persuade the beauty to give up all her secrets." He winked. "If you know what I mean."

In an instant, Tyr was across the room, forearm rammed into Freyr's throat. Barely breathing, he stared into Freyr's laughing blue eyes, whose smile never slipped off his handsome face.

"Still intend to keep all your secrets, my friend? Because I'm not above prying the information out of her." Freyr's eyes narrowed ever so slightly. "Not a lot of time left. Heard she saw the Orobus in action. Intel like that might help us prepare. Besides, you know me. Self-preservation is a priority, and I'll do whatever I can to keep myself alive another day."

"*Leave her alone.*" Tyr growled, feeling the bones in Freyr's throat whine as he pressed down even harder. "She's none of your concern. One day to rest and recoup, then she's heading west." Or rather, he was sending her west. *If he could convince her to leave.*

"Shhhee...ugh..." Tyr relaxed the pressure on the golden god's neck enough that Freyr could talk. "She *is* my concern because you've been locked in here staring at that damn schedule for five hours straight. Odin's checked out, and we can't afford to lose you too. *You've gotta* keep it together. If she's a distraction, send her away." Some of the light came back into Freyr's eyes, and they actually sparkled. "Or...let me handle her."

"You'll leave her alone," Tyr demanded. "She's not distracting me." *Five hours? Had he seriously been sitting here for five hours?*

"Then at least tell me who she is."

"Hunter, Hunter Wallace."

Freyr went limp beneath Tyr's hold. "The war chieftain's daughter?" A low whistle as Freyr blew out a long breath. "The Scottish princess, who they say is *possessed*? No shit? I've heard all the rumors, you know..."

Mir's sarcasm echoed from the doorway. "No shit." The redheaded god was already shaking his head as he stepped into the War Room. "She shouldn't be here, Tyr. Hunter Wallace is a menace."

Since Mir was the God of Wisdom and knew every ugly detail about Hunter's past, Tyr didn't bother disputing it.

Freyr's voice turned speculative. "No fucking wonder... You can let me go now, bro."

"Don't *bro* me." But Tyr released him and gave him a hand up. The fact that the truth was out in the open left him feeling on edge instead of relieved. Because Mir was right about Hunter. Sooner or later, this whole thing would blow up spectacularly.

"So...Hunter Wallace, huh?" Freyr rubbed his neck, curiosity written all over his face.

Best to shut *that* dangerous interest down quick, Tyr thought, as he redirected, "The Orobus and his army of the damned destroyed New York." Freyr's eyes widened, and Tyr motioned Mir closer as he continued to give them the rundown. "Hunter barely got out alive."

"No wonder she's pissed."

"Yeah. Losing your home will do that to you." Tyr shook his head. "Plus, she blames me for it."

Mir's lips quirked. "Of course she does. Well, she can add this to your ever-growing list of transgressions, right?"

Freyr looked between them, and then his voice turned serious. "Better run me through everything that's gone wrong between the two of you, Tyr. You know me. The more you tell me, the less likely I am to fuck things up."

Tyr didn't even try to fight the bitter smile twisting his lips. "You'll fuck it up, anyway."

Freyr beamed. "True enough. But not as badly as if I'm left in the dark. Besides, now I'm curious. Exactly what happened to New York? I *loved* that city. I used to know a girl there, well, a few girls, actually..." When Mir groaned, Freyr shut his mouth.

Tyr's voice turned flat as he ran it through, concentrating on the pertinent details. "The Orobus sent out a blast of magic that knocked out the power grid and most of the taller buildings, then a wave of Dark Elves swept in, picking off any mortal stragglers. Hel followed with her Grim."

At Mir's searching look, Tyr added, "The New York team fought back, taking heavy casualties. By her estimates, her team killed a couple thousand Grim and even more Dark Elves. But then the Orobus hit them with another surge of power. Managed to evac a few survivors, but was lucky to get out alive. She spent the last week fighting her way to us. She hit a few pockets of mortal resistance around the smaller cities, so the humans are fighting back, but they're vastly outnumbered." Tyr tapped a pile of papers. "Which backs up Loki's initial reports. Most of the Northeast is gone."

Tyr continued, "There's worse news. In three days, we'll bear the combined strength of the Orobus and all his armies, plus Hel and her Grim." He was already working out possible scenarios around that inevitability.

"Why would he come back here at all?" Freyr wondered out loud as Mir pondered the report.

Tyr met Freyr's gaze steadily. "Your guess is as good as mine. Could be the dolmens, or...us. It doesn't matter. Our job is to stop him. If he accesses the circle and opens a doorway to one of the other realms, he could unleash something even worse than the Dark Elves. We have to prevent that from happening."

"You know what?" Mir looked up at Freyr, his face thoughtful. "Screw the Orobus."

"Screw the Orobus?"

"Yeah, screw the Orobus. The real question is, why did Hunter Wallace come to *you*, Tyr?" Mir spun the map around, shoving it beneath Tyr's nose, his finger tracing the long, black line from New York to Chicago.

"Why would anyone travel *this* far...

"Just to see the person they hate most on this planet?"

3

THE DISPOSSESSED

Hunter counted the stones in the vaulted ceiling above her, set by masons back in 1920. If all that weight collapsed and buried them, her worries would be over. She sighed. *If only it were that easy.* A thousand years, a hundred wars, a million regrets, and she'd never felt like she did right now.

Weak. Useless. Defenseless.

Yet. Everything faded away when she'd set eyes on Tyr.

His familiar visage still strong and unflinching. Those dark, deep-set eyes still shrewd, yet steady. Tanned from millennia spent on battlefields. And his long, dark brown hair was tied back with a leather thong, exactly like it had been, a thousand years ago. *He hadn't changed at all.* Which pissed her off even more. The whole damn world coming to an end, and she was going to stew over *this*. The bastard who still held some infinite, subtle power over her.

She hated it. She hated *him* for it.

Flipping over, she stared out the window into the clouds, thinking about the first time she'd seen Tyr. He'd been in full armor, that long hair bound back by a gold circlet, mounted on a huge war horse that had shaken the ground when he'd galloped into their small village.

Her father, Domnall MacWallace, was the chieftain of a clan of mighty warriors, and even so, Tyr had bound her father with a sworn blood oath. *Forced* her da to swear fealty on bent knee, to fight in the War God's bloody vendetta against these demons he called the Grim. It was a forced fealty, sworn over too much whiskey and even more testosterone, but her father swore the oath just the same.

Tyr's bloody war stained the Alban fields black. True, she'd heard tales of these monsters, but never thought they'd reach her tiny village nor her quiet valley. But Tyr swore the demons were approaching, and curious, she'd followed against her father's orders, lagging behind the battle party, hoping to keep one eye on her father and the other on the God of War. What could she say? He was a dark and handsome stranger.

And she'd been curious.

The war band took a stand on a high cropping of rock, against a horde of invading Grim so large they'd taken her breath away. No explanation was given for why the monsters came to their little village that day. She'd never bothered to ask.

She'd only watched, torn between horror and fascination, flattened in the hillside grass as the swarm of monsters crested the rise before spilling down into the green valley where her village lay. The God of War raised his sword, bellowing a war cry, and the warriors surged after him. And then, the Grim began slaughtering the people she loved.

Her people.

Without thought, and certainly without any regard for her life, she'd swung herself up onto her horse and ridden straight into the melee. Picking up a sword from a dead solider, she'd hacked her way toward her father. She found Domnall Mac Wallace in the middle of the carnage, surveying his fallen men. And for the first time in her life, her da looked vulnerable. Frail. Old.

Sobbing, she'd reined her horse away. Away from all of that death. And ridden straight into Tyr. They'd circled each other for a moment. Wary strangers. *No*, she remembered, *it had been more than that.* Her hand hadn't left the grip of her sword. And that arrogant smile never left his face.

In the end, she'd galloped away, hating the war god for the dead clansmen strewn across that battlefield. For the broken man he'd left her for a father. Hated him for destroying everything in her perfect life.

She hated him more than she'd ever hated anything.

But more than that, Hunter despised herself for being too much of a coward to kill him, right then and there. *And later that night, when he'd sent for her?* Hunter squeezed her eyes shut. *Well. Everybody has regrets, don't they?*

"I'm sorry, I..."

Hunter shot off the bed, hand to her knife, crouching, face to face with a slip of a girl. Long, platinum hair framed a beautiful, waif-like face dominated by a pair of huge gray eyes that her gram would have said were 'tetched by the Fae.'

Hunter wouldn't have disagreed.

"Whoa, there. It's okay." The girl held out both hands to stop her and offered a soft, soothing smile. "Sorry. I knocked a couple of times. But I thought I'd better poke my head in and see if you needed anything." She stuck out a fine-boned hand. "I'm Celine."

Hunter took it. Cautiously. Friendship was something she judiciously avoided. For a multitude of reasons. "Hunter Wallace."

"Yeah, I heard. Freyr's been blabbing it all around. Can't keep his big mouth shut. I just... Look, are you hungry? Thought I'd see if you wanted to come and eat with us. In about an hour or so? We try to sit down together every couple of days. It helps."

"Helps what?"

"Keep us feeling...normal, I guess. When the whole world goes to shit, sometimes it's the little things that keep us connected, you know?"

"I do," Hunter whispered softly. As her humanity had faded away over the centuries, she'd done her best to hold on to what little she could. "Sure. I'll come and eat with you. Where?"

"War Room. It's down a floor, third door on the right. Follow the voices." Celine shrugged. "Not the ideal place, but it's the only table big enough to hold everyone. And the scouting party should be back by then." Now those gray eyes flashed with emotion. "Including my mate. See you!"

Celine slipped out of the room, stopping long enough to lay her hand on a folded pile of clothes beside the door. "Oh, I brought you these. Just in case you want to change. I didn't know..." Her depthless eyes swept Hunter from head to toe. "Yeah, you look...tired. So. Maybe a shower? And these might be more comfortable for dinner."

Hunter had forgotten what she looked like. Probably *smelled* like. She'd been fighting for days, then traveling nonstop for a week after that. With no sleep and certainly no showers. Her stomach growled. *Even less food.* "Yes, I believe I will clean up beforehand. My thanks to you." She managed an awkward bow.

Celine shook her head. "God, you'll fit right in with the rest of them. Well, I'll leave you to it."

As soon as the door closed, Hunter moved to the mirror. It had been so long since she'd even bothered, she was surprised at what was reflected back. Matted hair. Dark, black circles under her sloped, golden eyes, usually citrine in hue, were dulled by fatigue. In short, she looked like shit. "Great." She muttered. "Just great."

Still muttering, she ran the bath, hot as she could stand, and peeled off filthy clothes that had glued themselves to her like a second skin. Fading bruises, healing gashes, and teeth marks pebbled her body. Souvenirs of the battle to escape the city and the long, bloody slog to get here. She frowned. She should be healing faster, but then again, she *was* starving.

The light, airy clothing barely brushed against her skin after the heavy leathers, and her hair curled wildly around her face after the bath. Stomach grumbling, she headed down one floor, hesitated, then followed the noise.

4

*I*t had been so long.

That was Hunter's first thought. Centuries, but perhaps that was an exaggeration. *A century* perhaps, she corrected herself, since she'd shared a decent, common meal with strangers. Laughter. Conversation. Companionship. Why *had* it been so long? She reached for the doorknob even as her feet began to edge away from the din, her heart pounding a mile a minute.

Celine's small hand curled around her wrist and tugged. "There you are. Get in here." And then Hunter didn't have any choice, as she was pulled in by this creature who was stronger than she looked. Studiously avoiding Tyr's weighty gaze, she was yanked into a maelstrom of chattering laughter.

Celine giggled as she led her around the room and introduced her to everyone, the faces quickly becoming a blur. "So this is Fen, my mate." Hunter found herself staring at a broad, immense chest. Her gaze lifted to find a handsome face dominated by a pair of intense blue eyes and surrounded by a mane of black hair.

"A pleasure, Hunter." Fen pulled another couple into the group. "This is my pops, Loki, and his mate...er...wife, Morgane." Hunter shook hands all around, Morgane's strong grip nearly as calloused as her own, her bright green eyes weary yet watchful. And the way she moved, sleekly, as if her body was a weapon.

Here, Hunter thought, *was a woman who'd seen battle.*

"Glad you found your way home to us, Hunter. I heard you were a hell of a tracker for Rhiannon in New York." His voice dropped. "When you can, you'll have to give us the rundown on what happened to your team. We only got as far as Buffalo before Tyr recalled us." In Loki's brilliant blue eyes, she glimpsed the flash of pity before he was able to hide it. Her heart stuttered, thinking of all she'd lost. People she'd known for centuries. Most of them gone. A precious few survivors scattered.

Home to us.

Was this to be her new home, then? As something writhed in her gut at the very idea, she snapped, "At least you still *have* a home. Mine is gone. Because you let that *thing* escape." She shot a hard look at Tyr as she settled herself into the chair directly across from him.

Morgane's voice turned wary. "Loki only meant to welcome you, Hunter."

"I know what he meant. You have to understand that this is not, and never will be my home. It is *your* home. Mine was burned to the ground by this thing you're calling the Orobus. The only reason I've come is to help stop him. There's nothing else I want any part of."

Great. You could, literally, hear a pin drop. And...*this* was why she didn't share meals. Chagrin flooded through her at the look of shock on Celine's pale face. "Once he's defeated, I'll be on my way," she added lamely.

"You're assuming he *can* be defeated." Mir, his face hard and unforgiving, stepped up behind Tyr.

"*Everything* can be defeated." Hunter's voice was flat. "The only question is how." Her eyes flickered over the elegant, willowy woman standing at Mir's shoulder. "And whether you're willing to pay the price." For a moment, she swore she felt something...*powerful* leaching from the mortal. With a tilt of her head, Hunter caught the redhead's eye, held her curious gaze, felt a ripple of that power span across the room. There was a jolt of surprise when Mir stepped between them, blocking her view.

Interesting.

"Stop talking in riddles, Hunter. If the thing's a day or two out, then you'd better start explaining yourself. We could use new intel to prepare ourselves against him. Telling everyone what happened in NYC might be a good start." Mir ground the words out, his blue eyes flashing fire. Ah, he still despised her, then. Fine. *Feeling was mutual.*

Hunter frowned, her attention focused on the strange magic she'd felt emanating from the redhead. "All right, then. You want answers, I'll give them to you."

"My team... We thought we were prepared, but he decimated the city with a thought. Nothing could have braced us for his onslaught. Everyone stationed in Lower Manhattan and Brooklyn"—her voice faltered for a second before she got herself together—"was killed instantly by the initial wave of power he sent across the Hudson. Most of the mortals had nowhere to go; it was gridlock and they were hemmed in.

"We took up secondary positions in Midtown, Forest Park, and Queens. We only managed to hold those for about five hours. By the following day, we evacuated any mortal survivors north." She scanned the grave, pale faces. "There weren't many. Then a few of us went back in.

"By nightfall, the Dark Elves had overrun downtown, along with Hel and her Grim." Hunter had to force herself to get through this next part, as the rest of them sat in stunned silence. "We managed to maintain higher positions and used up what ammo we had to pick off hundreds of elves and Grim caught in the corridors between the gridlocked cars and the collapsed buildings. They took heavy casualties. We thought we'd made a dent in the enemy forces." She paused, as much to catch her breath as to get herself together. "But all we'd done was show the Orobus exactly where we were.

"I don't know how, but the monster sent another blast of power through our block. It was suffocating, a choking blackness that enveloped everything. We were blind. When I came to, I was the only one alive."

"How long were you out?"

"A few hours, at least. Hard to tell with the blanket of...shadow the creature laid over us. Once I came to, I made it back to base, organized the retreat, then hightailed here."

"Aaaand any fucking time now, you'll get to the point and explain your cryptic warning." Mir's face was flushed. "So out with it, what do you mean by there *being a price*?"

Call it a thousand years of experience, call it a sixth sense, but Hunter couldn't take her eyes off of the redhead. The woman's eyes were shifting all over the place, and it was obvious she knew something. Hunter smiled, betting she was right about both human nature and having a guilty conscious. "It seems to me you should ask your lover, Mir. Mayhap she knows more than she's telling you."

The woman at his side paled, right before flushing red.

"ENOUGH," Tyr shouted, his voice cutting through the bullshit like a knife. Mir burst out in a foul tirade, Sydney grasping his arm to stop him from going over the table after Hunter, who sat with her arms crossed, a taunting smile pasted on her face.

Silence to utter chaos. *This* was Hunter Wallace in a nutshell, Tyr raged silently. She was nitro glycerin. Dynamite. The Black Plague. Okay, that had actually been Hel on a day trip, but still, Hunter had the requisite skill set for total destruction. Even enjoyed it.

Ignoring her mocking little smile, Tyr attempted some damage control. Leaning in, he hissed, "Stop provoking Mir. Stirring things up does no good." In response, her smile only widened.

"Too late for that." Freyr muttered from the other end of the table among the hum of agreement.

Fine, if Hunter wanted to play, he could very well do the same. The smile that twisted Tyr's face was all teeth and no mirth. "But since you feel like you can come in here and start some shit, back up your accusation with more than just words. Sydney's part of this family. We trust her." Now his tone turned scathing. "Which is more than I can say for *you*."

They held each other's eyes for a long, strained moment before Hunter let out a hollow laugh. "Of course. My mistake." She offered a curt nod to the redhead. "I apologize, Sydney. I was completely out of line." Leaning back in her chair, she went on, "All I was *trying* to say is magic *always* demands a price. Something we all know to be true."

Tyr's gaze narrowed as Hunter continued, "The real question is why the creature is coming back at all? He must have good reason."

Lots of uncomfortable looks were exchanged before Loki finally explained, "There is a portal about a mile from here. The Orobus has been using it as a means to move between worlds and to bring his armies forth."

Now Hunter was nodding, her expression turning thoughtful. "It makes sense. He'd certainly need more troops. We hit him hard in New York, and he took some serious losses."

Keeping his eyes on her face, Tyr laid out the details, curious to how she'd react. "Except it's more than *just* a portal. It's a series of doorways, where each opening leads to a different world. Some of the worlds contain his armies, and from our recon, he's been breeding millions of them. Which is why we cannot allow him to open up *any* of those doors.

"Other doors seem to lead nowhere, and one leads to the prison the Orobus escaped. We cannot destroy them. We've already tried, but the explosives didn't make the slightest dent. They're protected by the creature's black magic."

A low, dark laugh issued as Hunter shook her head wonderingly. "The dark god created a hub. A central interchange to other realms, here in Chicago. No wonder he's heading back. My God, once he opens those portals..." She looked to Loki. "You're *certain* you tried everything to destroy them?"

"Threw everything we had at it," Loki assured her. "When the smoke cleared, the stone circle still stood." Tyr winced at Loki's revelation. Hunter Wallace and magical stone circles did not mix well.

"Wait? Stones?" In a second, her expression changed from thoughtful to furious as her head whipped to Tyr. "*You* said they were *portals.*"

"Which they are. A circle of ancient, standing stones, which are the Orobus's means of moving between realms. Which is *all* they are, Hunter. Don't make this into more than it is." When Hunter looked like she was about to explode, Tyr shrugged. Even though he knew what Hunter's issues were with the stones, he had bigger problems to deal with at the moment. Hunter would have to get in line. "The *stones* are not the issue. The issue is how to prepare ourselves for his forces once they arrive."

"And my sister," Fen pointed out. "Hel will certainly be with him, plenty of her Grim in tow." Leaning toward Hunter, he asked, "How many Grim would you say they have with them?"

"About three thousand, give or take," Hunter answered, her voice dropping. "And maybe two thousand Dark Elves. But if he hits Chicago like he hit New York..."

"He won't."

All eyes flew to Odin, sloppily propped up in the doorway.

"How can you be so sure?" Hunter asked, her eyes widening slightly as she took in Odin's disheveled appearance.

"Because that's not his game." Odin meandered into the room, an empty bottle of scotch hanging loosely from his hand. "He's toying with us, you see. And where's the fun in that if you wipe everyone away in one fell swoop?" Searching their faces, then the room, as if he'd never seen them before, his silver eyes were bleary. "This isn't the liquor room. Where is all the booze?"

Odin's normally crisp clothing was stained, his long white hair ragged as he swayed, raising an arm to shield his eyes from the overhead lights. "*Where* in the name of all that's holy is the damn scotch?"

Balder rounded the table and steered Odin back toward the door. "You're in the wrong corridor and on the wrong floor. *And* the Lag is all gone. You'll have to switch to Balvenie." Balder threw a backward glance to the others that was akin to *Gods, give me strength.* "Although my guess is, you're not going to notice."

When they'd cleared the door, Hunter posed a question for the room. "It seems obvious. If you know where the dark god's prison is, then shove him back inside."

There was laughter. A few loud snorts. A whole lot of head-shaking.

Tyr watched Hunter's gaze settle again on Syd. But to his surprise, Sydney was nodding, as if in total agreement. And when Hunter spoke again, her words were directed to the redhead. "*She* knows that's the only solution. Get him through the doorway into his prison, then destroy the portal. Send the thing back to hell."

"She's right," Sydney said, her voice small, her face still flushed pink. "I've worked out some possible scenarios, and it's really the best option."

Mir's voice turned sarcastic, as he leaned in until he and Hunter were nose to nose. "Oh...okay. Well, since you have all the answers, then why don't you tell me how? How in the fuck are we supposed to cram a primordial god back into his little box?"

She grinned, and this time, it did reach her eyes. "That's not my concern. However, once *you* manage to trap the monster, I will destroy the portals behind him."

"Finally, something you're fucking good at." Mir's mutter made her grin.

"Well...yes." Hunter's smile turned sharp. "Something I have *experience* with, anyway."

Mir gritted out, "If you can call almost ending the world...*experience.*"

"You are being overly dramatic, Mir." Hunter waved a dismissive hand. "It was but a..."

"Face it. You're a walking time bomb," Mir muttered.

"Enough bickering, you two," Tyr cut in. "Now that we have everyone's attention, yes, the rumors are true. Hunter is powerful enough to destroy the dolmens. The real trick will be luring the bastard through the correct doorway." Maybe this *would* work, after all. He'd been thinking of Hunter as a liability. Maybe it was time to start thinking of her as an asset. He turned to Hunter. "Any ideas?"

"Several," she told him, fingers drumming on the table. "None of which you'll like."

"Try me."

"Using someone as bait might work." Her smile turned mocking. "But remember what I said about there always being a price?" Tyr nodded slowly.

"Maybe this time it's not only the magic that will demand its due."

5

I n the aftermath of Hunter's pronouncement, a good-natured
argument broke out between Freyr and Thor, and Tyr leaned
back, letting the banter wash over him. At least the worst had
been avoided, and Mir and Hunter weren't at each other's throats.
Maybe this evening could be salvaged. *And maybe Odin had the right
idea, after all.* "You know what? Let's eat. And drink." He pulled over a
bottle of bourbon.

"Especially drink."

Catching Hunter's eyes, his throat tightened. There was, for a
moment, the slightest flash of something resembling compassion in
those penetrating, cat-like eyes. Clearly, he must look like roadkill if
she felt anything for him.

He was halfway through his glass when Celine sidled up next to
him and wrapped her arms around his neck. "Thanks for calling Fen
back early. I'm glad he's home." In response, Tyr shot the big, bad
wolf a smile over her shoulder.

From across the room, he felt the unspoken warning in Fenrir's
blue-eyed stare before the wolf finally turned away, as Loki whispered something in his ear.

"They'd done all they could do, sweetheart. Besides"—Tyr gave her hand a gentle pat—"he's better off here. He loves you to the moon and back, Celine."

"I know. I love him too. It's scary. The world's ending, and I wonder every day how much time we've got left." She turned those depthless eyes to Tyr. "But we have to talk about your friend, Hunter Wallace. She seems like trouble."

"You're not wrong, sweetheart, she's definitely trouble. But she's not exactly...my friend." He evaded as Celine slipped in beside him.

"I know. I had a dream about you two, a couple weeks ago." She leaned her elbows on the table, her gaze flipping between him and Hunter. "I saw you standing together on a field of blood. I knew who Hunter was, before she even showed up today."

"You couldn't have seen her. How is that even possible, Celine?"

"Sydney and Mir have this theory. They believe the Orobus created a new dimension when he came through and bent the magnetic fields. I'm able to go there, because he opened it up when he and I were connected psychically. Now I sometimes have visions." She shrugged her thin shoulders. "I don't like it."

She smiled sadly. "*And*, I should point out, Fen likes it even less."

Well, if that didn't give him the heebs, Tyr didn't know what did. "So Odin's gone blind, but you're having visions?"

She nodded, gaze turned downward, hands clasped in her lap. "Yup. Except I'm not sure what I'm seeing until it actually happens, if you know what I mean?"

Tyr didn't even know what to do with this. But if Celine had seen Hunter and him together... "All right. Describe this field to me. What did it look like? Could you tell where it was—Chicago, maybe?"

She glanced over her shoulder as if to make sure Fenrir was still laughing with Loki before continuing, her voice conspiratorial. "It was down in a valley, between some crazy high cliffs. There were a lot of dead...demons...Grim, scattered around you guys. Along with dead soldiers. And you and Hunter were circling each other on horses, looking like you were about to kill each other, or..."

"I get the picture." *What the hell?* "So tell me, was there more to this dream?" Tyr kept his voice steady and placidly calm while his internal radar went berserk. *Celine hadn't seen the future, she'd seen into the past.*

She nodded, growing considerably paler. This time, when Celine looked over, Hunter stared right back and their stare held. "She looked like a princess, all dressed up, perched up on this giant horse, but then, she turned...into something else."

"What did she turn into?"

Her eyes never left Hunter. "I watched her turn into the Orobus."

His hand shook when he poured the last of the bourbon into his glass, the amber liquid overflowing the rim. *Yep, just when you thought things were as bad as they could get.* "It was only a dream, Celine."

"Maybe," Celine murmured. "But there's more. Hunter talked to me after she turned into the Orobus, Tyr. She *told* me things." This conversation was taking a turn he didn't like. Tyr evaluated the room. Fen was still yukking it up with Loki, Hunter was surveying the entry points to the room for weaknesses, and Mir was focused on them like he knew exactly what this was about.

"Okay. Go on." There was a tightness to his voice that even the whiskey couldn't smooth out, along with a sense of impending doom.

Celine walked him through it, remembering. "It *was* Hunter, but she was all tangled up in the Orobus, if that makes any sense. Like there was this awful cancer infecting her, waiting to get out. But on the outside, she still looked like a fairy princess."

If only you knew.

"She said she was a part of the whole. But he would come for her someday. She also said...that you *made* her, Tyr."

Yup. He had to shut this down quick. "Celine, honey..."

Celine's voice turned high. "What did you *make* her into, Tyr?"

"Yes Tyr, why don't you tell all of these fine people, these *friends* of yours, what happened that night you used your magic on me? What you turned me into?" It shouldn't have surprised him when he heard that low, husky voice of Hunter's right behind him.

Hunter's voice turned hard. "Handy, isn't it, that there happens to be a cursed stone circle, *right here in Chicago?* Funny you never mentioned that little tidbit when I arrived. Must have slipped your mind."

TYR SQUEEZED his eyes shut and prayed for patience. He didn't blame Hunter, really, for being pissed off. Nor did he blame her for hating him. Hell, he hated himself. But seriously, did they have to do this in front of everyone?

OF COURSE THEY DID.

SHE WAS HUNTER FUCKING WALLACE, and this was how she did *everything.*

Big. Loud. Over the top.

As emotions warred within him, he spun to face her. Met those raging, wildfire eyes of hers. And felt this momentous *shift* inside himself. He'd always felt this mix of emotions around her. Love. Hate. These feelings were so tightly wound together that somehow, over the years, they'd simply become the force that pulled them together. Just as they would, inevitably, be the things that drove them apart. But for now...

As THE BAND of immortal brothers and the women they loved looked on with widening eyes, Tyr explained, "Long story short, Hunter killed me after I forced her father and her clan to fight a losing war against a Grim invasion. Most of them died. When she killed me, the blast from the release of my magic killed her as well. I resurrected us both. But the old magic I used—"

· · ·

HUNTER CUT IN, "We were on hallowed ground. On my family's burial grounds, which just so happened to be a cursed circle of stones..."

"AND MY SPELL pulled some ancient, evil spirit up out of the ground that night. Then, when I combined the spell with my blood, the only way to save Hunter was to..."

"SEAL IT INSIDE OF ME. FOREVER." She hissed through her bared teeth.

"BETTER I SHOULD HAVE LEFT you to die?" Tyr countered.

"DOUBLE-EDGED SWORD, IF YOU ASK ME." Her voice was so low it was practically a growl.

"TRUTH." He nodded solemnly. "The magic I used afforded you a degree of immortality. But the spirit that surged up out of the earth and possessed you?" He explained to the now-silent crowd. "Well, the spirit came with some interesting side effects."

"INTERESTING?" Hunter's face had gone rigid. "That's what you choose to call this?" She waved a hand over her body. "You cursed me, asshole. For a thousand years, I've been cursed, and you want to whitewash your mistake by calling what you did to me...interesting?"

HUNTER FELT a million regrets rising up in her as she faced off with

Tyr. But he'd gotten most of it right, as usual. She'd been alive and walking for all these years. Because of him. She was also cursed. Because of him.

He was her savior and jailor.

Her love and hate.

She'd been stretched thin between the two for so damn long that she felt the tension, like exhaustion, in her very bones. Perhaps she had become the battle itself. Certainly there wasn't anything left of the chieftain's daughter she'd been when she'd ridden away from him a thousand years ago, wondering what an immortal god's lips tasted like.

And when she came back down out of her head, Tyr was staring at her so intently, and he looked so...*tired*, she thought with a jolt. The sight of him recalled how her father looked in the middle of that battlefield, surrounded by dead soldiers. *He looks fragile.* This indefatigable being, this one constant in her life looked defeatable. Hunter frowned. She didn't like that. Not one bit.

She needed him to be the wall she could throw herself against, over and over again.

The one that would never, ever break.

Tyr grasped her arm. "We need to talk. You and me. Now."

She managed to nod. Because all of a sudden, words just wouldn't come.

A sort of guttering hopelessness swelled inside her. As if this final, historic confrontation she'd waited so long for was going to break her goddamned heart.

Tyr strode out of the room, practically towing her along. Away from the silent speculation, the judging eyes, the exposing of all their long-held secrets.

"In here." Huge double doors swung inward to silence. An echoing vastness swallowed them, seeming to suck her dry. "This used to be Odin's. But since he's off drinking somewhere..." Tyr's warning echoed into the dark corners. "Just...stay away from the fucking throne."

Against the grandness of the marble, the sheer vastness of the space, she only noticed the little things. His bloody knuckles. His red-rimmed eyes. His thin shirt stretched too tightly across muscle and bone. *Damn him.* She needed him to be the monster she loved to hate. The relentless, unbreakable killing machine. Instead he had the audacity to look...vulnerable.

"*Tyr...*" His name came out softly, sounding almost sentimental.

She tried again. "Tyr." *Better.* "There's too much between us to be made right. There are too many mistakes between us to undo them all. You know it as well as I do."

He watched her for a long moment, then spoke. "When I first saw you that day, I thought you were weak. I thought you were helpless. I thought... Look at this young, mortal girl in her lovely dress. She's so *pretty.* So *breakable.*" The smile she saw on his normally expression-less face was mirthless and a little regretful before disappearing completely. "I thought wrong. About everything."

"Tyr...I..."

He scrubbed a hand through his hair, so hard she heard the rasp. "When you came to me that night, Hunter? When we were...together, you know I would give anything to undo what happened?" And yet, they hadn't been *together.* Not like that. Not *ever* like that. No, they'd been *together* for another reason entirely, that fateful night.

"You *know* that, right?" His eyes, along with his voice, were pleading.

Hunter paused *This* was what she'd wanted her entire life. Him, weak and begging, preferably on his knees before her. All of his defenses down, nothing left of the invincible god he'd once been. And then? She'd wipe that arrogant smile right off his face. *And she'd enjoy every wicked moment of it.*

Except now that the moment was here, it felt empty. And all of her vengefulness, all of her hatred, the culmination of everything seemed ugly. "I don't understand what happened. I was just so angry...*so angry*...that night I met you at the circle."

"Aye. You were. Angry and beautiful and utterly captivating. But still...mortal. Which is why I thought to bed you and go on my way afterwards. Which is the only reason I let you get too close."

"While all I wanted was to put my knife through your heart." She still, to this day, remembered it. Felt the slick, easy slide of the blade between his ribs, into his chest cavity, as she drove the hilt home. She'd tasted the cool satisfaction of revenge. She'd locked eyes with him at that very moment, whispering, "For my father, my brethren, and my blood." Before yanking her knife free while his blood coated her hands.

Oh, the feeling had been glorious. Until a second later, when a burst of energy surged out of his body, knocking her backward against a rock, snapping her neck. Still, she'd savored vengeance.

Just not long enough.

"And you did. Get your revenge." Pride flashed in his eyes for a second before he tamped it back down, and she thought she must have imagined it. "But I couldn't let you die, Hunter. It wasn't *in* me to let such a magnificent creature die."

She shook her head as his quiet pledge echoed around the chamber. "You should have. I've lived an abnormal life."

"You've lived an *extraordinary* life."

"According to an immortal, perhaps." She had to shake this melancholy feeling and get on with what she'd come here to ask. God knows she'd waited long enough for it. "But I'm only human, Tyr."

He scoffed. "You haven't been human for a thousand years."

"No, I haven't." She stared up at him. "What am I, Tyr?" In all of her scenarios, all of her imaginings, she'd never once imagined this. That they might talk. *Just talk.* About that night. What their choices had done to them for all these years.

He blinked in surprise. "You are Hunter Wallace. Daughter of the last chieftain of the Picts. Captain of the New York team, and one of the finest trackers I know."

"I came here because I hate you," she said softly. "And I came for my final piece of revenge."

Just as softly, he whispered, "If you shove that sword in my heart tonight, Hunter, you might get what you came for."

A quick fear shot through her, even as she shook her head back and forth. "That's not... You misunderstand me," she stammered. "That is not what I came here to do." She drew her brows together in confusion at the sudden tangle of feelings that assaulted her. "I didn't come here to kill *you*." True, she still felt a kernel of hatred. Maybe she always would. But seeing him, being this close to him, hatred faded away.

Tyr circled behind her. "What did you mean when you asked, what you were? Surely, after all this time, you *know*? What does this thing inside of you *feel* like?"

She sighed. Of course he'd wonder. Despite everything, Tyr was, first and foremost, a warrior, with the weight of the world on his shoulders. She was yet another problem on his doorstep.

Hunter turned, countering, "What happened that night, when you brought me back to life? What did you *do*, exactly?"

"I can't tell you." Hands on her hips, she glared until he finally explained. "I used some half-remembered magic to heal your body before your life spark faded completely. The spell, mixed with my blood, should have taken nature's energy from the earth, and transferred it to you, restoring your life. But I didn't get it right, not the words, nor the order in which I performed it. Add to that, you recall where we were?"

She shuddered. "The circle. Which had been a sacrificial site centuries before. Atrocities were performed there. Awful, pagan things."

Tyr nodded. "Whatever I pulled out of the ground was primitive, and it was evil, Hunter. I should have moved your body, but there wasn't enough time. Then my blood mixed with the spell, complicating things further. Black magic and blood magic mixed together. You ask me what kind of magic I used?" He spread his hands helplessly. "In truth, I don't know."

"Whatever I am now, it's not normal."

"That's not true," Tyr demurred.

She considered him, chewing her lip. "You are the only person who can undo what was done to me. And give me what I want."

Face shadowed, he asked carefully, "What are you proposing?"

"You need something. I need something as well." Her gaze was unwavering. "I would like to make a deal with you, Tyr."

FOR YEARS, she'd weighed this. This choice, against the thousand unnatural years she'd lived, and the fifty or so she'd been due had she lived the mortal life gifted to her by nature.

She was tired. Years upon years of loneliness. Outliving everyone she'd ever known. Letting them get close, only to watch them wither away and die. Losing her grasp of time itself, as decades, even centuries raced past.

This past week, during her mad scramble here, she'd tried to come up with a way to solve her problem. And just now, in the meeting, it had been presented to her on a silver platter. A means of maneuvering Tyr into doing what needed done.

"I swear, I will help you trap the creature and then destroy the gateway behind it. Once that is done..." She took a deep, steadying breath, her eyes never leaving his face. "Once the Orobus is dead, you will undo the blood spell and allow me to die.

"Failing that, you will kill me out right."

TYR'S HEART STOPPED. Or maybe time stopped. For all these years, the world had been a tolerable place because Hunter had been somewhere in it, alive and breathing. Hating him. Which had been okay too. Except...

He'd never imagined she'd ask this of him. Never imagined she'd yearn for death. Not when he'd worked so hard to give her life and to ensure she kept it. But now, her demand hanging in the air between them, she seemed oddly at peace. For too long a moment he regarded her, never breaking the resolved stare of those intense golden eyes before making his decision.

He didn't have any intention of keeping his word.

So when she stretched out a steady hand, he gripped her palm and lied straight to her face. "Deal."

6

Her hand in Tyr's, Hunter felt a weight slide off her.

Free. She was almost free.

Put the monster back in its cage and then this endless, lonely existence would finally be over. For a moment, she allowed herself the simple pleasure of taking in Tyr's handsome face. And handsome, he was. With the perfectly carved features of the gods, only marred by a single, faint scar, he was certainly too serious. Definitely too uncompromising. But there was no denying his dark beauty.

She knew his visage, in many ways, better than her own. Had spent hours and hours staring at that beautiful face. Alone, tucked into a cave in the Highlands, just the two of them. When she'd had nothing but time.

Of course, he'd never known.

After the night she'd died and Tyr resurrected her, he left her unconscious on her father's doorstep. She hadn't watched him leave, hadn't spoken a word to him, nor he to her. Just woken up and he'd been gone.

But he'd trapped something inside of her. Something monstrous.

The next thing Hunter remembered was staring at the side of the mountain, at the smoking crater where her father's castle used to be. At the piles of smoldering, dead bodies strewn around her. A roiling, terrible energy burned inside her, tearing its way out of her belly. She'd thought at first she was dying, but what she experienced was only her new, horrifying reality. It was weeks, months later before Tyr found her again, wandering the Highlands.

He'd never told her how he'd located her, only taken her far away, to a small, out of the way cave, and kept her there while the consuming darkness ate her from the inside out. She'd begged him, some days, to kill her.

But he always refused.

In time, her head cleared. In time, her mind began to work again.

He coaxed her back to life. Urged her to eat, to bathe, to embrace humanity once again. To shove that consuming blackness down within herself, to control it. To *force* it to submit to her will. He'd never left her, not once, not in all of that time.

And Tyr never knew she sat over him, night after night, in the dark. Half mad and certainly half wild, trying hard to re-discover herself in the tangled mess he'd created when he'd brought her back to life. For all those months, his face became the only thing grounding her to this world. For centuries after, she'd pondered the why's of it.

Even now, her hand in his, she was still pondering it.

7

The next day, Tyr fought to maintain his focus on the incoming invasion.

The Orobus and Elves and Grim. *Oh my.*

They were about be hit by a sledgehammer, and they weren't even close to prepared. But because this whole mess fell in his lap, they would be. No matter what, by the time that bastard arrived, they'd be ready for him. "Where are we? Can anyone give me a solid timetable?"

Loki's expression tightened. "Yesterday, after I transformed, I flew out and scoped out the incoming army. Even after their losses, it's still an immense legion. Not very organized, but the first ground troops are only a day out. Thor, where do you expect his main entry point to be?"

Thor walked over, pointed to a spot on the map, then dragged his finger up through the center. "South end of the city. Then straight up the beltway would be my best guess. After that, Lake Shore to Millennium Park, terminating at the circle. Hate to say it, but I agree with Hunter's initial assessment. He's coming to gather troops."

Tyr's tone turned thoughtful. "If I were in his shoes, I'd secure the entire area around the circle, first thing. Send in legions of Dark Elves in as shock troops to infiltrate the city, then set up a perimeter around the stones. Secure the entire area with patrols."

"Are we sure about that?" His arms braced wide on the table, Loki focused on the grid of the city map, tapping the place Tyr marked as the most sensible access point. "Could be he's just coming to kick our asses."

Tyr had spent most of the night pondering this exact question and come up with only one possibility. He'd like to think he was right. "I'm sure. Look, he needs fresh troops. He took heavy losses during this campaign. Lost plenty of Dark Elves and Grim on the way there and back." Tyr nodded, almost to himself. "He's coming for reinforcements. This is the only place he can find them."

"One benefit is, if the army of the damned is smaller, we'll stand a better chance," Balder pointed out, while Fen nodded in agreement. "At least during this initial attack."

"True." Loki said, eyes gleaming. "But those odds will only last until they reach the circle. Once they get those portals open and begin emptying the armies from Svartlheim onto this world..."

"It's over." Tyr ran his hand through his hair, deliberating. "But he'll still need time to do it, ground patrols to secure the site, time to bring those armies through."

"Most likely Hel and her Grim will be used as reinforcements, since she doesn't rely on the portals to transport her Grim," Loki added, the map forgotten at the moment. "So our prime objective is keeping that stone circle secure."

"Can't destroy it," Vali reminded them. "Speaking of which, our munitions supply is running low. We need to restock. The military depot is close. And abandoned."

"Then our objective is to blockade the Orobus from the circle at all costs. Defend the stones for as long as we can. This will push us to our limits, given how stretched thin we are. I could use more soldiers." Tyr exhaled, the sound more of a groan. "Fen, has Celine seen anything that might give us a timetable?"

The look Fen shot him clearly said *yes, asshole, of course she has.* But his voice remained even as he said instead, "We need to talk."

Tyr could guess what this was about.

Resignation in his voice, Tyr waved for him to continue. "Just say it, Fen. It'll all come out in the end. The way I see it, we've got a day left until shit hits the fan." Tyr spread his arms wide. "Out with it. We've got no secrets in this room."

Fen scanned the table, meeting each and every pair of eyes. "Celine saw Hunter turn into the Orobus in a vision. Mir says she's capable of leveling a city block, should she ever lose control. She acted aggressively at dinner last night, and then there are the rumors we've heard over the years..." Fen leveled his stare at Tyr. "I don't think she can be trusted. Neither does Mir. So until we're sure she's not a threat, I say she goes." He traded glances with Loki. "Not with my mate, *our mates* under the same roof. You're not putting them in danger."

"Damn it. That's not fair. Maybe she's not good with people, but Hunter risked her life to bring us intel. She's willing to fight with us." Tyr realized his hands grasping the back of the chair were sweaty.

"She was a trusted member of the New York team for over a *hundred* years. One of Rhiannon's captains, for the gods' sake. She's also the best damn tracker I know." He would have gone on, but looking around the table, Tyr found nothing but a mixture of suspicion, sympathy, and condemnation on their faces. He sucked in a breath before saying, "Then we put it to a vote."

They voted. Twice. Since there were six of them, the vote was split, and unless they brought the women into it, it would stay that way.

"Don't I get a vote too?" Amidst the utter silence, Hunter stepped in, nodding once to Tyr, her face completely unreadable, yet set like steel. How much she'd heard, he didn't know, but he figured it was enough.

"You know what? I'll make it easy for you." She solidly met their stares, one by one, not a hint of hesitation in her gaze. "I say...I go. I was heading out anyway. And I'll cover more ground alone." She flashed a too-bright smile. "I'll be gone tonight. Then you boys can get back to your war games."

Rounding the table, Tyr caught her arm. "Don't do this. You don't have to leave, we'll work *something* out." If he hadn't known her as he did, he would have sworn her eyes were bright from tears.

"I won't stay where I'm not wanted. I'll leave in a few hours, as soon as it's dark." She notched her chin higher. "You heard them. They're worried about their mates. And I can't say I blame them." Out of nowhere, she leaned into him, all soft against his hard lines. "But don't think for a single second I'm going very far, *or* that our deal is off. I'll fulfill my end of the bargain."

Tyr's eyes slid half closed as he breathed her in.

"And then you'll be fulfilling yours."

HOURS LATER, lying on the bed, Hunter was busy despising her weaknesses.

She'd almost done it. She'd almost trusted him. Imagined she might learn to live here, fight this war side by side with him. She'd never, ever learn, would she? She'd been softening around the edges, but that was only exhaustion mixed with this new, hateful sentimentality that kept cropping up whenever she was around Tyr.

It must be this weariness that seeped into her very bones.

She was just getting up when someone knocked. "Come in." She'd been expecting Tyr. Hoping for him. If only to tell him to go to hell, one last time. Her eyebrows popped up when she saw who it was.

"I'm pregnant." Celine slipped in, chin wobbly, and full of apologies. "It's why Fen's acting like this. He's worried. And a little crazy. Once I told him about my dreams, he went into overprotective mode. I'm really sorry, Hunter. I don't want you to leave."

Hunter shrugged. "I'm the one who voted and broke the tie." There was some, small satisfaction in that. Hunter began dressing, jabbed her small knife into her boot. "I'm the one who decided to go. So at least they didn't *make* me leave."

"I heard. Why?" Celine cocked her head. "Freyr says you've lived alone for like a thousand years. Is that true?"

"I'm going to shut Freyr up for good," she muttered. *But yes, pretty much.* She'd tried to get along with people, she really had. But it had always been too complicated and too messy. "Look, it's better if I head out. Safer for everyone."

"I know you worry about this strange power inside you. Do you really want to find out what you are?" Celine's eyes seemed to grow deeper by the minute, turning into bottomless lakes. "Because I can show you."

Curiosity prickled. *How did Celine know what was going on in her head?* Caution, though, kept her tongue silent.

"I can show you because I'm a Dreamwalker," Celine explained, matter-of-factly, gliding further into the room. "There's a place I found in the Otherworld. I call it the Dreaming. I can take you there. The answers you're looking for are there."

An odd fear shivered though Hunter. "I think it's really best if you just let me go." She glanced toward the door, but it was closed. She didn't remember Celine shutting it.

Celine bit her lip. "It's my fault Fen wants you out of here. I feel *responsible* for all of this. At least let me try to help?" Her eyes pleaded, *begging* Hunter to let her do this, and Hunter softened. "Please? Helping might make me feel less guilty," Celine prodded.

In truth, Hunter was curious.

And deep down inside, she knew she might be something awful.

But she had to know for sure.

"Come on, this will only take a minute. Sit over here." Celine pointed. "And I'll sit here." Face to face with the diminutive creature, a soft feeling of contentment washed over her, along with Celine's words.

"Now close your eyes. I'll lead you in. Just try to relax." With her eyes closed, Hunter let Celine's soft laughter wash over her. "I've never done this before, so it might not work, but if it does...now just relax."

As Celine's voice faded, Hunter floated in nothingness. Gone was the hard floor beneath her and the soaring ceiling overhead. Instead, her world turned white and wispy. When a small cool hand slipped into hers, her eyes flew open.

"There you are." To Hunter's astonishment, they were floating in a fog, against a nondescript landscape of ghostly gray. Wisps of smoke or clouds floated all around them, and the air—it smelled like rain or wet limestone.

"Is this a dream? Are we in a dream?" Hunter whispered.

"It's an actual place. For me, at least." Celine squeezed and Hunter felt a sharp, quick pressure on her hand. "See? You feel things in here. Not as real as anything outside and I don't know exactly which world we're on. We could be close to the Underworld, but I sure hope not." Celine shuddered. "We want to stay out of there."

"It feels warm in here."

"Does it? It feels cold to me. All right." Celine met her eyes steadily. "Are you ready for this, Hunter? Close your eyes and think about the place inside of you that's different. The place that changed, when Tyr brought you back to life. The place that's dark."

Had Tyr told her? Hunter wondered. *But how could he? Even he didn't know the full extent of her darkness.* "How do you know about that?" she whispered.

"I've been seeing you in my visions for weeks and weeks. If you really want to understand this power inside you, open yourself up and let it out, it's the only way to know for sure. Just let go."

Hunter hesitated. When she'd lost control before, the destruction she'd wreaked had been so awful, she lived with the memories still. If it hadn't been for Tyr...

"No, I can't. Celine, what's in me is terrible, it's so terrible, you don't understand..."

"Hunter, we're not in the physical world. We are in the *Dreaming.* Look around you. You can't do any harm in here. Go ahead. Give yourself over to it."

Still, Hunter hesitated. This girl *could not know* the strength of the power inside of her. Suddenly, she was all alone and then, from behind, Celine's low voice crooned silkily into Hunter's ear, "Let go,

Hunter. How long has it been since you were truly free? Let it out. Show us what you are. Why hide yourself?"

Why indeed?

Hunter felt the quick stab of anger. She was only in this mess because she'd been in the wrong place at the wrong time. *And because you killed a god.* Well, yes, there was that. She might shoulder a *bit* of the blame. Still, it would be nice to let down her guard. Just for a few, precious seconds.

"C'mon Hunter, relax." Celine coaxed gently from somewhere behind her. "Let it out. Let us *see* you."

But still, fear pricked at Hunter. Memories of *before* washed over her. The smoking crater, the ruined castle. The dead villagers. While a wrongness about this place played on the outside edge of her instincts.

Caution raised its head, and she whirled around, finding nothing behind her except swirling mists. "First, tell me exactly why you want this so badly," she countered, searching the fog for any sign of Celine. "And then, perhaps, I'll decide whether to show myself to you."

Somewhere in the mist, Celine chuckled, a cunning, wild laugh edged with madness. Hunter ducked, her hand going for her knives, just as a dark form rose up, from which a raging voice issued,

"Don't you understand, my child? I already know who you are.

"You are me, and I am you."

8

Heart hammering, intuition prickling, Hunter lunged up off the bed and stood for a second in the middle of the room, finding her bearings. She was not, as she remembered, dressed in her fighting leathers but was still in the loose borrowed clothing. Celine wasn't with her, and sunlight was streaming in all around her.

What in the hell?

The door flew open with such force that the crash reverberated through the room. Celine swayed on her feet, half dressed, wild-eyed and panting in the doorway. "I just...you and I just...oh my God...I..." Her pale eyes flew around the room, bouncing off everything before finally settling on Hunter. "You and I were...."

Somehow, Celine's sudden appearance, combined with the fact she'd obviously just woken up, made everything fall into place. Hunter's heart pounded even faster as she realized what had *almost happened. What she had almost done...* Hunter sheathed her knives and caught her breath. "Yes. Yes, I remember it all. That was...quite disturbing." *To say the least.*

Settling back on the bed, Hunter eyed the diminutive blonde.

"Are congratulations in order, then?" she asked, her gaze dipping to Celine's stomach.

Celine's mouth fell open. "Oh my God, *it really was real.* How is that even possible? Do you remember all of it?"

"I do." Since she didn't want to have this conversation in front of everyone, Hunter crossed over and pulled Celine into the room, shutting the door. "So how much of that was you?"

"I wasn't doing it on purpose, just so you know," Celine told her. "I just laid down. I've been so tired these past few weeks." She offered a wan smile, hand brushing her stomach. "And then somehow, we were together in my dream. Everything was fine until... How did you even know?" Her gaze turned speculative. "When did you figure out *he* was there too?"

"At some point the atmosphere felt...different. Evil, almost. As if it weren't you doing the asking. As if you were worn as a costume." Hunter braced herself. "That was the God of Chaos?"

"Yes, it was. He took control."

"Explain to me exactly what he felt like."

Celine shuddered. "Relentless. Definitely overwhelming. And he wanted you to lose control. It was as if he wanted to see what might happen, once you did." Her voice grew reedy.

Hunter's stomach lurched. "I know," she muttered, suddenly frantic. "I *know* that's what he wanted. He used the Dreaming and your abilities to maneuver me into lowering my guard." A shaking started somewhere in her knees. "And that was before he said—*you are me*—"

"*And I am you,*" Celine finished, her eyes wide.

Hunter tried to quell the growing horror inside of her. It seemed she finally did have a name. And she didn't like it one bit.

"There's something else you should know." Celine's bottom lip wobbled. "This isn't my first brush with the Orobus. He's been in my dreams before."

Hunter began to strip quickly, panic building along with Celine's questions.

"But this time he seemed different. This time, when he manipulated us, he was trying to accomplish something. What did he want you to *do*, Hunter?"

Hunter tugged on her pants, reasoning this near-disaster was the final push out the door she needed. "If the Orobus had succeeded just now, if he'd tricked me into releasing my power, the blast would have leveled this entire building, perhaps the city block. And there was a second when I considered it. You see, it's happened before, and unless I'm very careful, it could happen again."

Hunter stripped off the loose blouse and pulled on the jacket. "I *have* to leave right now. Fenrir was right to be worried. Nobody's safe around me. Especially now."

She needed time to think. Space to work through this disturbing turn of events.

You are me, and I am you.

If that message meant what she thought it did, then she was thoroughly screwed. It also meant the Orobus was heading straight for *her*. And she'd best put as much space between herself and the Tower as she could.

Celine grabbed her arm, and there was a surprising amount of strength in those slender fingers. "You can't go out there. There's nowhere to even go, Hunter. The city's falling apart, and it's dangerous."

"Don't be ridiculous. It simply means I have an entire city at my disposal. And playing hide and seek was always one of my specialties," she added wryly. If this thing thought she'd just lie down and allow herself to be cornered like a rat, he hadn't studied history. *At least, not her history.*

"But you'll be a sitting duck out there."

Hunter fixed Celine with a steady stare. "No, actually I won't be." She tucked another knife in her right boot. Checked both guns. She'd need some ammo but had scoped out the armory on the way in, and she'd swing by and take what she needed on the way out.

"It's the Orobus who'd better watch *his* back."

9

Tyr stationed Balder at the south end of the city. Vali on the west side, in case the God of Chaos swept in through the suburbs. Thor at the pier, just in case the bastard could swim. He didn't ever want to be accused of underestimating the enemy.

Looking at the maps, the video feeds, the logistics, the hours and hours of planning, his brain rattled around in his skull. It'd be tonight, possibly tomorrow, when the combined forces slammed down on them. Mir strung some magical warning systems together, so when the bastard broke through his wards, at least they'd know.

Not that Tyr was focused on their impending doom.

No, at the moment, his mental bandwidth was used up on a worry of another sort.

He'd sensed Hunter, the second she'd left the building. Knew she was currently on the south end, close to Balder's position, probably setting up a secondary sightline. Waiting for her opportunity. Of course, if he had his way, he'd keep her close. But it wasn't up to him, never had been. From the first second he'd seen her, it had been like the Fates had conspired in some cosmic plan to both throw them together and tear them apart.

Tyr ground his teeth. She *had* been close. For two entire days. And what had they done? Circled each other like jackals. When he *should* have had her in his bed. Fuck this war. Fuck the God of Chaos. Fuck the world. After everything, they'd ended up right where they'd begun.

On opposite sides.

"Fuck."

"Yeah. That about sums it up. Given any thought to how we're going to draw the God of Chaos down to the circle? Because none of this will matter if we can't toast his ass within the first few hours of the attack."

Mir ambled in, his gaze ruthless as he proposed, "If only we had something the creature wanted."

"What in the fuck are you talking about?" Tyr *had* to get his head back in the game. They only had a few hours left before they were hip deep in blood, and until then, all of this rested on his shoulders. "Could you possibly be any vaguer?"

"What if we *did* have what he wanted?" Mir pushed, "Would you leverage it?"

"Of course I'd use it. Are you fucking crazy? I'd do anything...*anything* to kill that bastard." Tyr concentrated on positioning, found they were shorthanded. "Look, what we really need are more hands on deck, and a rocket launcher or two might help, but sure, tell me what the fucker wants." He dragged his hand through his hair, deciding to move Vali further south, praying the break in formation wasn't going to prove fatal.

"I'm dead serious, Tyr. If we had something that would draw him to us like a magnet, would you use it as bait?" Mir took a step closer. "Would you?" he demanded, his finger drilling into Tyr's chest.

Tyr's internal warning system went off a minute too late. "What exactly *is* this something?"

"I just had a little chat with Celine and Fen. Regarding visions." Even Mir looked unhappy about it. "And the visions she's been having about Hunter. And the Orobus. But before you fly off the..."

"No." Tyr swung his head steadily side to side. "Let me amend that. *Fuck no.*" Everything inside of Tyr shut down. Locked down tight as all the little pieces fell into place. As clues from these past few days —what was inside of her, the death wish Hunter seemed to have— began to suddenly make more sense. "Don't say it. Don't even think it."

"Think this through for a minute."

"Damn it, Tyr. She's out there. Alone. And that thing's gunning straight for us. Celine's visions haven't been wrong. Not so far. Even you can't argue with that. And she's had a new one."

Tyr couldn't even think, couldn't even breathe as Mir said, "Celine said she and Hunter were together in her dream. And the Orobus *talked* to Hunter. And he told her..." Mir's mouth tightened.

"Don't you even finish that sentence," Tyr gritted out. "You've already pissed me off, so just shut up right the fuck now."

"Celine said the thing told Hunter, *'You are me, and I am you.'*"

"That sounds like a mind fuck to me," Tyr said. "And it isn't proof of anything. Ever thought that maybe this thing is trying to distract us? Orchestrating some diversion to pull us away, while he razes Chicago to the ground?" As Mir remained silent, Tyr chuckled. "I thought not. That's why I'm in charge of this war, and you're in charge of...well, pretty much everything else." Tyr snarled, "Now get out of my way."

He would have been gone, except Mir braced his hand against his chest. "Look. This way you can control the situation, Tyr. Let's pull her back in. If she shares some connection to him, and you've got to admit that's a possibility, keeping her close is better than her being out there alone."

Tyr barked out a short, bitter laugh. "*Control the situation?* You don't know Hunter. You don't know *anything* about her. And why the hell are you so sure this thing's gunning for her, anyway?"

From the doorway, Celine's soft voice said, "Because we were both pulled into the same dream. And the Orobus was after her. Not me. Her."

"Bullshit," he said flatly. "This is bullshit. It was only a dream."

Whirling, he made for the door, was out in the hall when Celine's voice stopped him cold. "There was a lot more to it, Tyr, and you've got to calm down and listen. The God of Chaos tried to get Hunter to reveal her powers to him. I believe he wanted to confirm she possessed a sliver of his energy. But she said something terrible would happen if she did." Celine added, "He's coming for her, Tyr, whether you like it or not."

He'd never seen what he'd pulled out of the ground that night. It had felt, in some way, as ancient as time itself. It had certainly been evil. But he'd sealed the darkness inside of her just the same. Because with that hideous force had come life. He'd considered it, at the time, a small price to pay. "Still doesn't—"

"We talked...afterwards. We discussed everything that happened in the dream. And Hunter was so shaken up by it, she left. But before she did, she said if she'd lost control, the blast would have destroyed this building, maybe even the block. Said she'd done it before. Is that true?"

"I don't know what you mean," Tyr murmured.

Now it was Mir who laughed. "Bullshit. You know *exactly* what she's asking. Rumor is, Hunter destroyed an entire mountainside once. My question is, why would the God of Chaos be after her in the first place?" Tyr barely felt the punch Mir landed on his shoulder, nor heard the question that followed. "Talk to us, asshole, or you'll wish you had."

So there were times in one's very, very long life when things came to a head. This was one of them. "She's the opposite of creation."

"So she's destruction?" Mir smirked. "Yeah, I've heard the rumors."

"Not exactly. She's more of a black hole. If she..." God, was he actually going to break his word? He'd *sworn* never to speak of this. He chose his words carefully. "After Hunter died, I used an old pagan binding spell to save her. Before she woke up, I took her back to her father, thinking I'd leave her, maybe ride back someday and find her again, and... Fuck, I didn't know what I thought. She was still unconscious when I left.

"It was weeks later when I heard what happened. Whispers of a castle disappearing. Along with the entire clan, the village beside it, most of the loch, and the upland crags guarding the valley. I rode back, and when I reached it... I couldn't believe my eyes. Everything was gone, except for a great, smoking black crater. The castle. The mountain. And over four hundred people. Erased.

"I found her wandering the Highlands. Out of her mind. Darkness oozing from her pores. Begging me to kill her." Tyr rubbed his face, feeling moisture there. "Her name was Charlotte. She'd been a beautiful, beloved daughter of a once-great king. By the time I found her, there was nothing left. She was begging for mercy, for death. I couldn't give her either.

"She was easy enough to find. In her wake, everything died. It was as if she consumed life itself as she passed. Fields of heather were black, forests turned to skeletons, flocks of sheep became carcasses. And the mortals..." Tyr didn't bother finishing.

"The same as the God of Chaos," Mir murmured.

"I ended up trapping her like an animal. Took her to the mountains. Since my blood was in her, blood magic protected me, I suppose. I even controlled her to a certain extent. I kept her away from anything living. I used every spell I knew, every bit of magic I could summon, to seal that thing away, inside of her."

"How long?"

"Months, I suppose. I never kept track. She certainly couldn't. It took time, but she became herself again. Or as close to herself as she could get."

"You should have killed her."

Tyr nodded faintly. "Perhaps. She begged me for it enough times."

"This time, there was no home to take her back to. She remembered nothing of the castle, the village, what had happened. What she'd done. So I told her that I'd done it. The God of War had yearned for vengeance. Demanded his due. And she believed me."

"You lied." Celine's voice turned disbelieving. "Why would you tell her that, Tyr?"

He shrugged. "I'm easy to hate, especially back then. She'd never been whole if she knew the truth of what she'd done. And since I was the one who cursed her in the first place..."

"You were the one to blame," she finished for him.

"I *am* the one to blame. Like you said. I should have let her die." And yet, if they killed the Orobus and Hunter had her way, he'd have to keep his word. "But I couldn't."

"After that, we've stayed on opposite sides of the continent. Opposite sides of the world, when we were able. But I always knew exactly where she was." Tyr wasn't even sure when he finished speaking, only that Celine's eyes were brimming with tears. He was sure his heart had never hurt quite so much.

Mir rolled his shoulders. "Let's go get your girl. Get her on board. If she manages to draw the bastard to the circle, we'll push him through the door. After that, I don't give a fuck if she leaves a crater the size of the Grand Canyon behind. Let her finish him off. Maybe he'll take whatever's inside Hunter with him when he goes."

"And Ava?" Celine reminded them.

"And Ava too. We've got enough of his poison floating around here. It's time to get rid of him for good. Maybe even take care of Hel and her demons."

"Too much to hope for." *Plus, there was still their little deal to contend with.* "If I'm going to get her, I'm going alone."

"Not a good idea, my man."

"Non-negotiable. She won't trust anyone else." Tyr almost smiled. "Not that she trusts me, but at least she won't kill me on sight." Anything was possible.

Mir followed him down to the weapons room, helped outfit him with body armor, weapons, and a killer pair of knives. "Where is she?" Tyr asked, not really needing confirmation on his hunch but wanting to make conversation to fill the silence.

"Last I heard she was just north of Balder's position. Been there most of the day."

Tyr closed his eyes, sending feelers out for her. *Yeah, that felt about right.* She was tired, bone-dead exhausted, but still managed to be on full alert.

"She hasn't moved, which I can't believe. Balder's been shifting position every half an hour."

Tyr shot him an amused glance. "You don't know her. Like I told you, she's the best damn tracker alive. She'll sit there and wait until the end of time, if that's what it takes."

"The problem is, he'll be gunning straight for her." Mir picked up a radio, muttered into it. "Hey shithead, any movement?"

Balder's voice sounded tinny and distorted. "Not yet. Some movement to the east, but it could be nothing."

Tyr checked his vest, pulled his shirt down over it. Tugged a beanie down over his head. "I'm headed his way. Tell him not to cap my ass by mistake." Since Balder was still jumpy after being tortured in the Underworld for thousands of years, it was a definite possibility.

"Tyr's coming to you. Hunter's a few hundred feet north of your position." Mir's eyes met his over the com. "Probably somewhere high and dry."

"I'll be there in a minute."

"Tyr's on his way. Don't shoot him by mistake. I'm not wasting my time healing his cranky old ass," Mir said into the crackling com unit. "FYI, the God of Chaos will be heading straight for your position. Stay sharp."

10

As it turned out, Hunter liked Chicago.

Not that she'd admit that to anyone. But the way the wind whipped in off the lake, smelling of the water, reminded her of home. Old home, the way she liked to remember Scotland. Alba, as they'd called it back then. These stone pillars were her rocky granite crags, the blue lake her beloved loch. And Chicago was greener than New York, where every inch had been asphalted within an inch of its life. She eased the cramp in her leg, the crick in her back. She was about a hundred yards from Balder, and could practically smell him. "You, my friend, need a bath."

She barely felt the cold that bit through her leathers, barely felt anything around her, so engrossed she was in mulling over the developments of the past days. There had been a certain sense of hope when she thought she might discover what she was. A sense that with a name, everything would fall neatly into place, and her life would become a thing of order and, therefore, easily managed.

"I am you, and you are me." She frowned. "Fat chance of that. You are you and I am who I've always been. We are not, and never will be, the same."

She was a war chieftain's daughter. And nothing, not even this all-powerful creature, would ever take *that* away from her.

TYR CROUCHED about a hundred feet from Hunter's position. Observing.

Some might call it stalking, but he preferred the other. Made it seem, well, more respectable. She sat, long legs dangling over the nothingness dropping a thousand feet below her, without so much as a twitch, until he caught the slightest movement of her torso, followed by a backward rolling of her shoulders. Inwardly, he groaned. He'd best get on with this.

"Not exactly a walk in the park to find you up here." He went with a casual tone, hoping to not spook her. "And I have better things to do right now than chase you down."

"Do you know what your problem is, Tyr?"

No, but he was pretty sure he was about to find out.

"You took the long way up. The south elevator shaft is wide open, the cables intact. It's faster than the east stairwell." She turned that golden stare on him, and he felt its crackling bite all the way to his very marrow. "And you never know quite how to speak to me, do you? But since you've been sitting there behind that wall for over an hour, just spit it out already. You've certainly had enough time to figure out what you want to say."

True, except the words were still tangled up in his throat. "How long have you known I was here?"

"An hour. You sounded like a rhino coming up those stairs with your boots." That shrewd gaze drilled straight through him. "And before you ask, no, I haven't seen anything. Big flock of birds stirred up about two hours ago. But that could have been anything."

"Why did you vote yourself off the island, Hunter?"

"Because it was best for everyone."

"For who? For you? For everyone else? Tell me, who were you

trying to protect? We're all big boys and girls. We've seen a lot of shit in these past months. I'm pretty sure we can handle—"

Her voice was cool when she answered. "You know full well that you can't handle what's inside of me, Tyr. This god... He played a mind trick on me, in that vision with Celine. And he almost fooled me. Except for a vague feeling of...*wrongness* about the whole scene, I almost bought it."

Her voice broke, then rose. "What do you think would have happened if I'd let go? What would have happened to your precious Tower? Your friends? Let's not forget what I can do, nor what I *have* done." Hunter leaned her head back. "I'm so tired. I can't do this anymore. Life. A thousand years is too damn long. Let me help you finish this, and then you can let me rest." He realized her eyes were squeezed tight. "I just want to rest."

He'd never really thought about what her life was like.

For him, immortality had been a cakewalk. At first. Sure, there'd been a rough eon or two here and there, but he'd had his brothers, and trips to Asgard, and wars with the Titans and so forth to break things up. He'd never considered what a mortal life would be like, stretched out over a millennium. "Has it really been so bad?"

She shot him a sideways look. "I've been *alone*, Tyr." Her voice had this fragile edge he hadn't heard since those months in the mountains, when it was just the two of them. His feet were rooted to the floor as she continued. "At first, I was afraid of being around anyone else. Afraid of myself, of what I might do to others by mistake. Then, it became habit. I missed people at first, so much. I thought about my father, my clan. Then I thought about them less and less. Then came the day I knew..."

Tyr smelled her tears as he approached, crouched down so they almost touched. Over everything else, the fact she'd remained isolated for so long tore his heart to shreds. "I knew whatever I'd been that day we met on the battlefield, I was no more. I'd lost my humanity. And I'd never get it back. After that, it was easy to be alone."

"Look, Hunter. Come back." *No, not quite right.*

"Come back *with me*. Stay..."

Her head swiveled around, golden eyes locked on tight.

"...*with* me. This time, I *want* you there. I *need* to know you're safe. Fuck what's inside of you. I trust you to keep it locked down tight. Just"—he indicated the network of blown out windows and twisted beams around them—"let me take you somewhere that's not here."

"You want me somewhere safe?" A strange little smile played on the corners of her mouth. "You want me to *stay* with you?"

Fuck yes. "Hunter..." Her name was a plea and a thousand things wrapped up in that one little word, and he would have poured out his heart to her in that moment, both of them dangling precariously over this yawning emptiness. Had the flock of starlings not chosen that particular moment to overrun the entire blown-out building.

The birds swarmed through the broken windows, weaving through beams and gutted walls, streaming past in a blur, filling the space with the dry-brush rattle of wings, forcing Tyr to grasp the nearest beam for support. Their passage gave him the strangest sensation of falling.

And when they were gone, so was Hunter.

Casting about, he sensed her several stories below and descending fast. Running for the elevator shaft and cursing missed opportunities, he leapt, grasped the still shaking cable, and fell like a bullet, the cable heating up against his palm. "Damn it. I *will* have my say," he muttered as his feet hit the bottom of the pit with a boom.

He honed onto her location immediately. She was already outside. "What the hell, Hunter?" He followed, as if she were a magnet and he steel. Rubber banded together, where she went, he followed. Back and forth, forever and ever.

He turned onto East 100th and paused. The damn trees lining the street were full to overflowing with the flock of birds, the street full of their shrieking calls, the sound deafening. Hunter was just ahead, and she surveyed the trees as well, the cawing an ear-splitting din around them.

"Stop, will you?" he yelled as she slowed. *Just for a minute, woman.* He thought crossly. If only to make his case. Maybe getting her into bed was too far a reach for one day's work, but if he could get her home, that would be enough.

As their eyes met, and he felt that now-familiar kick in the gut he felt at the sight of her, a look of horror crossed her face. That foreign expression drew out the moment, even as a feeling of utter dread crawled up his spine. A tingling blackness crept over him, as if the dark hands of death gripped his shoulders, ready to pull him down underground. In the time it took for Hunter to open her mouth and scream a warning, Tyr's feet were swept from underneath him, the city around him splintered apart, and darkness stretched out into infinity.

11

Hunter stood in the now-silent street. It was empty. The birds, *if they had even been birds*, were gone. She didn't know how long it had been since Tyr vanished right before her eyes, in a swirl of dark malevolence she could still feel as if it were a poison eating away at her insides, but panic bloomed at his absence.

I took him away. To show you what you had to lose.

The words echoed around her head, the Orobus's taunting tone both graveyard cold and birthday happy. A cat with a new toy. Hunter shuddered. She'd hoped for a level playing field this time around. She'd counted on gaining some advantage, since they had prior warning of his approach. She, like Tyr, had been wrong on both counts. "All right, you bastard. Where are you? What do you want from me?"

Come to the circle and meet. Face to pretty face. We trade.

She had no idea where this circle was, only that it was located close to the Tower. She'd find it though, and then? This *thing* would be sorry. "I'll be there. Give me an hour."

Half as much. I know how fast you are.

Hunter cast about the city for Tyr and found nothing. But the creature was right about one thing. She *was* fast. Tightening her pack, she began to race along the lake, heading straight into downtown.

TWENTY MINUTES later and the dolmens loomed huge overhead.

Her family's circle had been more modest, a few strategically placed standing stones with a raised, stone altar in the center. The very altar she'd snapped her neck against, in fact, the night Tyr had brought her back to life. Thankfully, there was no altar in sight, so her neck seemed safe enough at the moment. Switching position, she evaluated the largest structure. It towered over the rest, appearing more like a hut than a doorway, with no apparent openings for anything to gain access. But one thing was for sure, the whole cursed place felt wrong.

Not that the power inside of her cared.

The moment she'd looked in this direction, the elemental darkness within her began to claw. To twist. To fight its way out of her. As if it knew exactly where she was headed. Which meant she was nearly exhausted with the effort to contain it. Which had been the Orobus's plan all along, she realized.

Why fight the enemy when you could have them fight themselves?

She had to give the creature props. This was a good tactic and one she'd employed herself, many times before.

Plus, she'd been twisted into knots since the second Tyr disappeared. Which was ridiculous. Tyr was a big boy. A warrior. The *God of War*, for heaven's sake. Why she was wasting her time worrying about him was beyond her. The man could take care of himself.

Scanning the blind spots, she wondered aloud, "Where are you?"

She'd picked the high ground for this approach, skirting huge chunks of white rubble. On the other side of the circle, the water stretched out, evenly blue under a brilliant sky. Senses on alert, she expected at least a faint tingling from the creature's proximity, but felt...nothing. If she hadn't known better, she would have sworn she was the only living thing here, but she wasn't. She couldn't be. *This* was where he had wanted her.

Which meant the Orobus was here too.

A quick scan turned up no sign of Tyr, along with a quick flash of anger, or possibly sheer aggravation. How had the man managed to get himself snatched off the street in broad daylight? They weren't *complete* amateurs, after all. She even flirted with the possibility that he'd done it on purpose, for the sheer sake *of* irritating her.

The dolmens cast long shadows across the pit, curving upward, toward the edges, toward her position. Noting the location of those shadows and realizing her advantage, Hunter settled her back against a chunk of rubble. "Should have done your homework. Now let's see how you fare against me."

Hunter turned into shadow herself, flitting from stone to stone, working her way down, never letting so much as a sliver of sun touch her. This trick of hers had cost many a man his life, becoming the darkness. Even though she doubted her illusions would work on this creature, it might get her close.

Close enough to free Tyr. Or to kill the creature.

With a burst of speed, she shot down the incline with a shower of gravel, surprised to reach the bottom unscathed. Bracing her hand against the nearest stone, it stirred beneath her palm, as if it were awakening. Or felt the faintest recognition of kinship.

This place was filled with primeval power. The kind from which she'd been reborn.

And it seemed the stones knew it as inside the formation a faint light bloomed, as if a portal were opening, a hazy, lazily spinning doorway growing brighter as the city behind her darkened.

There was a lingering, evil silence within these stones, a corruption to them, as if the blood of the innocents soaked them. Lives had been stolen inside this circle. And would be again.

The sun began to set, slanting the long shadows of the city across the ground at her feet, their shadows intermingling with the shadows cast by the dolmens, until a grid formed, and Hunter realized she stood at the center of a shadowy net. The back of her neck prickling, Hunter spun, finding nothing but dying sunlight and dust hanging like spendthrift in the air. "Where are you?"

Gotcha.

The voice crept out of the shadows. Along with a vague, shifting shape that might have been the creature and was certainly the most malevolent thing she'd ever sensed. In answer, the power trapped inside her clawed for escape.

"Oh I don't know about that." Hunter's words held the lazy, confident cadence that comes when you are certain you have the upper hand.

She had to admit, this was the perfect opportunity. Her and the creature, alone together in the bowl of darkness, her power practically begging to be unleashed. All she had to do was turn herself loose and smoke his ass. Deed done. And once she located Tyr afterwards, he would kill her. As promised. If there was one thing she could count on, it was for Tyr to keep his word.

"It looks like a perfect evening to me." Even with Grim seeping out of the darkness like a swarm of black spiders, she was enjoying a certain amount of brashness in her current situation. "You burned my city." Rage pushed her a step forward. "You tore down my home." Arrogance, yet another. "And then, you bastard, you made a huge mistake."

I never make mistakes, girl. I make moves, and I always win.

She should have heard the laughter that outlined his every word. Should have but was too wrapped up in her own hubris to notice. In a massive reversal of fortune, the kind that leaves you speechless, the long shadows morphed into a physical, tangible web of magic, closing in around her and scooping her up with the Grim, like so many mackerel in a net. The sky disappeared as she fought against the weight of the monsters, their slick, writhing bodies as they were all crushed together, tighter and tighter.

As a final middle finger salute, the shadows obscuring the Orobus retreated, revealing Tyr, broken and bloodied, lying at the creature's feet.

Shit. If she unleashed her power right now, the blast would eradicate everything in the vicinity. Including Tyr. If she didn't, the creature would eradicate everything. Including Tyr.

In her history of spectacular failings, this debacle was in her top three. As Grim after Grim piled on top of her, crushing the air out of her lungs, her vision faded, and Hunter amended that estimation.

No, definitely in the top two.

"Come and get me, you bastard." Hunter panted as claws scrambled over her, not digging in too deeply. At the moment, she was simply another impediment for them to avoid, not an enemy for them to destroy. As long as they were all in the same boat, she'd remain relatively safe from their gnashing jaws. "I know you want to." At some point, the Orobus would *have* to approach. Predator to prey, he would come closer to claim what he wanted.

She'd be ready when the time came.

Covered in the demons, she gagged on the stench of rotting things, blood and gore, the sickly sweetness repelling. But covered in them, she was also hidden, and used the opportunity to worm her way to the edge of the shadow-net, work her arm through an opening. Ever so slowly, Hunter inched her way toward freedom. There was a certain sick fascination in scrambling over creatures bred to kill you, while they shielded your escape from the monster poised to destroy you. But paradoxes aside, the smallest sense of hope ignited when she dug her nails into stone and pulled herself free of the net of twisting, flailing bodies.

There would be a matter of seconds—optimistically, moments—before the Orobus realized she was free. Skirting the writhing creatures, she lunged toward Tyr. Momentum drove her straight into him, bowling them into a tight knot, and entangled, they tumbled toward the open dolmen and stopped just before the light-filled doorway. Hunter leaned him carefully against the back of the dolmen.

It's just like you to think you have a chance. The creature's deep voice echoed against the stone, amplified by the basin. *When there is nowhere to go.*

"*You* are a walking cliché," Hunter muttered, tipping Tyr's head up, worried. For a god, he was bleeding. A lot. Too much, she realized. "And you, Tyr... What's happened to you?" A flicker of pain crossed his blood-slicked face, and he winced when she shifted him upward. "I need to look at your back."

When she did, her heart almost stopped. "How did he do this to you?" She groaned, easing him back, brushing hair sticky with blood from his forehead. "And why aren't you healing?"

"Can't." The word was soft and indistinct, but it paralyzed her.

"Yes, yes you can. You *have* to. Heal yourself. You're a god. *Do it.* I need you, Tyr. I need you to get up and help me get you out of here."

He cannot, girl. I'm draining away his power. Sucking it from him, like marrow from a bone. The creature's taunting, sing-song words wound around the stones. As if the creature saw her disbelieving face, he laughed before adding, *I speak the truth. You don't believe me? Ask him yourself. If he can answer. He has a few moments left.*

Hunter gripped the lapels of Tyr's coat. "Tell me the bastard's lying. Heal yourself, damn it, and help me out." Tyr attempted a wan smile.

"Sorry to disappoint, but it's the truth." Tyr's voice grew faint. "Don't know how, but I think I'm dying."

The Orobus expanded until his darkness swallowed up the world, the sky above, his words hanging on the air. *Before he expires, I want you to know this.* The space around Hunter vibrated with the thing's vile satisfaction. *The God of War is only be the first to fall. And I have you to thank for it.*

Tyr was fading away right in front of her, blood pouring out of so many places, his face grayed away to white. As seconds stretched out impossibly to moments, Hunter searched for a way out. A loophole, an opening, a last chance. Anything to grasp at, to save them. And found nothing.

For just a second, she let herself experience it.

The frustration that she'd been beaten.

And then it passed, because she knew that another second would doom them both.

And so, with her arm across his throat, and her eyes locked on the Orobus, Hunter Wallace braced her feet on the ground and yanked Tyr backward through the spinning opening and into some other world.

12

Hunter expected *something* on the other side.

But not this.

She spun on her heel, instincts prickling. She'd dropped them into the middle of utter desolation. Unless the Orobus materialized out of thin air behind them, they were alone. Yet, she'd expected a doorway, a small dolmen on this side. *Something* to mark where they'd come through.

Nothing at all.

When Tyr moaned at her feet, she crouched down and lay a soothing hand on his shoulder.

Trouble was something she was used to. But this was madness.

As much as she hated to do it, she needed answers, so she gave Tyr a gentle shake. "Tyr, wake up. Can you please open your eyes for me?" When he only moaned, she shook him again, harder this time. When his eyes opened, they were foggy with pain. "Hey." She tried to smile. "There you are. I need you, Tyr. I really need you."

"Sure, babe." He offered her a weak smile. "Whatcha need?" He struggled up onto one elbow, then collapsed, never taking his eyes off her. The smell of death hung on him, as panic began its spiraling climb within her. "Hunter?" His words were slurred. "You...okay?"

She realized her face was wet and scrubbed furiously at her cheeks. "Can you tell me where we are?" Seeing Tyr like this, broken and battered, made her feel...scared. And she hadn't been scared in as long as she could remember.

"I'm not sure." He pushed himself up, and the effort cost him. "If I didn't know better..." The look he gave her was accusing. *What did you do, Hunter?*

"What I had to," she said flatly. "I had to get us away from him, and I didn't know what else to do, so I pulled us both through an open doorway. This is where we ended up." She indicated their surroundings. "It's just...I have no idea which world we're on. And I have a bad feeling..."

"We're on Svartlheim." Tyr began shaking. "This is bad, Hunter."

"I know. I know, Tyr," she said, chewing her lip. "I didn't have a choice. The Orobus had us trapped, he was draining your magic, and there wasn't anywhere to go. Except through." She glanced around. "At least we're alone. So far." Her gaze lifted, then settled on the horizon, where mountains rose from the edge of the flat plain. "Maybe if we can get to the mountains, maybe then..."

Tyr pushed up, then fell, his body crumbling as Hunter caught him by the arm, easing him back down. "You're right, Hunter." Tyr's voice turned gentle, wheedling, "Promise me? Get to the mountains. Understand?" She nodded in agreement, her gaze swinging between the far-off mountains and the long, open plain stretching between them. "Okay, good." Relief flooded his voice as he gazed up at her. A light, cold rain started to fall as he mumbled, his voice weak as he added, "Stick to the eastern face... Weather's coming from the west. You've gotta stay dry." Her heart stilled. "Stay alive longer that way. Nod if you understand."

His expression was so tranquil. Determined, yet peaceful. A masterpiece of stubbornness, which had always been his main problem. "Are you even listening? You *have* to reach...mountains by nightfall. Don't stop... Keep going...till you make it."

As the implications of his command hit her, she realized the truth.

She loved him.

This was the moment she'd dreaded. The moment she'd lived for. The one she'd wanted for so long. The mighty god, completely at her mercy. And when Tyr moaned and slumped over, unconscious, she finally understood what connected them.

It wasn't hate and revenge. It never had been.

It was something far more binding.

As the drizzle turned into a solid downpour, she grasped Tyr's coat with both hands and pulled him across the rocky ground until she located a dry spot under a cantilevered, half-buried rock. Pushing him underneath it, she wrapped herself around him, set her back to the wind and rain, and prayed to whatever gods were listening to throw her a bone.

TYR WOKE UP, hurting like a bitch, but warmer than he'd been in a long, long time. Confused for a minute, he wondered why his face was smashed into a hard wall, and why it was so dark. The atmosphere felt heavy and stank of brimstone and something even more rotten. He tried to move. Gods, he hurt. In ways he hadn't been aware it was possible to ache. The smell of blood was overwhelming, and his face felt stiff, his eyes practically glued shut. But to his back? Whatever *that* was felt warm, *and* soft *and* heavenly. Shifting, he pushed against the softness and froze when it started mumbling.

"Tyr, stop moving around." That was Hunter's voice. That meant Hunter's body was pressed against his. All those aches and pains disappeared as every nerve ending woke up in a tingling firestorm. Where the hell was he? A jumble of fuzzy, disjointed images flashed through his mind as the acrid smell of brimstone fully penetrated his senses. As he shot up and his head made contact with the rock overhead, he cursed. "*Fuck.*"

"I *told* you to stop moving around." There was an early morning huskiness to Hunter's voice, a rough-around-the-edges growl that shivered straight through him. "You'll open up the gashes on your back. They've just finally closed."

Carefully he rolled over, lingering on her face for a moment before taking in the broken landscape that stretched out behind them. "How did I get up here?"

"I dragged you up here. Sorry." She offered an apologetic smile. "I know it probably hurt, but it was raining, and..." She gave a little shrug. "This was better than nothing." In slow motion, her hand reached out and pushed his hair over to the side, stroking the side of his face along the way. He closed his eyes. Her touch... After all these years, it felt like a benediction.

"How did we get here, Hunter?" Because there was no doubt about where they were. His last, clear memory, the one that was as sharp as glass, was standing in that street, watching her face tighten in horror. After that, things must have gone very, very badly. "Do you know where we are?"

"You said Svartlheim last night, but I was hoping that maybe..." Her eyes were apologetic. "I didn't have a choice, Tyr."

"I know, love." What really surprised him was that the rock-strewn field around them wasn't already swarming with Dark Elves and whatever else the Orobus had decided to breed on this godforsaken planet. Just because they were safe now, didn't mean they'd be safe for long. They had to find high ground. "Can you make it to those mountains?"

Hunter nodded. "I could have made it last night. I'm not leaving you. We're going together."

When he set his jaw, she simply smiled and stroked his face again. "We go together. Or not at all." She circled behind him and he felt gentle, capable hands running over his back. "This is good, you're getting your strength back. You've healed up some, these may be closed enough for some light travel. And I have a bit of food."

"Water?"

Her eyes slid away from his and over to her small black pack. She tugged it open and pulled out two flimsy plastic bottles.

"Not enough. A bottle and a half. But maybe if we ration it..." She sighed as she offered him one bottle and he took a tentative sip.

Tyr looked to the mountains again. He'd only been here once before, and even the Underworld hadn't left him with such a bad taste in his mouth. "The water may be clean enough in the higher elevations for us to safely drink." *If they were lucky.*

She screwed the cap on the bottle and shot him a carefree, easy smile. "Then we'd best get moving, right?"

Resistance had always been Hunter Wallace's trademark, and as she shouldered the pack, Tyr pondered the difference. There was a kind of calm composure to her today, a lovely sort of peace that he'd never seen before. As if all the thorns had been plucked away. He wasn't sure he was comfortable with the sudden change. "We should be able to make the foothills by dark. We'll have better luck finding shelter there. Did you sleep at all last night?"

"I slept just fine, Tyr. Why do you ask?"

The bright, clear smile she threw him was also something he'd never seen before.

Not ever.

13

"It's been two days."

"Yeah, I can count, asshole. As well as you. What do you propose we do?" Mir drummed his fingers on the table, worry coursing an irrational, incessant beat through his chest as he watched Thor wear a groove into the floor. Reaching up a hand, Mir attempted to massage the anxiety away. No such luck.

"First Odin, now Tyr."

"Odin's on a bender. There's a big difference." Thor's pacing stopped.

"Again, not a news flash. What do you propose we do about it?" Mir glowered darkly at the lot of them. Just like Odin or Tyr would have. If they'd actually been here. Fuckers.

"We *could* actually go look for them." Fenrir stalked into the room. "You know, search and rescue shit? It *has* been two days."

"Again, not a fucking news flash."

"Look, we know he left and went looking for Hunter. Might have even found her, according to Balder. Then nada."

Mir joined Thor in the pacing. Maybe movement would help. "You covered the entire area south of the highway all the way down to the basin quadrant?" He stopped. "You sure?"

Thor gave him a look that clearly said *he was fucking sure.* "Of course we did. Three times. No sign of either of them. I'm telling you, Mir, it's like they vanished off the face of the Earth."

Two days. And no sign of the Orobus, either. Nor Hel and her Grim. No attack, no invasion. But Mir knew the bastard was here somewhere. *He had to be.* And if Tyr was missing, that meant one of two things. He was either dead or taken prisoner. If he was a prisoner, he could be anywhere, but... "Fenrir, you're going to have to do something for me."

When Celine came in a few moments later, Fen gripped her arm, his face set in what could only be called rage. "She's here, but she's not going to..."

Celine laid a gentle hand on his arm before turning to Mir and the others. "Fen's just worried, is all. And I want to help. What can I do, Mir?" At Fen's low, rumbling growl, she shot her mate a stern look. "We *do* want to help, don't we?"

Fen gave her a curt, reluctant snarl. She plunked her hands on her hips and rolled her eyes. "Good. It's settled. I'm helping, you're not happy about it. I get it. Let's move on."

Mir debated, his gaze shifting from the anger contorting Fen's face to the determination setting Celine's. "Okay, here's the thing. It's like Tyr disappeared, and we can't find any sign of him. So that either means—"

"He's dead." Celine's eyes were depthless.

"Or he's been taken," Mir added, while Thor and Freyr settled back along the wall, well out of Fenrir's path.

"All right, then." Celine sat at the table while Fen filled in the entire space behind her. "What's your plan? How do you want me to find him?"

"I need you to go into the Dreaming." At Fen's loud menacing growl, he held out both hands. "*Only* to see if Tyr's there. We've got to confirm he's still alive. If he is, then we'll figure out how to locate him and bring him home." Mir hoped like hell *that* was true, but he couldn't help the drop in his voice as he added, "If he's not, well, let's just say we'll need to change our focus."

"I'll find him, Mir." She offered up a sad smile. "You do realize, he'll be there whether he's alive or dead. So I'll find him no matter what."

Mir pulled out the chair and sat next to her. "There's something else. We haven't seen Hunter since she left. Tyr went out looking for her and may have found her. There's a chance—"

"They're together?" Celine clapped her hands together in excitement. "That's great, Mir. And actually, that'll make this easier. Since we've connected before in the Dreaming," she explained. "I know for sure I can locate Hunter, just let me try."

Mir hoped so. "Celine, we don't have a lot of time. The Orobus is here in the city." The hammer was about to fall, he could just feel it. Gods, he wished Odin and Tyr were here. His team was being whittled away, one at a time, and their loss left him vulnerable, like the too-brittle point of a knife.

Sucking in a deep breath, Mir held Fen's uncompromising stare before he uttered his next question. "I've gotta ask, Celine. Have you felt him? Is he close?" As the atmosphere of the room chilled down, Mir watched her eyes turn a guarded, flat gray.

Her distressed expression was a dead giveaway, but Mir gave her moment to answer. "I've felt...something. And I was almost sure it was him."

Fen's hands crept down over her shoulders, gripping tight.

"But yes, you're probably right. It *must* be him, even though there's no sign of him yet. Fen said the whole army was supposed to arrive yesterday."

Fen's grip on her shoulders loosened as he smoothed his hands down her arms.

"But I've got to be honest, Mir. There's a problem with me helping you," Celine whispered, her eyes going wide.

"I know. We have a shit ton of problems. What I have to find out is how close he is. Can you tell me that?" Mir leaned in and took her hand as Fen growled a low warning. "Can you feel him?"

She shuddered.

"Anything, Celine. I'll take anything right about now. Even your best guess."

After a moment, during which her hand trembled in his, Celine murmured, "He's way out over the lake. But he feels different to me this time. If I didn't know any better, I'd say..." Her voice wavered. "That he's angry."

"How can you tell?"

"Because I can't seem to pin him down at all. He's spread out. It's almost like he's... I dunno, *looking around* for something. But there's so much damn emotion masking his intentions, I just can't get a clear feel for what he's up to." She shook her head. "Rage and searching, that's all I got. At least he's not attacking us, right?"

"That's right." Fen kissed the top of the head. "And now you go to bed for a while, angel." The look he threw Mir's way said she'd be taking the damn nap, no matter how little time they had left. Mir scanned her face, noticing she did look unusually tired.

"Thanks sweetheart, you know I wouldn't have asked if I had any other options."

"I know that." Celine squeezed his arm. "And so does Fen. It's just..." The smile spread over her face. "I'm not sure how much longer I can help you with this super clandestine spy stuff, Mir. Which is *the problem* I was talking about." She beamed her sunny smile up to the wolf before turning it on the rest of them. "We might as well tell him, Fen, everyone will know soon enough, anyhow.

"So...how do you feel about being an uncle, Mir?"

Mir closed his eyes, sweat blooming on his face. He wondered if the universe was in on some kind of cosmic joke where he was the punch line.

A baby? How was he supposed to keep a baby safe, when he couldn't even keep the rest of them alive?

As Thor whooped about finding scotch and cigars, and Freyr swung Celine off her feet in a giant hug, Mir felt quiet desperation unfurl. The kind when you know there's no hope, but the stakes just got impossibly higher. But while a sad, bittersweet joy shot through him, Fen waited—his eyes hopeful and eager.

So instead of putting all of that into words, Mir simply clapped his hand on Fen's shoulder and told him exactly what he needed to hear.

"Hell yeah, we'd all love to be uncles."

14

Trudging toward the looming mountains, Tyr had to admit there was a sort of regal beauty to this place. Punctuated by sharp craggy peaks, they'd almost reached the foothills rising from the edge of the bleak, open plain that stretched out behind them.

At least it would be a beautiful place to die.

Tyr stumbled as they made their way over the windswept rubble. Night would be here soon, and he didn't want to think what the dark brought with it. "Another twenty minutes, Hunter, then we find a place to hole up." Beyond words, she simply nodded, focused on the long crack along the towering stone wall above them. The goal for the last few hours had been to reach that dark crevice.

Twenty minutes later, as he hooked his fingers around the edges of a rock to pull himself up another few feet, he wondered if they'd make it through this night. They had to. They simply had to.

"Almost there, Hunter." Having her with him was the only thing that kept him moving. Call it pride, or simple stubbornness, he'd be godsdamned if he'd leave her alone out here.

"Oh, Tyr." That hint of pity in her voice was all it took for the final burst of adrenaline that pushed him to the top. Fuck if he'd let her feel sorry for him. Fuck if he'd let her think he couldn't climb to the top of this little fucking hill.

He felt like a bleached bone carcass left too long in the sun by the time he heaved his broken body up and over the ledge, but by the gods, he'd made it. Hearing her scrambling up the rocks behind him, he worked to keep his breathing effortless, even while he wanted to force oxygen in and out of his lungs like a bellows.

Hunter flung herself alongside him in the dirt. When her arm crept over his chest, and she nestled into his side, he felt a longing that he thought exhaustion would have wiped out. Damn, even under all the dirt and sweat and blood, she still did it for him.

"Hunter, we have to get ourselves under cover, we're too exposed." Tyr picked up her hand, and it was limp as a fish. She was out. Groaning, he clambered upright. Right now they were sitting ducks. Otherwise known as dead.

Searching the darkness of the shallow cave, there was a chance something lurked in the depths, but since none of his senses screamed at him to run, and with night falling fast, options were limited. Besides, he was still being driven by this overwhelming need to see her safe. Stooping, he gathered her in his arms and stumbled into the darkness.

Tyr kept his tree stumps of legs moving until he found the back of the crevasse. It was all he could do to put his back against the rock and slide down, arms still wrapped around Hunter. Warm against him, he felt more connected to her than ever, bound together in complete darkness. And when she curled around him, relaxed against him in a way he'd only imagined, his eyes slipped closed.

He woke to the thinnest sliver of light. Well, that and the hunger pains threatening to gnaw a hole inside of him. He didn't move a muscle, though. He still had Hunter in his arms, and there was no way he would squander a second of this. Against her softness, even his pain faded away as he took his time, searching every detail of the peaceful face nestled on his chest.

But as much as he hated to wake her, they had serious problems. Neither of them were going to last much longer without food and water. Tyr ran his fingers down the side of her face, despising the grime and sweat that clung to her skin. The contact sent shocks of electricity up through his body, and he shifted closer, hypnotized as her eyes flickered open, and those gold-flecked orbs darkened when she focused on him. "Good morning." Tyr smiled, fully expecting her to push away, and was shocked when she simply leaned farther into his touch.

"Morning, Tyr." Gods, he loved that dusky, early-morning undercurrent to her voice; it was sexy and rough and made him hard as hell. And since the curve of her ass was currently pressing down on him when his cock jumped, her smile instantly shifted from sweet to knowing. Shit. Moving out from under her, he stood and quickly backed away.

"You don't have to leave, Tyr. I kind of liked having you underneath me." Her face looked innocent as hell, but those words, coupled with that seductive voice.... Hands unfurling, Tyr stopped himself, the beast within him hammering to be unleashed. Yeah, he stopped himself cold. Before he took her right there. In the dirt, in a cave, on the darkest world of them all.

Hell to the no.

Hunter was a *princess*. A chieftain's daughter. She deserved a castle. A throne. A whole fucking kingdom. And who was he? Definitely not the God of anything, anymore. A no-name nobody. And as injured as he was? A liability, to boot.

Tyr cleared his throat, his chest heaving, turning so he didn't have to face her. "Now that you're awake, we have problems. For one, we need food. And water. I'll take a look outside." He couldn't bear to turn around but felt her gaze boring into him. When she finally did speak, she sounded like she was fighting for composure.

"I've got three protein bars. That's one apiece. And one for us to split, later." Her voice turned apologetic. "And only half a bottle of water left." That was when he heard the tears in her voice. "Oh God. I'm so sorry, Tyr. There isn't enough. I should have..."

"Don't apologize. It won't do any good, anyway." Just before he stepped out, he added gruffly, "You've got nothing to be sorry for, trust me."

The day, such that it was, dawned a slate gray. It was raining in long, slanting torrents, staining everything a shiny blackish-blue. Thank the gods. They needed this water or they wouldn't survive the day, protein bars or no. Tyr gathered a handful, touched his tongue to it. It was brackish, and tasted like the depths of hell, but it was potable. "Hunter, come out here, we've got water." The flat, closed look on her face as she ducked out into the rain cut his heart, but the tears that trembled her lips destroyed him. Telling himself this was for the best, he pulled her alongside him and kept his voice flat and business-like. "Drink as much as you can right now, then fill up the bottles until they're full. I'm not sure how long this will last. We need to drink while we can, and then we'll eat."

She silently obeyed, and after a couple hesitant sips, turned her face upwards into the rain, letting it mix with the tears spilling down her face as he tried to think about what came next.

THE RAIN on her face was freezing, but at least Tyr couldn't see her crying. She'd nearly made a total fool of herself, and the one, single time she'd picked to let her guard down had backfired. And it hurt. It more than hurt. The rejection confused her, and she didn't know what to do next. She didn't understand it. She'd *felt* his desire, knew this thing between them was real. Yet he'd backed away from her like she had the plague.

She scooped more of the sulpher-like water into her mouth, choking the bitter stuff down. If she wanted to survive, *this* was what was necessary. As was food. As was movement. She had to shove all of this unnecessary emotional baggage aside. This was why she'd always stayed away from people. They only became liabilities, she thought crossly.

She felt him beside her, she felt him *everywhere*, she realized, growing crosser and crosser by the minute. Stalking back into the cave, she took the two thin bars out of the pack. Silently, she handed one to Tyr before opening her own, forcing herself to chew slowly.

"We're in trouble here, Hunter."

Yes, she was well aware of that. In so many ways.

"This world has no food, and lots of Dark Elves. I was here once, long ago, and I remember there *is* a doorway up in the mountains. But to get there..." Tyr shook his head, licking his fingers as if savoring those last, final calories. "We'd have to travel a hundred miles. Perhaps hundreds of miles. I don't even know where we are. I don't know where we came through. I don't know where to go." Suddenly everything made sense. Because beneath those words, she heard so much more.

I don't know how to get us back home.

I don't know how to save you.

"And that's okay." Strangely enough, despite their dire situation, relief flooded through her. She suddenly felt as if everything she'd ever done had led her to this world, to this moment, to this man. And no matter what happened next, Hunter realized she didn't want to be anywhere else.

"You didn't bring us here. I did. I made the decision, impulsive and stupid as it was. If this is anyone's fault, then that person would be me." She felt him move closer and closed her eyes, praying for just a touch. "So don't blame yourself. Blame me." A bitter smile crossed her face. "You've always said I was a walking disaster."

"It's not like you weren't warned."

The rain slowed, and when his arms finally did close around her, pulling her into him, every place they touched, warmth flowed back in.

"Shit, Hunter, none of this is your fault." His lips pressed against her ear, causing little sparks of electricity to travel along her spine. "You saved my life with your stupid stunt."

"Well. At least we can agree on one thing, I suppose."

But leaning back into him, feeling that muscular body against hers, the one she'd thought of for so damn long, she figured if she was going to be stuck here, in the middle of nowhere, Tyr was definitely the person she'd have picked to spend her last few days with.

They stiffened at the same time as movement across the valley caught their eye. Something had caught their scent.

More than a single something, as the shadows merged, then formed a solid line, the point of it heading straight for them.

15

———————

"Uhhh, Mir, we got a shit show down here."

Mir stalked down the hallway, heading for the Throne Room as he listened to Thor's somewhat sketchy report. "Just tell me what you're seeing."

"Um, okay." Thor's voice issued thinly from the little black com unit. "So...if a thunderstorm was on the ground, that's sorta what this looks like. Plus, if you covered it all in oil and added in a bunch of tornadoes. Oh, and detonated a nuclear bomb in the center."

Over the static of the com, Thor added, "And we've got tons of patrols down here, looks like Dark Elves skulking around. A group of about ten just passed right by me. Fuck, they stink so bad..."

"Stick to the report, you're breaking up."

"Yup, okay. The Orobus has moved in off the lake and taken up position over the stone circle." There was a pause, the crackle of wind, and then, "I've got a couple hundred elves, maybe two hundred Grim on-site. And the Orobus is currently the size of three football fields."

"Get your ass back here, Thor. Right now."

"Roger that shit."

CELINE RUBBED HER BELLY. She'd be showing in a few weeks, but for now, all she felt was tired. And a little sick. And a little hungry, she thought, thinking longingly of ice cream and chocolate. Or strawberries and peanut butter. She wasn't entirely sure.

Add to that, this weird mix of nervous anticipation and fear. She was a mess.

"You ready?"

Mir had a walkie-talkie in his hand, faint staticky distortion still trickling out of it. At her questioning glance, he quickly flicked the button off before leading her toward the Throne Room. Fen was waiting for them, bristling with hostility. Actually showed a hint of fang when he spotted Mir at her side.

But he loved her, so he'd go along with this crazy plan.

She hoped.

Even though she still didn't understand what she was doing here. Even if she *could* locate Tyr and Hunter in the Dreaming, there was no way to bring them home. So knowing where they were did no good.

Once the huge doors closed behind them, Mir led the way over to an ornately carved arch between two columns, set in a shadowed alcove of the enormous room. "So when the Tower was being built, Odin created this archway as a portal. He also warded this room, so only he can activate the doorway. He sometimes used this to travel between worlds. And to bring others here."

Beside him, Sydney gave Celine an encouraging nod as she picked up the story, "Hel, for instance. But since it's warded, it only works for Odin because it's coded for his specific brand of magic. Good news is, we've figured out how to manipulate Odin's wards. Mir can negate them for a short period of time, and once you find Tyr and Hunter in the Dreaming, we can use my magic to bring all of you back."

Celine felt the faintest ray of hope that the plan *might* work.

"And if Odin gets wind of this?"

"Balder's keeping an eye on him at the moment, so we're good," Mir muttered. "As long as the scotch holds out, we've got the room to ourselves."

Fen spread blankets on the floor in front of the archway and fluffed up a pillow, before taking her hand and leading her over. "You're going to lie down, and you're going to relax. But at the first sign...*any* sign at all of the God of Chaos, or any kind of trouble, I'm pulling you out of there. Understand?"

She rose up to her tiptoes to kiss his cheek. "I got this, Fen. I'm getting them out of there." Her smile turned hard as she pointed to Mir. "But it's up to *you* to get us home safely, hear me?"

"Great. No pressure."

She lay down, closed her eyes, and went in to get her friends.

As always, the Dreaming was winding labyrinth, a world devoid of landmarks. But none of that mattered. Celine didn't need landmarks. She only needed... "Ahh, there you are." Who needed landmarks when you had love to follow?

Tyr and Hunter were twined together with their backs against a wall, both very much alive. All good.

Celine pushed farther into the physical realm, finally stepping through a thick, ghostly veil onto a rocky ledge overtop a sea of jagged rocks. Somewhere ahead of her, hidden in the darkness, she sensed them. Her feet dragging slightly on the uneven, rocky floor, she crept farther into the low, narrow cave, where the air smelled foul and the very nature of the place seemed saturated with evil. All bad.

They looked fast asleep, and she would have sworn they were, until Tyr's eyes cracked open to slits. She noticed the knife in his hand, just before Hunter's head swiveled, and she snapped,

"What in the holy hell are you doing here, Celine?"

TEN MINUTES LATER, Celine was explaining Mir's crazy plan.

The problem was, neither of them were buying it.

"You *cannot* be here. You *have* to go back, Celine." Hunter was frantic, on the verge of hysteria.

Tyr doubled down on that order. "You *are* going back. This is no place for you."

When Celine shook her head, Hunter grasped her hands. "You *know* you can't be here." She didn't break their stare. "You know it's not just you at risk, Celine. Don't be stupid. Go home. We're done for and we've made our peace with that."

Celine grinned. "Nonsense. Mir and Syd figured out how to bring both of you home." The grin faded slightly. "There's just one catch. You'll need to fall asleep."

"This is crazy, Celine. You know how things went wrong last time." Not that Hunter was wrong. The Orobus showing up right now *was* the last thing they all needed. But she had to at least try. Besides, she was here. That was half the battle, right?

"We can make it work. Let *me* do this, Hunter. Tyr, tell her to quit arguing and wasting time." Celine looked over at the dark haired god. "We've done stuff like this before."

Tyr growled. "Nothing remotely like this, Celine. You've got to get the hell out of here. And you don't have much time." He hobbled to the cave opening, scanning the rocky incline that led to their lair and limped slowly back. "They're coming and now I've lost sight of them. No telling how close they are."

Hunter explained quickly as Celine's heart began to pound. "Look, we're stuck here, Celine. But you're not. Get home while you still can. Tyr's sure there's a wave of Dark Elves coming. More than we can fight off. So go back the way you came…"

Celine shook her head vehemently. "Even more reason to try this. I'm not leaving you two."

"Oh yes you are." With a shove, Hunter pushed her backwards through the slight distortion shimmering in the air and Celine felt the cool wash of the portal as she passed through. But she stayed on the rocky ledge in the cave.

Celine put her hands on her hips. "I already told you, I'm not going back alone." Hunter looked helplessly to Tyr for help.

"Celine, honey..." Tyr limped over. "C'mon, you know you've got to get home. There's nothing you can do for us, we're toast. Head home, sweetheart. We'll hold out as long as we can."

"Look, I think we can hold out until tomorrow. We've got the high ground," Hunter lied. "Go back to the Tower and get reinforcements. We'll be waiting."

"Stop stalling, Hunter. This isn't the time to be stubborn. How long do we have, Tyr?"

"Don't know." He'd positioned himself at the opening, legs spread, his big body a flesh and blood barrier between them and whatever was coming. "I can't hear them, but they're stealthy. In the darkness I can't gauge the distance, so who the hell knows?" Tyr shook his head, the sudden movement forcing him to brace a hand against the wall.

Celine grit her teeth at their stubbornness. "Just trust me, damn it. All I need the two of you to do is asleep. It's not that hard, just hang onto me and fall asleep. And then we'll all go back together."

"How the hell are you supposed to do that?"

"Syd and Mir figured out how to use the portal in Odin's Throne Room," Celine explained. "Or, at least, they figured out how to fix Odin's magic so they could use the portal. Or something like that, I'm not good with the magicky part of this plan. But I do know how to pull you out of this realm and into the real one. If only you just..."

"Yeah, I heard you. Fall asleep." Tyr murmured, his gaze fixed on the darkness outside. The vaguest sound of scuffling carried up to them on the wind.

"Time for debate is over. Lay down...here." Celine indicated a place in the dirt. "And Hunter, lay next to him...here."

Hunter laid down and gave Tyr a look that dared him to disobey. He gimped over and lowered himself painfully to the ground, awkwardly laid himself next to Hunter.

"Good. Now...close your eyes. You both have to relax." Hunter's hand crept into Tyr's, his larger one enfolding hers as Celine told them, "I need you both to relax. Really try to relax." Her voice hitched slightly as the sound of falling stone echoed through the cave. "That's good. Relax. You're so tired. So tired and you *have* to sleep. Let your-self go to sleep."

To her surprise, Celine watched sleep take hold of them, quicker than she'd thought it would, which was good. Just as Tyr's eyes shut, feet thudded on stone outside, and she knew time had run out. Wrap-ping her fingers firmly in theirs, and squeezing her eyes closed, she drew a couple deep, calming breaths.

"Fen, you'd better be on it, my love, or we are in deep shit."

Celine forced herself into the Dreaming. When the first, cold tendrils of the place wrapped their fingers around her, she breathed out a sigh of relief. Against the sounds of scratching and snarling, Celine yanked the three of them through the portal and into the Dreaming, just as sharp, black claws reached for them.

Once inside the misty realm, Celine got her bearings. While they hadn't exactly worked out the deets on how to get back, she'd been secretly hoping for some direct conduit between both realms. Keeping her hands firmly intertwined with theirs, she started along a meandering path. Dodging the countless specters and half-formed monsters, she made slow progress, feeling more and more lost with every step she took. *Who needed landmarks when you had love to follow?*

Love to follow.

Of course. All she had to do was find her mate.

Fen was a complete and utter mess. A jumble of worry and alpha male protectiveness mixed in with all that love blazing in his big, huge heart. And all she had to do was follow him home, like a giant, blinking homing beacon.

And Syd and Mir were doing their part as well, because as she drew closer to Fen, the mists began to whirl and dissipate, swirl apart. Until they formed a ghostly doorway.

Keeping her hands firmly entwined with Tyr and Hunter, she tugged them along, trying to figure out how this whole thing would work. One step took her right up to the ever-changing doorway. The next one took her straight through it.

And when she next opened her eyes, she stared up into Fen's big blue ones.

16

Waking up, the first thing Tyr noticed was Hunter's absence.

Then the lack of brimstone attacking his senses.

Mir's face swam into his line of vision, outlined against the halo of fluorescent light. Tyr blinked up at him. "I can't believe you came up with such a stupid plan." Then a small smile crossed his face. "And I can't believe it fucking worked. We were dead. Wouldn't have made it another day." The thought sobered him up fast. "Another hour, most likely."

Christ. It had been so close. For both of them. "Where's Hunter? I have to see her." He went to swing his legs over the edge of the bed, and then collapsed, surprised he hadn't passed out completely.

"Uh, yeah, you aren't going anywhere right now." Mir's face floated back into sight. "You've lost a shit-ton of blood. You were dehydrated, had a serious concussion, and three broken ribs. It nearly depleted my magic, healing your sorry ass, especially the gashes on your back. You, my friend, were a disaster." His face was serious. "Honestly, I can't believe you survived. Either of you."

"Only because of Celine. And you and Syd." Tyr winced when he thought again about how close it had been. They had given up when

Celine had stepped through that portal. He'd wrapped Hunter in his arms and been waiting for the first wave of monsters to pour through that opening. They'd resigned themselves to it. Maybe they'd even been good with it. Mostly. Sure, he'd had regrets, but still....

Tyr pushed up to his elbows. Slower. This time the room stayed where it was supposed to be. "I've got to see her." He knew he was a stubborn asshole, but there was some driving imperative inside of him. Suddenly, he couldn't recall the exact color of her eyes. He did know he wouldn't rest until he saw her.

"Look, she's in better shape than you. I'll bring her to you. She's been asking..." Mir looked out the window. "Anyhow, I'll get her. You'll be golden by tomorrow *if* you take it easy, but if you fall on your fucking face, I'm leaving you there, do you hear me?"

Tyr figured it would be bad enough that Hunter would see him helpless. Finding him flat on the floor with his ass in the air would definitely be ten times worse. "I'm staying in bed. Fear not, oh Wise One."

"Fuck you."

"Yeah. Fuck you too." *Gods, it felt good to be back.*

Tyr sat up straighter, stuffing pillows behind him, then shifted again, rearranging the blankets. What was he? A sixteen-year-old girl? They'd known each other for a thousand years. Been enemies for most of that time. So what was with this sudden case of nerves? The longer Mir was gone, the longer he waited, the more weirded out he became. He was the God of War for the gods' sake, *he* called the fucking shots. He....

Whatever skittering, random, bullshit thoughts his brain was firing off disappeared into the nether regions the second Hunter strode into the room. Tyr had spent countless hours with her. Nursed her back to health from maddened, soulless animal to woman. Had thought they'd die together on that godforsaken cliff in that godforsaken world. And still, she took his breath away. Every. Single. Fucking. Time.

Hunter paused, shut the door behind her, put her back against it, waiting for him to say something. *Do something.* Fingers curling into the blankets, Tyr hardened his heart. She was a princess. And in truth, he wasn't worthy of her. Never had been. And after the beating he'd taken, she probably thought he was worthless.

"Are you quite finished feeling sorry for yourself?"

"You don't have any idea of what I'm thinking."

"I can practically hear every word, Tyr." Her voice softened. "You are *not* weak. You would have died to keep me safe." She focused those riveting eyes upon him, and his heart stuttered.

"Truth is, I would have died too quickly and too easily to be much help to anyone, least of all you."

"If you'd only stop..."

"Damn it, Hunter..."

But she went on as if he wasn't even in the room. "Do you know what that cave reminded me of, Tyr?" Her voice took on a dreamy tone, the kind that meant she was somewhere else, far, far away. "It reminded me of the cave in the Highlands. The one where you took me so I wouldn't destroy everything I touched. Do you remember?"

Tyr held his breath. For so long, he'd believed her so out of her mind, she hadn't realized where she was nor what she'd done. *He'd banked on it*, as a matter of fact.

"It was so beautiful, do you remember? The heather was just coming out, and the sky was so blue, at least on the clear days. When the storms would blow through, it would get cold and you'd build a fire in that little pit. But you stayed with me. You never left. *That's* what these past few days reminded me of, Tyr. Of all those months we spent together in the Highlands." Her voice took on a vulnerability he'd never heard, or never allowed himself to hear, perhaps. "It's the only time I was ever at peace. Even though I was a mess. Even though I'd done...terrible things."

His breath just wouldn't come. He thought she didn't know.

He thought she didn't remember.

"But then you took me home, and you *did* leave me." Now there was a shimmer of tears in the words. "And I never saw you again. *I* was the one who finally had to come and find *you*."

"Hunter..." How could he convince her? She was better off

without him. He'd thought she'd find someone. Had watched, and waited, and wondered long enough for it to become some kind of mystery that she hadn't.

"But I haven't." She smiled at him, a blazing, piercing smile that cut right through to the heart of him. "Do you want to know why I never found anyone?" She took a step closer to his bed, and he realized he wasn't nearly as battered and bruised as he had supposed. "Because I already found you. Or you found me, on that battlefield, long ago. It doesn't really matter, in the end. I should have given myself to you that night. God knows I wanted to. But what I wanted even more was to hurt you, which led to an eternity of... Whatever *this* is that we've been doing. This eternal back and forth. This messed up dance we've done for centuries.

"It's going to end. Right now."

In her extraordinary eyes, passion blazed like a firestorm, and for once in his miserable life, Tyr didn't have anything to say. He knew if he tried to get out of bed, he'd end up on his ass. So he did the only thing he could. He opened both arms to her.

"I can't tell you why, either. I can only tell you, I won't wait another second."

"Come here, love."

Crushed against him, Hunter filled up every hard, bruised edge he had, and he didn't even care that his ribs hurt when he eased her down onto the bed. Tucked into his arms, he buried his face in her hair, and felt, for the first time in forever, the Fates smiling down upon him.

17

It turns out blood loss, broken ribs, and a concussion don't stand a chance when you've got the love of your life wrapped in your arms.

But the fuckers sure conspired against him when he went to stand up. "Whoa, slow down, Tyr." The entire room whirled as Hunter laid a firm hand against his chest and pushed him back down. Anger and resentment made his hackles rise, as he waited for the inevitable. For her to tell him he was weak and injured and fuck knows what else.

"We have all night, you know. No sense in rushing anything." Her smile beguiled as she slid out of her jacket, the weapon-laden leather landing on the floor with a solid clunk. She put a hand to her waistband, then paused, her eyes meeting his purposefully. "Unless you *want* to wait any longer?"

"Fuck no." The words slid out of him, as every drop of blood in his body rushed to his cock. But he was done talking. He was busy looking. Hunter was a lean, honed, killing machine. Every inch of her was breathtaking. His perfect match. As she shimmied out of her leather pants and kicked them to the side of the room, she stole his breath away. Given the fact he spent the majority of his life on battlefields, he'd never wanted a soft, pliable woman.

No, *this* woman was who he wanted.

Always had, always would.

She was perfect. *They* were perfect.

Sinking her teeth into her bottom lip, Hunter looked him over, her gaze gobbling up every square inch of him, every bit as greedy as he was staring at her. When her fingers curled into loose fists, and her breaths quickened, Tyr asked, "Like what you see, princess?"

"Oh, I do," she whispered, stepping closer. "I very much do." Another step and she closed the space, almost within touching distance. Except Tyr stayed put. Ever so slowly, she reached out and pressed a fingertip to his throat, then traced it down, over his collarbone, between his pecs, down along his abdomen and over the angry, still-healing scars, and lower still, to where the sheet tented up.

"I tried, you know." A half-smile crossed her face. "I tried not to fall in love with you. But I don't think I was ever successful. I might have loved you from the very beginning. All of that hate, it was some form of twisted love, but I never wanted to admit it."

"What about now?" Tyr asked, now sure where this was all going.

"Now it's just love." And in truth, that's what shone in her golden eyes, brilliant and clear. Love with a hint of tears.

Now Tyr did move, circling her wrist with his hand, drawing her in. "Then we're even. Because I've loved you ever since the day I saw you on that horse in front of your father's castle. So before we waste any *more* time, I believe you started something. Care to finish it?" A long, slow blink and then a creamy smile spread across her face.

Climbing up onto the bed, she pointed out, "I'm not sure I should be starting anything with an invalid. Maybe the real question is, are you up for it?" Hauling her across him, Tyr groaned at the lovely friction of her body on his while need surged through his veins.

He wanted her. Now.

Hand tangled in her hair, he drew her into a gentle kiss. Slowly and sweetly, taking his time, stroking her velvety lips with his tongue. After fantasizing for so long about what she tasted like, she tasted like nectar. So luscious, he drove his tongue between her teeth and she sucked him in, devouring him with the kiss, her body twisting to align with his, hips grinding up and down along his cock. One hand braced on his chest, she reared back.

"God, Tyr, I want you so damn bad. *Right now.*"

He pulled her head down, kissed her again, feeling her body quake. Breaking away from her pink mouth, he stared hard into her eyes. "I've waited long enough for this," he told her. "I'm taking my fucking time tonight. Which means I'll give you whatever you want, angel. But it'll be together. You okay with that?"

She managed a faint nod, her eyes darkening to amber, her pelvis rocking up and down against his. His hands wrapped around her hips, stopped her while she groaned. "Now, now, none of that, you are going to wait for me."

"Tyyyyrrr." She drew out his name as he slowly rolled her to the side, his ribs aching. The next second, he had her exactly where he wanted her, spread out beneath him, her hair a black curtain across the white pillow, a thin camisole and a slip of black panties the only thing between him and paradise. His only question was where to begin.

"Why are you looking at me like that?" she asked softly.

"Like what?"

"Like you've never seen me before."

"Because I've imagined this moment for so long. And now that it's finally here, I want to savor every second of it." Tyr slid a finger beneath the bottom edge of the camisole, meeting her eyes solidly before he began easing it up. Her skin... It was like satin. No, it *was* satin. Creamy, ivory satin, revealed a bit at a time, his fingers skimming over every perfect square inch, the slow, deliberate contact making her writhe beneath his touch. When he finally cupped her breast, his thumb brushing her nipple, she gasped and arched into his touch, mouth open, eyes closed.

"Raise your arms." He ordered gruffly. She complied, and using both hands, he drew the cami up over her head, his hips pinning her down to the bed. He couldn't take his eyes from her, even though his ribs were groaning, head beginning to spin. Exposed to him, he brushed a hand along her curves, and her nipples peaked in its wake, before dropping to her lips and kissing her again, his tongue lazily tracing her teeth, then her lips. When he drove his tongue in deep and hard, Hunter took him, all of him, with the same sort of ferocity and gave back just as good, then moaned in frustration when he withdrew.

True, his head was spinning. His ribs, half-healed or not, were screaming. But he'd be damned if he wouldn't finish this. And the way Hunter looked beneath him, creamy perfection, he couldn't have stopped if he'd tried.

Dropping his head, he sucked in one nipple, then the other, teeth closing down on them, pressing ever so slightly, the slight catch in her breath all he needed to keep on going until she was panting. Skimming his lips up her neck and settling back on her mouth, he couldn't get enough. Taste enough. Fast enough.

"Tyyyr. Please." She moaned again, her voice trembling, dangerously on edge.

He released her wrists. "You keep your hands up over your head. Don't move. Not a muscle." Eyes half closed, she managed a half nod, her expression dazed. Slipping a hand under her panties, he found her soaking. "Fuck, Hunter. You're so damn wet." He slid a finger up between her center, then slid his finger into his mouth while she watched. "Damn, you taste good."

Her eyes fluttered opened ever so slightly as she moaned, "Please don't make me wait. I can't, I just...can't. Please."

And that was it.

Drawing down her panties, Tyr knelt between her thighs, pressing them wider with his palms, until she was completely bared to him. Arms stretched over her head, legs spread, completely at his mercy, Tyr slid his hand beneath her ass, lifted her to his mouth and feasted. His tongue found her nub, spun it in a circle, and pressed down.

Almost instantly, Hunter exploded, her fingers digging into the top of his head, her scream bouncing off the walls. Part of Tyr's brain wondered if the door was locked.

Part of him didn't give two shits.

When she finally settled, her body turned pliant and soft, he licked her one last time, the salty sweetness coating his tongue, and trailed kisses up her stomach, pausing on her breasts. Her hands cupped his face, pulling him back to her mouth. "I want you inside of me, damn it. Now."

Every breath he took was ragged, rough. Every second seemed drawn out. For as long as they'd waited, for everything between them, things were about to change. Irretrievably.

Forever.

Bracing an elbow, he positioned himself at her entrance, slid the head of his cock through her wet, velvety heat. And then slowly sank into her, feeling her stretch and stretch to accommodate his girth. And he kept sliding in, inch by inch, his eyes never once leaving her face, the most exotic, beautiful creature he'd ever seen.

She felt exquisite.

～

FINALLY.

When Tyr entered her, when Hunter had him inside her, he filled her up. So much so she felt completely and totally taken. Which was exactly what she needed.

Then he slowly pulled out and thrust back in. Friction building, he kept the pace, slow and sweet, every long, steady stroke amping up the wildfire blazing at her core. Her head rocked back, and pleasure shivered down her spine while Tyr's fingers dug into her ass for better leverage.

"I've got to go slow, angel. Not in the best shape for this at the moment." Helping to brace up his shoulders, she widened her legs as he rode her in long strokes, each one deeper than the one before, one elbow next to her head, his other hand wrapped around her hip. She felt his arm tremble, sweat slide down the curve of his back, the effort costing him. But he didn't, couldn't stop. Not even as she shuddered beneath him, his name on her lips.

Languidly he fucked her, in an unhurried, thorough rhythm

before driving himself into her and groaning out something, maybe her name, before rolling at the last possible moment so he didn't crush her, and collapsed.

Little jolts of pleasure continued to shoot through her, sending her body spontaneously jerking, her heart beating a mile a minute, even as Tyr pulled her up against him, spooning her from behind, nestling into the curve of her ass.

And oddly enough, it didn't feel weird.

He felt perfect.

18

"**Y**ou need a little light over there?"

Tyr watched Hunter pad across the room in the near-dark, to where he sat hunched over a pile of papers at the small table, trying to see. She embraced him from behind, the contact sending jolts through him as she ran her fingers through his too-long hair.

"Sorry, I didn't mean to wake you. You should get some more sleep." Leaning back, looking at her, Tyr couldn't believe his luck. The woman of his dreams, wrapped in a sheet from *his* bed, was in his bedroom, naked. It was like Christmas and his birthday and every holiday known to man, all on the same day.

"*You're* the one who should come back to bed," she whispered, her tongue dipping into his ear.

They'd been in bed. And on the floor. And in the shower, the sink, the desk, and the window seat. Twice. Damn. "If you don't get some sleep, Tyr, you won't heal quickly enough."

Quick enough to fight. Quick enough to make a difference.

Tyr could fill in the blanks just fine.

As if sensing the frustration radiating off of him, Hunter's voice grew insistent. "Just come to bed, Tyr." With the barest glance at the piles of paperwork spread across the desk, she slipped into his lap, smoothing a hand across his chest.

"I have to evaluate this new intel Thor brought from the site, Hunter. I wish we had more time. But we don't. Not enough time, angel. The Orobus is here, and sooner or later, he'll figure out you're back. Now I've figured a way out of this mess, but it's full of holes. I need a few more hours to tighten it up.

"My priority—the most important thing—is to lock the bastard down. Before he comes gunning for you again. And to do that, I've got to work out the kinks in this plan." He tucked her in tightly against his throat. "I'm not letting him take you away from me." They fit together as if the gods themselves had tailored them for each other.

She sighed. "I know. It's just...we wasted so much time, Tyr. Why did we waste so much time?"

"Because we're both stubborn, bullheaded, obstinate—"

"Okay, I get it." She chuffed out a low laugh, her hands cupping his face as she rose. "I don't need a whole bunch of examples of how we failed. I'd give anything for a few, peaceful days together. But you really need to sleep, Tyr. Just a couple of hours, my love." Her eyes were dreamy and inviting as she dragged him toward the bed.

And to his chagrin, Tyr went with no complaint.

AN HOUR LATER, while Tyr slept, Hunter studied Thor's reports. Especially worrying was the drone footage over the stone circle. The Orobus spread itself over the eastern bank of the lakeshore like a plague, covering everything from the old Shedd Aquarium down to the edge of Soldier Field.

Finally she pulled out Tyr's notes, the hand drawn routes, his lists of pros and cons. His *plan*. And came to the conclusion that Tyr was on the money. But for this to work, the creature had to be smaller. More controllable. This being was too large, too disembodied. Too... nonphysical. Picking up the neatly scripted, detailed account of what

Thor had felt—the rage, the out-of-control anger—the Orobus was also too unpredictable.

She liked predictable. Take any creature. They all wanted *something*. Food, usually. Figure out what that was, and you knew, for the most part, what that animal would do next. Where it would go next. The key to its behavior.

Fortunately, she knew what the Orobus wanted.

The creature's sheer size was the problem. In this body, there was no way to force him through the doorway and lock him in his prison. Figuring out how to concentrate him into something small enough to fit through the portal was the key. Pulling one of Tyr's shirts over her head, Hunter crept out of the room and headed for the one person who might have answers.

Hunter knocked on Mir and Sydney's door, hesitating the second before her knuckles made contact with the thick oak. It wasn't like her to second guess herself, but her actions were complicated by feelings she wasn't used to. And while she might prefer the surgical neatness of her old life, that existence came with plenty of cold, hard edges. She shivered, remembering the warm bed and the warm man waiting in it, and rapped again.

"Give me a fucking minute, will you?" *Mir sure was a grump in the morning.* Which totally figured, since it was actually the middle of the night, she realized belatedly as he flung the door open. "Well. Surprise, surprise. You lovebirds out of sugar?"

"What? Sugar? No. *What?*" The whole *lovebirds* thing threw her off completely, and whatever she was planning to say went out the window in a tangle of confusion. She really had to get a handle on this human interaction stuff. "I actually came..." She cleared her throat. "I came to talk to Sydney. While I know we didn't get off on the right foot..."

"You mean you insulted her and then threw her under the bus in front of everyone?"

"Yes. Yes, that is what I mean. *What I did.* And I'm sorry." Hunter ran through possible apology scenarios. Excuses aside, they didn't change the fact that she'd been an asshole. So she left it at that and waited while Mir's cold, contemptuous gaze ground her down.

"Well, don't stand there blocking the door, Mir. Let her in." Sydney smiled at her with all the force of a mega-watt spotlight, waving a hand dismissively in the air. "And don't worry about what happened in the War Room. We all get off to a rocky start, it's just the nature of these guys. Gods. Whatever." She laughed, the sound ringing brightly. "Or maybe it's just because the world's ending, and it doesn't really matter anymore. So, what can we do for you, Hunter?"

Hunter spread the paperwork across the table, gave them both a moment. "This plan of Tyr's—I need to know how viable you think it is. If we can lure the Orobus into the correct dolmen, how confident are you that your magic will lock that door behind it?"

Sydney hesitated for a moment before answering, "Obviously, you've seen Thor's reports. The newest pictures. I'd say the plan *would* be viable, if only he was smaller. But since he's so vast... I just don't think we can do it."

"But if he took a smaller form?" Hunter pushed. "Could you make this work? There's a lot of moving parts, but if you had enough time to set all of this up, and everything went right, *and* the Orobus was in the circle, could you make this happen?"

Mir shuffled through the papers, took another look. "Yes. Problem is, any time now he's going to open up those doors and pull his armies through. And we can't get close enough to stop him. I don't understand why he hasn't done it already."

"Because that's not his main priority at the moment." Hunter blew out the breath she'd been holding. "He's looking for something he lost. He's looking for me and Tyr."

As they stared, Hunter merely shrugged. "Celine brought us home through a back door. My guess is, he's still searching for us on Svartlheim. It's keeping him busy, at the moment. But sooner than later he's going to figure out we're back on earth. And when he does, he'll come for me." And after reading through Tyr's plan, Hunter realized he'd arrived at the same conclusion.

"You could be right," Mir mused. "But if he's looking for you, then he's keyed in on his energy signature. It's probably only a matter of time before he senses you."

"Except he's spread out and uncontrolled, and he's not focused," Hunter pointed out. "Which is working to our advantage at the moment. It would give us time to get things in place. Before I did my thing."

"Exactly what are you saying?" Intent, Sydney searched Hunter's face, then Mir's. "What are you two talking about?"

"I'm saying the Orobus's size is *not* a problem. *It's an opportunity.*" Hunter leaned in, tapping the papers. "One I intend to exploit to the fullest." Hunter met Mir's eyes, seeing understanding dawn in them as Sydney's mouth formed a perfect little "O."

"That gives me a few hours, right?"

He nodded, his face grave. "Tyr... Once Tyr discovers what you've done, he's going to lose his shit."

She knew that. Knew it and didn't see another way.

"Care to let me in on what you intend to do?"

"If I knew, I would. But I haven't even seen this thing yet, not in his current form. I need to get a feel for what we're dealing with. Scout the area, figure out the best means of approaching the problem. Once I have a clear idea, I'll call it in." She offered him the barest smile. "I do have a few tricks up my sleeve, you know."

"Not against him, you don't."

Hunter tried to ignore the warning. "Once he's out of the area, Sydney, how long will it take to get everyone set up?" She was almost spent, but if she only had to lead the creature on a chase for a few hours...

Sydney shook her head, set the papers to the side, then turned to her laptop. "Considering everything Tyr wants in place?" She clicked the keyboard, pulled up a report. "I'd say less than an hour. If we work fast."

"Don't forget about the patrols. Thor mentioned plenty of Dark Elves and Grim stationed around the area as protection. We'll have to deal with them before we can set up."

Syd furiously tapped the keyboard. "Already have, and if we put

Fen and Thor on the patrols, we should still be able to get it done in less than an hour."

Something in Hunter relaxed. "All right." *They might pull this off.* "Let me scope out the situation. I'll evaluate, then head back in, and we can regroup here in an hour. You can double-check my route, which will give you enough time get everything staged. Once he's clear of the area, you put everything in place, then I come in from behind and wipe the circle out."

"I'm sending up a drone. I want this on video," Mir told her. "For posterity, of course." He added with a smirk.

"What kind of power are we talking about here?" Sydney asked, curious.

"Oh, you know, the kind that levels entire cities," Mir muttered, "or mountains."

"Yes," Hunter agreed. "*That* kind. Also, the kind that could raze the circle to the ground. *After* you lock the Orobus up. Eradicating the stones should remove any possibility of him returning to this world. Providing you concur, of course." She raised her eyebrows at Sydney, whose eyes grew bigger.

"Oh, I agree," Sydney murmured after some thought. "*If* we manage to do our part, how thorough a job are we talking?"

"Dust particles," Mir muttered.

Hunter didn't bother to reply.

"Wow," Sydney said, her thoughts obviously far away. When she finally glanced up at Hunter, the girl had a glint in her eye that Hunter could only call morbid curiosity, before it faded away. "I wish we had more time to talk, I have so many questions..." Sydney shook her head, red hair spilling all around. "But yeah. Theoretically, this is the best solution for permanently locking the monster away. A group effort, combining all of our powers." She dropped her voice, leaned in, and whispered, "We'll need to get Ava on board."

Mir shook his head so hard, Hunter thought it might fall off. "Syd, we've been over this a million times. *Not* a good idea."

"We *need* to get her on board. I have this idea... She's critical to luring the Orobus into the dolmen." Sydney snapped her gaze over to

Hunter again. "Actually, I'm surprised *you* didn't suggest it in the first place."

"I don't even *know* who Ava is," Hunter told the redhead, noting Mir's tight, pissed off expression.

"Ah, well, that explains it." Sydney's voice turned speculative. "Because if you *knew* about Ava, then you would have already..." Her voice trailed off, as she finally saw Mir's face.

"Care to tell me who Ava is?" Hunter asked, her own curiosity sparking.

"Morgane's sister, she lives upstairs. And I'm just surprised, I guess." Syd shrugged. "You know, since she's *exactly* like you."

Stunned, Hunter's gaze snapped to Mir's face. Set in stone. As if he was wishing he could take back every word coming out of Sydney's mouth. "Oh, really?" Hunter asked, not liking the direction this conversation was headed. "*How* is she like me? Semi-immortal? A fighter?"

"A royal pain in the ass?" Mir added softly.

"Oh no," Sydney said, leaning in. "She has the same power in her that you do. Whether it's from the Orobus, nobody knows. You know, since she *never comes downstairs*. But whatever it is, it kind of makes the hair on the back of my neck stand up, you know?" Sydney sucked in a breath. "Like I said, I'm just surprised you didn't know about her. I'd have thought you'd sensed her."

"And how, exactly would I do that?" Hunter's tone turned coolly dangerous.

"Like I do when I meet one of my kind." This time, when Sydney held her eyes, Hunter noted the pure, molten power burning in those green orbs. "I'm a witch. I sense magic flowing in another witch or warlock. It calls to me. Because their magic speaks directly to mine."

"You're a witch?" Hunter repeated, feeling like a fool for doing so. It had been a lifetime, a mortal lifetime at least, since she'd run across a *real* witch, but now that Sydney was this close, Hunter recognized the raw, unbridled magic in the air.

"Yup." Sydney's smile faltered. "Even though I tried my damndest not to be."

Sydney went on, "But enough about that. So we know where the Orobus needs to be imprisoned, and now we know we can destroy the circle, once he's inside. But I really don't like this idea of yours."

"Let me worry about that. Once he's trapped, I'll release my power and vaporize the site. Everyone will have to be clear, of course." Hunter paused, estimating the range of destruction. She'd never loosed the power, not of her own accord. Hard to say what would happen. But it was a fair assumption to assume there'd be nothing left. "Destroying the stones will destroy the portals, correct?"

"I'm positive. The spatial interference that occurs within each dolmen doesn't occur outside of them, nor does it occur independently of them. Safe to assume, and my tests confirm this, once the dolmens cease to exist, so will the doorways. I'll use magic to lock the gate behind him, then you will essentially remove the door itself. And there will be no way for the God of Chaos to reconstruct another portal."

"Where did this one come from in the first place?"

"They..." Sydney shook her head apologetically. "It was me, actually, who dug up the circle, out of a peat bog in what was once Neolithic Ireland. My crazy old professor had been having these visions, and it turned out he was being controlled by the God of Chaos."

Something inside Hunter chilled at the words. "How did he use your professor?"

"The Orobus planted compulsions in him, told him the location of the circle. Used his expertise and his contacts to transport the stones back here, get them set up at the Field Museum. But the professor became delusional and unpredictable. It was like he broke down under the pressure or something."

"How did you get involved?"

Sydney shuddered. Immediately Mir went to her, "I'm right here, baby." As his arms wrapped around her, she went on, her voice shaky.

"The professor called me in on the project. I'm the one who excavated the circle in Ireland. I was the one who erected them and arranged them in the proper sequence.

"Then, the creature took me over and used me to spy on Mir and everyone here. I don't remember...much." She dropped her eyes so fast, Hunter knew that was mostly a lie. "What I do remember was both fascinating and horrifying. *Mostly* horrifying. That's why I'm doing everything I can to try to figure out how to stop him.

"There are a lot of us, Hunter, who've been used to do his bidding. Me, Celine—thousands of others, probably, over the eons—each of us putting him closer to his goal.

"The point is, everything he does gets him closer to what he wants."

"And what do you believe he wants?" Hunter asked.

"At first, I thought he wanted to wipe everything away. Like what your power is capable of.

"But I've come up with a new theory, especially after what happened in New York. He didn't destroy this city, though he easily could have. He was imprisoned by the very first of the gods, according to their lexicon of faith. And he's so fixated on Odin, on eliminating these other immortal beings. I believe he means to supplant them. I think he means to become the One God."

"So the Orobus has a god complex?"

"He started out as nothing but chaos. My guess is he likes the order he's discovered in the natural world, the order to power. We've established he enjoys having an audience. And he's amassing armies, creatures to control."

"He has Hel working with him as his demonic general," Mir pointed out.

"He does," Sydney agreed. "She's probably guiding him, planting seeds, manipulating him in her own way." She shuddered. "It would be in her best interest to do so. And from my brief, yet dramatic encounter with her, that would fit."

"All right," Hunter told them, rising. "I'm heading down there to take a look around. Tyr's still sleeping, I'll try to be back before he wakes. If I'm not, he'll be on the warpath by breakfast." She tipped her head down. "Sorry in advance. But if I mean to get down there..."

"Then you'd better leave now." Mir finished for her.

19

Finally, Hunter had a definitive plan of action.

She knew, deep in her bones, it was the right one. She also knew, just as deeply, that it was the last thing she wanted to do. She'd been sitting here in a room touched only by moonbeams, watching Tyr sleep. She'd stolen these last, precious moments with him. And she'd never give them back because she was taking them with her when she went.

He'd always thought she'd been nothing but a mad animal, those days in the cave up on the mountain. But she'd been so much more. She'd been freed. Of society. Of the world itself. All the while, learning to control the terrible, quicksilver power imprisoned within her. As he patiently coaxed her back into this world of theirs, taught her how to live and breathe and see and feel like the human she'd once been, she'd fallen completely and utterly in love with him. And so, when he'd abandoned her next to the decimated castle, her heart had broken in some irreparable way.

It was a wondrous thing to love him again.

To know she'd take this feeling with her to the next place, wherever that might be.

Turning, Hunter left the room, slipped through the silent hall-
ways of the Tower and out into the dark streets of Chicago.

Because while her heart belonged to the sleeping god,

The Orobus held her soul.

20

I am you, and you are me.

Well, the Orobus was certainly huge. Hunter watched the thing spin beneath her, an enormous psychic abyss, crackling with the occasional flash of blue-black energy, spread out over a mind-boggling area.

Whatever Tyr had pulled up out of the ground and infused into her was definitely part of this dark god. She recognized the connection now, though she wished to deny it. Some kind of primordial life force, the bond between them was undeniable. Clearly, it was how the Orobus knew to use Tyr. Her love would be used against her again if she wasn't careful.

Well, *she* would not allow either of them to be manipulated. Perched on the edge of what had once been a grand hotel, Hunter searched the darkness for the core of the creature's power. She couldn't find one. Thor had not exaggerated in his report. In fact, he had vastly understated the situation.

Or the thing was growing at an alarming rate of speed.

"Funny, I thought I'd find you here."

The last person she'd thought would be sneaking around, snuck up behind her. Well, she'd heard him coming for about ten minutes but had wanted the company. She was just surprised. "Isn't this a bit below your pay grade?"

"Oh, I don't know. Pretty girl under a new moon, maybe my night's looking up." Freyr's smile didn't quite reach his beautiful eyes, and a cold, icy feeling swept through her. So he'd not come here to chat.

"It'll be dawn in an hour, and the moon's at a quarter. You'd best get to the point, Freyr. We're past time for pussyfooting around."

"All right. Mir sent me for backup. Such that I am. He and Syd are working out some minor details before he goes to the rest of the group with the plan, so he figured a second set of eyes down here might help."

"He sent you to ensure I don't do anything stupid."

"Yes," Freyr muttered. "That's pretty much it." His beautiful face tightened. "Since you seem to have an uncanny ability to cause trouble wherever you go, Hunter, he figured it wouldn't hurt. You almost got Tyr killed. The God of War, for fuck's sake. Care to explain what you're planning?"

"We're coming up with a strategy to stop that thing." She hedged. Seeing the full scope of the creature had her questioning their sanity right about now. "And besides, this doesn't seem like your scene. I thought all you ever did was look pretty and chase women?" As the words escaped her mouth, she winced. Men and their egos. Her and her mouth. This would probably not end well.

"Are you calling me a whore?"

She heard a hint of ire at the insult.

"Just because you chose to go through life a nun doesn't give you the right to criticize how I live mine. I happen to like sex. *And women.* So watch the judgy attitude."

Shit. He was totally right. "I'm sorry. What I *meant* to say was..."

"What you meant to say is... Freyr, why are you out here, when you normally would have chosen the safest path and stayed home watching DVD's in bed with a bag of snacks and a cold beer?" Crossing his arms, he stared her down, and for the very first time, she saw something beyond the staggering beauty, something more like quiet strength.

"Yes. *That* would have been a much better choice of words. So why are you here?"

"Not exactly sure. I guess I had to see this for myself." Freyr's gaze skimmed the scene below them, his eyes widening slightly. "Footage doesn't quite do it justice, does it?"

"Not one bit."

The blond god *was* an incredible specimen, she noted. So handsome he didn't even look real, as if a soft glow enveloped him from head to toe, the faintest hint of magic emanating from his pores. And that mane of hair—every color of blonde—from the purest sunshine to the deepest amber picked up the faint moon glow in the air.

"Done gaping?" he taunted, eyes still focused below. "None of this matters, you know. It's all just window dressing, really."

For a moment, Hunter scanned the gloom, the buildings, before she realized Freyr was talking about himself.

"I was born this way, as were my sisters and brothers before me. But it doesn't matter," he insisted again. "My whole life, I've done nothing but rely on my looks to get me by. And now? *This* world doesn't care about beauty." He nodded to the roiling cloud of black below them. "*He* certainly doesn't."

"There's an old saying, you know. 'The more beautiful the face, the more fatal it's bite.' You'd do well to remember it."

"Are you sure that wasn't about the Medusa?" He finally looked at her, and his eyes, practically the same shade as hers, were bleak.

"No, but the principle is the same, Freyr. If you want to change, be whatever you want to be. Just become something different. You're a *god*, for heaven's sake, just do it."

"*Now* you sound like a sound bite."

"Maybe, but still. Whatever's holding you back, get past it, get over it, or get through it." Hunter sighed, turning back to the monster beneath them. "*Something* brought you down here, besides Mir's orders. What was it?" But her words echoed away into the dark. And nothing but silence echoed back.

"Freyr? Don't walk away from me." She forced herself not to shout after him. "I need you. We need each other right now. There aren't many of us left." It went against everything she'd believed in, but this was the only way they would survive. Together. Apart, the Orobus would pick them off, one by one.

Relief flickered to life when Freyr strode out of the shadows. "Fine. I'll listen to your inspirational speech. But keep it short. I can't do anything about my short attention span."

"What did bring you down here?" she prodded. "You could have checked on me and ghosted back out. There's no reason for you to speak to me. Unless you wanted to. So, what do you want?"

"To help." The gold in his eyes seemed alight. "I mean, *really* help. Not in the half-assed way I usually do." Freyr moved in. "Simply following orders isn't doing it for me anymore. Maybe it's time I stepped up. Made a difference."

"Wow, look at who's giving me a run for motivational speaker of the year."

"Fuck off," Freyr muttered good-naturedly.

"You first," Hunter told him. "Now, as to why we're both here."

A tilt of that gorgeous face had blond hair spilling over his shoulder. *Annoying, really.*

"Go ahead, I'm all ears."

"I'm down here because of something Sydney said." Hunter paused, unsure how to lay it out, since things hardly made sense even to her. "Her theory is the Orobus wants to replace you—the gods—by becoming one himself." She snuck another look through the blown-out window behind them. "I'd like to prevent that from happening."

"I'm with you so far."

"But we have the obvious problem. He's too big right now for us to handle." Hunter met Freyr's gaze steadily. "But I've found a solution."

Freyr's eyes narrowed. "I'm not going to like this, am I?"

Hunter shook her head. "Not one bit." At his nod, she continued, "Being stationary allows him to spread himself thinly over the site, effectively guarding it. And shutting us out, since nothing can get past his defenses. But if he was on the move? He'd have to condense himself down, streamline himself for travel. Especially if he was forced to pursue something."

"What do you suggest?"

You are me, and I am you.

"He wants this little piece of dark power inside of me. He'll follow me out of the city. To move, and move quickly, he'll have to compress himself into a form that can be easily transported. Which also means..."

"Easily contained."

She nodded. "Exactly. And once I draw him away, it will give everyone time to set up around the site, put Tyr's plan into action. Mir and Syd are already working out logistics. There are variables, of course. You'll have to eliminate any Grim and elves stationed down there. And I have no idea how long you'll have to operate. But I'll buy you as much time as I can."

"That's the upside. Now, tell me what the downside is. 'Cause there's always a downside." Freyr's brilliant eyes narrowed down to slits. "Wait. Tyr has no idea you're down here, does he?"

Ignoring the question completely, Hunter plowed ahead. "As far as drawing him back, if you threaten the circle, say...tried to blow up the stones?"

"We already tried that. There's some kind of protection on them. We tried to get through them but no luck."

"You only have to *threaten* them. Its primitive logic. If his lair is threatened, in any way, even if he *knows* it's secure, he'll be compelled to check. The instinct will be hardwired into him." She searched her gut and knew she was right about this. "*Trust* me, he'll come back. If all goes well, you'll be ready, he'll be in a smaller form. I'll circle in from behind, wiping the entire structure off the map, the second Sydney locks the portal with her magic. If anything seems off, or goes wrong, then we abort and regroup back at the Tower."

"Nope. You are not going to lead that thing out of the city and leave me, *ME*, to tell Tyr what you've done. That's your plan? It is, isn't it? You're going to chicken shit it out of here and leave me to do your dirty work. Well let me tell you something, sweetheart, I'm not fucking doing it."

"It's the only way this will work, Freyr. If I head back to the Tower now, there's no way Tyr will let me do this. He'll take one look at the size of this thing and shut the plan down. Look, I know this isn't fair, and I know it puts you in a bad spot..."

"A bad spot, is that seriously what you call this?"

His voice took on a high, mocking tone, "Oh by the way Tyr, I let your girlfriend lead the monster who's about to destroy the world out of the city, dead on her heels. But yeah, I'm here, safe and sound, to deliver her message. Oh, and by the way, do you want to loose your deadly God of War powers on me now or later?" he scoffed. "How's that? Did I get it right?"

Yes, that was certainly accurate. "I don't have a choice."

"The hell you don't. We head back to the Tower, and we work as a *team*. We come up with something that doesn't get you killed and me with my beautiful ass getting a serious beat down. Deal?"

As Hunter moved blindingly fast and used a quick jab to the temple to knock Freyr out, lowering him gently to the ground so he didn't, as he put it, damage his beautiful ass, Hunter wished, for once, that she could just do things the easy way. She sighed.

But no, things just never worked out the way you wanted them to.

21

Hunter had never been in this position before.

Which was saying something, considering how old she was.

But as her breaths turned jerky and uneven and her chest felt about to burst, she was pretty sure she was the prey in her current situation. The need to flee was overwhelming. The sheer size of the thing she was up against was like nothing she'd ever faced before. Then there was this strange kinship she felt with the monster, as if like called to like. *That* feeling she fought with every fiber of her being.

Skirting the shadowy outer edge of the Orobus, she muttered, "I must be crazy," before edging closer, her heart beating out of control.

At some point, she hoped, the monster would sense her. Sense their sameness. Just as he had before. And at that point, she was betting on two things. The creature would take a moment to gather himself together. The problem with sentience is that action is tempered by reasoning. And that critical moment of indecision would buy her time to escape.

If they were wrong, and this being was ruled by instinct alone, she'd be dead in a heartbeat.

A step closer, then another. The roiling movement slowed near her, as if recognizing a familiar presence. *Yes,* she thought, *yes, here I am, right here.*

See me. *See me.*

The suddenness with which the creature stopped, and recognized, and seemingly latched onto her was startling. And frightening.

Just as quickly, Hunter raced along the path she'd carefully chosen. A route both convoluted enough to slow the Orobus down and direct enough to take her out of the city. She was determined to draw him far enough away that it would buy the gods and humans time to prepare. A grim smile played over her face as she raced below the highway, jumped into the hot-wired pickup she'd left running, and flew along the twisted labyrinth of streets and tunnels.

Behind her, the concrete rumbled overhead. He was following.

She only prayed he'd go where she led.

22

Freyr woke with hard concrete underneath him and a cold, vile breeze above. It smelled faintly of brimstone and evil, and he rubbed his head, wincing. "Damn you to hell, Hunter."

He rolled over against the low wall, broken glass crunching beneath him. The massive cloud that made up the Orobus was still down there, swirling in all of its hellish, black glory, and he figured Hunter was there, somewhere. Probably putting her reckless scheme into action.

And his ass in a fucking sling.

One more look had him ghosting back to the Tower, where he dumped himself directly into Tyr's room, not giving a shit about propriety or anything else at the moment. Which was good, because Tyr sat up, groggy yet expectant, probably expecting to bang his lover. Except that was *so* not going to happen.

"Hey." Freyr reached out and prodded the god to get his attention. It was like poking an iron anvil. "We've got to talk."

"What the fuck, Freyr?" Tyr yelled, launching himself out of bed. "What are you doing, ghosting straight into my bedroom? Are you crazy?"

"Yeah, you're going to want to put on some clothes for this."
Keeping his eyes averted, Freyr hunted around the room and finally
spotted the half full bottle of bourbon. Grabbing it, he thankfully
swigged down a few mouthfuls. Gods, his head was *killing* him. That
woman had a mean right hook. "*Clothes*, Tyr, for fuck's sake."

The God of War had seen better days, his body battered and
covered in an array of spectacular bruising, some of it fading to green,
and on his abdomen the marks were dark purple, a sure sign of deep
kidney damage. Freyr perked up. Maybe Tyr wasn't in any shape to
deliver a severe beat down, after all.

"So I have some news. And before you go ape shit on me, first, I
only went to take a look around. Secondly, it was on Mir's orders."
Freyr took another swig of the Weller. "So this *totally* wasn't my fault."
Handing the bottle over, he nodded. "You'd better finish this off."

Tyr set the bottle aside with such careful precision, Freyr knew
exactly where *this* discussion was heading. "Where is Hunter? And
you'd better tell me she's still in the building, or you and me have a
problem."

Then Tyr sniffed. Cocked his head at Freyr, a dangerous glint in
his eye. Then sniffed again. Far too late, Freyr's sixth sense, the one
that normally kept his ass out of danger, went off. "It can't be. You...
You bastard." Tyr's eyes went round, then filled with so much rage that
Freyr didn't know how they didn't overflow.

Freyr backed away, quickly "Whoa, wait, you've got this all
wrong..."

Next thing he knew agony exploded through him as the hard
stone floor made instant, painful contact with his back and shoulders. A full two-fifty of muscle hit him like a battering ram. "I didn't
mean to. I swear. I didn't..." *Would he seriously never learn?* "I didn't
touch her, Tyr. I swear, didn't lay a finger on her..."

Worse, that sounded much, much worse.

As Tyr continued beating the ever-loving shit out of him, Freyr's
brain rattled around for an explanation that wouldn't end up getting
him killed. "She's drawing the God of Chaos out of the city," he
babbled as Tyr's fist sank into his gut. "I only went down there

because Mir sent me to keep an eye on her. And FYI, killing me isn't going to bring her back."

There was a second when he thought the pounding might continue, but then the fists stopped, and he sagged in relief. Pain was not something he wanted to become acquainted with on an intimate basis. "Shit. I thought you were about to kill me."

"Thought so too." Tyr was out of breath, head hanging down between his enormous shoulders, blood seeping from wounds that had opened back up. "You're bleeding."

"Yeah, well, so are you."

Freyr rubbed a hand across his face, surprised by the salty, coppery taste in his mouth. "Again. This was totally *not* my fault. Hunter knocked me out and took matters into her own hands. I tried to talk her out of it, I really did, but..." When Tyr's head snapped up, Freyr held out a hand to stop the oncoming attack. He was tired of getting his ass handed to him, and he also preferred having all his teeth.

"Damn it, Tyr, she went after the Orobus by herself. She knocked me out to do it." Thankfully the bastard stayed where he was. "My head fucking hurts, and I ruined my favorite jeans. So for once, just listen." Surprisingly, Tyr did exactly that.

"Start explaining pretty damn fast, asshole." Tyr yanked on pants, then boots, and a shirt. Then headed for the door. "And while you're at it, tell me why Mir sent you after her in the first place."

Succinctly, Freyr explained. And he made it quick. Mostly because Tyr was pissed and partly because his head did actually hurt, he ran the debacle down, point by miserable point. By the time he'd finished, they'd reached Mir's room and picked up Vali and Thor in their wake, which was a huge plus because Tyr hardly ever killed anyone in front of an audience.

They'd barely crossed the threshold, Mir sliding his chair back, eyes shrewd as he sized up the God of War's disheveled, furious disposition. "Ah. I see you're caught up. And from the looks of it, Hunter did exactly what I thought she would. Let me guess, she slipped past you and is already on the move?"

Freyr just nodded while Tyr began barking out orders, "Thor. Find Loki and Fen, tell them we're moving up the schedule. Thor, you and Morgane on weapons. Vali, you and Balder are on munitions." He had to hand it to him, Tyr didn't hesitate one bit. "Load up one of the older trucks, enough for a medium-sized explosion. I'm not wasting resources, but the blast has to be believable enough to convince the bastard to come back."

While Tyr organized, Mir caught everyone else up. Once they were on the same page, he threw the whole mess back to Freyr, who finished with—

"Last I saw, the damn thing was still on-site. But Hunter must have been down there somewhere, because the Orobus was starting to morph and get smaller. I figured the smart thing was to get back here as fast as I could and tell Tyr what Hunter was up to." He noticed Tyr got really quiet, and Vali pounded away down the hall, leaving just the three of them.

Tyr whirled to him. "So why the fuck did you let her go?" So apparently, he hadn't listened to a word Freyr had said.

"I'm not the one who let her out of the Tower," Freyr pointed out. "Look, I tried to talk some sense into her, Tyr, I really did. But she sucker punched me, and next thing I knew, I'm waking up, watching the God of Chaos condense himself down into this little evil ball of darkness."

"So she was right?" Mir mused. "He *did* follow her."

"Looked like it." Freyr leaned against the counter, head pounding. "Seems like she's got the bastard all figured out. She leads him out. Then we lure him back. She suggested staging an explosion, seemed pretty sure that would draw him back to the site, especially if his lair was threatened." He looked at Tyr, his battered mess of a body, and offered, "Look, I'm fucking sorry. I begged her to stay. Said we needed to work as a team. I wish she would have listened."

"So do I."

Freyr glanced up as Sydney rushed in, laptop in hand. As soon as she spotted Tyr, her face dropped. So apparently, she knew what was going down. Freyr prodded. "So Tyr, can we even pull this off?"

"She jumped the gun by about four hours. But yeah, if Hunter draws him far enough away, we'll still have time to get set up. We'll fill the old Ranger with whatever explosives we have left, park close by, and detonate it, which *should* bring the bastard flying back. But we have a small problem." Tyr glanced at Mir and Syd as if looking for confirmation. "We still haven't worked out a solid method to lure the thing into the prison."

"Well, I'll tell you this." Ava stepped in the room, her eyes wary. "He won't go through willingly. Not unless you offer him something he really, really wants. And even if you manage that, then you'd better be sure she"—Ava shot Sydney a hard, knowing glance—"can damn well lock the door behind him. Or believe me, he'll be pissed. Big and pissed off and on the rampage."

Lots of mumbling.

"Where do you think Hunter's taking him?" Mir asked, his gaze focused on Tyr.

"She'd draw him away from the more populated areas, so somewhere rural. Maybe upstate, but possibly west. Freyr, did she say anything about which direction?"

"No, we didn't exactly get that far before she hit me over the head."

"West," Celine said from the doorway. "He's heading west and moving fast. Sorry, Fen went to help load the truck, so I came down. I felt him leave the city, all of a sudden." She firmed her mouth. "He's heading west, I'm sure of it."

"You mean to tell me this thing is now chasing Hunter across Illinois?"

Uncomfortable looks were exchanged all around.

"She seemed sure she could lead him out of the city and make it back here in time," Freyr assured Tyr, hoping to ease his mind. "Look, she has a good idea of what she's up against." He paused, scanning Tyr's face. "Better than any of us, actually."

"There's a good reason for that," Mir murmured. "Still doesn't answer the question why she's gone vigilante all of a sudden."

"She's doing this to keep the rest of us out of his grasp."

"And why the hell would she do that?"

Tyr's voice was gruff, his words deliberate as he explained, his gaze downcast. "The Orobus snatched me off the street. Like I was a nothing. Used me as bait to draw her down to the circle. Then almost killed me. Said he would do the same to all of us. The only reason I'm alive is because she pulled us through the portal. Otherwise, he'd have all of her power. As well as mine."

"So he *does* want her power." Sydney gasped softly, her hand grasping Mir's.

Tyr nodded gravely. "It's what he's chasing, right now."

"That little piece of himself, sealed up inside of her." Ava startled at the revelation, her gaze swinging over to Tyr and locking on. "The Orobus recognizes her as a kindred soul."

TYR WAS A MESS. Every fiber of his being was aching to fly out of here and pick up Hunter's trail. But he had a duty to make sure this narrow window of opportunity—the one Hunter was risking her life to create —was capitalized on. Which was why he was only half listening when Freyr chimed in.

"That's exactly what she said, right before she knocked my ass out. She told me she's got a little of himself inside of her, and that's why he'd follow her."

Of course she knew the creature would follow her. Tyr gritted his teeth; there'd be time enough for anger later. "And did Hunter happen to explain what would happen if the God of Chaos caught her? That he'd take that little piece of power back for himself?" Tyr's voice roughened. "No, because she's impossibly reckless."

"Just like her to leave me out of the plan," he grumbled. "I would have stopped her." He spun away, the blank wall a welcome haven from the looks on everyone's faces. But years spent on battlefields had taught him a thing or two.

"We're moving up the timetable, is all." Tyr spoke as if to himself. "And she's faster than he is. Smarter, too. She'll out maneuver him.

She'll be okay." Turning back, he said, "Freyr, go see where we're at. We need to be completely set up in twenty, minimum. That includes the charges, surveillance, and recon." A mental tally came up short on manpower, but they'd have to make do.

When Freyr didn't move, Tyr roared, "What the hell is wrong with you? She's buying us time, and we're wasting it."

Sydney spoke quickly. "Tyr's right. We can't allow Hunter to get too far away. The faster we draw him back, the better. And I've got an idea for luring him to the prison." Biting her lip, she glanced over at Ava. "But it's risky, and it means Ava and I will have to get close." When Mir started to protest, she stopped him with a shake of her head. "We don't have the luxury of choices right now. None of us. We all do what's necessary. Give Ava and me a couple of minutes, and then we'll tell you if what I'm thinking is even possible."

Freyr cut in. "I'll get us set up. I'm thinking the pickup should be parked at the east end?"

Tyr dipped his head in agreement and added, "If I know Hunter, she'll head back into the city once she's sure she's clear. It won't take her long, so we need to be in position."

Freyr hesitated in the doorway. "*Where* should we position ourselves? If we knew which direction the Orobus was coming, it would help."

Tyr considered.

North. Hunter was hardwired to head north. She would lure him away, then circle back around. *And she was smart*. She was clever and smart and she'd backtrack on the bastard. Make sure the creature couldn't trace her scent, Tyr realized. The tight, constricting knot on his heart relaxed just enough that he could actually feel blood begin to flow.

"North," he told Freyr. "She's heading north, and she'll have him running in circles by now. She'll maintain a tight perimeter and won't put too much distance between herself and the circle."

"Good," Freyr said as he left, "by the time we blow the truck, she shouldn't have any problems making it back here in time."

The moment he was gone, Tyr turned to Sydney. Ava was already across the room, thrown in a chair, feet on the table. "All right ladies, you have one minute to convince me."

"*Lady*," Ava said. "And I have no idea what the plan is."

"The Orobus showed...some *interest* in Ava, when they crossed paths a month ago." Sydney gestured wildly, talking fast, "And Ava can control the darkness, right? So all she has to do is to bait the trap, per se, wrap her shadows around the prison, enough so the Orobus senses her. All I need is for him to get close."

"How close?" Mir asked, his voice gruff.

"Maybe fifteen feet or so. And he'll have to be *inside* the circle."

"Why inside?" Tyr asked.

"Because we'll be on the outside."

Mir made a low, grumbly sound.

"I'll create a chamber, of sorts. A magical cylinder, a circle of magic encompassing the large dolmen but with a roof and a bottom this time. There will be one tiny opening, and I need him near it."

"Fifteen feet?" Tyr queried, now curious.

"Yes. I believe he'll approach, just to check out Ava. He's *very* interested in her, you see."

Ava shuddered visibly, her foot bobbing nervously as she pointed out, "I've noticed I don't get a vote in this. Just so you know, I'm doing this under protest."

Sydney went on, her voice lilting with excitement, "I've seen what you can do with your shadows, Ava, and you won't even have to be *that* close. Like...only thirty feet or so." Sydney seemed satisfied that was plenty of room between Ava and an evil, primordial god.

"For your information, that's way too close," Ava mumbled, her left foot joggling a mile a minute now.

"Nonsense," Sydney said, "we'll all be right there, and once he's within ten feet of you, start withdrawing. He'll follow you to the dolmen, and then I'll create a cylinder of magic. Then your part is finished."

"And then what?" Mir's tone was sour.

"I'm going to burn all the air out of the chamber. At such a high temperature...."

"You know, this could actually work." Mir sounded surprised.

"Of course it will work, doofus," Syd muttered. "I've been working on this theory for days and days. I have this all figured out." She patted Ava's hand. "You'll be perfectly safe. I'll be right beside you the entire time."

Tyr rubbed his temple in frustration. "Let's just say, for the sake of argument, I am *not* a rocket scientist. What in the fuck are you two talking about?"

"I'll create a vacuum chamber inside the magical cylinder I form around the dolmen. In his current non-physical form, once he's close enough, the force of the vacuum will pull him into the chamber. Then I'll use my magic, casting the spell to contain him. Then Hunter will raze the entire circle to the ground."

Tyr had to admit, it *sounded* convincing. He hated Syd and Ava would be so close, but... Here was a solution to the one problem they'd never been able to solve. "How strong will this vacuum be?"

"My fire burns at over a million degrees. Any hotter and everything would evaporate. I can only manage that for about a second. But that'll be enough. Trust me, as long as he's within fifteen feet of the opening, he'll be pulled through in a flash." She smiled. "It will look like he disappperated." She looked between them. "Like in the book? You know... Never mind."

"What about everything else?" Tyr calculated. There would be nine of them there, and he wasn't about to risk a single life. "What about us? How will we remain safe?"

"My magic will protect us. I'll be the closest because I'm casting the spell. Once he's contained, we'll evacuate to a safe distance, and Hunter can wipe everything thing out, all the way down to bare earth." She paused for effect. "And good riddance."

As Syd watched him, holding her breath, Tyr wondered at the change in their fortunes. A couple of months ago, none of them even knew each other. Now here they were, immortal and mortal magic combining to save the world. Hopefully. Mir offered the shallowest of nods, and Tyr cleared his throat. "Okay. We go with your plan. For now." He looked at Ava. "You good with this? Nobody will think any less of you if you back out. We'll find another way to get him close to the dolmen."

"Naw," she said, sliding her boots off the table. "I'll go. I'm just not crazy about getting so close to something that feels like a barrel of evil, if you get my drift?" She walked over to join them. "Besides, Morgane's already on her way to the site. I can't be the only one left behind, it'd make me look bad."

"Okay. Group effort, it is."

He was humming with an energy he hadn't felt in a while. It felt electric. It felt dangerous. Other than the tingle of fear that, somehow, Hunter might have underestimated her opponent, he was anticipating this. They had a good plan. They had magic, luck, and timing on their side. No one could ask for better odds.

By the time they reached the garage, Vali and Balder were gone, and Morgane was just leaving. "Great timing. You missed loading up the vehicles, but that's cool." When she spotted Ava, she grinned. "Hey sis, wanna ride shotgun? Loki and everyone already headed out, but you can ride with me." Ava, Mir, and Celine loaded in and with a squeal of tires, they took off.

Tyr grabbed one of the Hummers, swinging himself into the driver's seat. Freyr hopped in the other side. "Everyone out?"

"Yeah. Enough explosives in the truck to make a big hole, not enough to deplete our stores. Fen and Celine are already in position, far enough away the danger is minimal, and according to their first reports, the site is quiet."

Tyr felt anticipation amp up a notch higher.

"This will work," Freyr reassured him. "We all ran it through, and considering the options, it's a solid plan. Worst-case scenario? Things go south and we bail. All we've expended are some munitions."

Tyr didn't feel like reminding him today could go a whole lot worse than that, considering there was no time to organize. He liked guarantees. Not that there were any on the battlefield.

"When do I tell Vali to hit the button?"

Tyr romped the curb and cut across Lakeshore, heading for the museum campus. "We'll be there in three minutes. Hunter might already be circling back." He checked his TIG watch. "Give me a minute to park, and then another minute to get under cover. Then tell them to blow it."

Freyr pulled out the com unit. The whole place was eerily quiet. The crunch of gravel the only sound as Tyr navigated the vehicle around the hunks of what used to be the Field Museum while they made their way down toward the pit that held the circle of stone dolmens. "Park here." He pointed to a spot behind the remainder of a retaining wall.

In the distance, he watched Loki and Fen appear out of nowhere, decimate a patrol of Dark Elves, and disappear just as quickly. Tyr swung the vehicle in and they got out, Freyr raising the com to his mouth. A second later, the entire site was lit by the yellow glare of fire before the roar of the explosion hit them, the sound deafening as it tore across the open spit of land.

Another small troop of Dark Elves came tearing across the rubble field, feet kicking up gravel. Tyr rose up in front of them, took two of them out, while Freyr circled behind and cut down another. The fourth made a swipe for Freyr's throat, and Tyr gutted him. Off in the distance, a few Grim scuttled out of the shadows, then disappeared, the smoke swallowing them up.

"We've got a few pockets of Grim up here on the north end." Thor's voice cracked out of the com. "Taking care of them now."

"All right." Freyr spoke into the com, his voice low. "Make it quick. Morgane and Celine have eyes all the way along the corridor. Trust me. They'll see anything coming and give us a head's up."

Settling in, Tyr put his back to the stone, jammed his hands into his pockets and began counting down the seconds.

23

Circling back from the north, Hunter planned to ditch the truck outside a million-dollar mansion in Evanston. She sensed the Orobus barely twenty minutes behind her, and she meant to maintain that distance.

Once morning dawned, she intended to be working her way to the circle, ready to do her part and take her lumps from a pissed off Tyr.

She shivered. "He is going to be sooo angry with me."

She hadn't exactly picked the house strategically. She was almost out of gas, and she didn't want to get too far away from the city. In other words, she was out of options, and this was the best she could do. Not that it was *awful* she thought, surveying the terrain as she crested the long drive. The house was immense, mostly glass, and the big break wall might prove useful if things went south. The water meant no human casualties, and the surrounding structures appeared abandoned.

Her plan, such that it was, was to hold the Orobus here long enough for Tyr to set off the explosion to draw the thing back. Once that happened, the God of Chaos would fly back to Chicago. She'd follow, a safe distance behind.

Except she'd used most of her gas.

And she had no other transportation.

She sighed. Surely one of these huge garages had an extra sports car or two in them. She couldn't believe she'd run out of gas. Her head wasn't in the game. Her concentration was focused on a certain unyielding god, who she imagined had steam coming out of both ears right about now. *I should have said goodbye.* Nope, he would have tied her to the bed. That thought made her tingle. *I should have at least left a note,* she amended.

Next time, she reminded herself, she'd do better next time.

There had to be a learning curve for this kind of stuff, right? Some sort of step-by-step manual on how not to screw relationships up so badly?

Dropping her head to the steering wheel as she inched up the drive, Hunter's eyes burned, and her head throbbed. She'd been through the wringer these last few days but still had enough juice to finish this thing. *Too many people depended on her to finish this.* She thought of them now, tentatively, as a sort of extended kind of family. Between them and the fate of the world, well, it was no wonder a girl's shoulders felt a bit heavy.

Glancing in the rearview, she frowned at what she left behind her.

She'd done her best, laying bread crumbs for the Orobus to follow.

Letting just enough of her darkness escape for the creature to sense, enticing him farther northward. The tiniest whisper of fearsome power was crucial for this to work, but God, it hurt her heart as she killed everything she passed.

"It's for a good cause," she'd assured herself. Now, from the rearview, she was not so sure. The once-lush yard blackened to moldy gray, trees turned skeletal, birds dropped from the sky. But as the pestilence spread, her target followed.

Opening herself up a bit further, she allowed another flicker of deadly energy to escape. Once she had planted enough of herself here, he'd circle. Until Tyr and the others called him back. Then they'd have their chance. Possibly their only chance.

"And then, I'm going to burn you down."

Stepping out of the truck, Hunter watched in sick fascination as shadows spun out from her body, burning deep, black trenches out through the grass, then floated over the water, bringing silver fish to the surface. A bone-deep shudder spasmed through her as she closed herself down, the effort causing pain to shoot through her, the power clawing against her insides.

"Not a chance," she muttered, stalking across the blackened, dead yard, then into the skeletal tree line. It wasn't long before she reached fresh, green woodland, the dense undergrowth hiding her, thorns raking at her skin as she settled in to wait. Long minutes passed, the breeze rattling the leaves, the lapping of the waves on the shore just beyond them, rhythmic and almost soothing.

It took her a moment to realize that not all the shadows were from the early dawn.

Something cool and oily flowed over her. Like the wind, the touch of the creature was all but invisible, his clutching grasp curious and infinitely evil. Silently, Hunter drew out a knife, knowing, rationally, it wouldn't help.

The thing was here, and he was covering the entire site in a strangling blanket of fume.

Afraid to even breathe, Hunter stilled and watched the world disappear before her eyes as the Orobus wrapped her in his shadowy grasp. For a few long seconds, she was alone with only her own heartbeats and the smothering dark. And ever so slowly, a fingernail scraped its way along her cheek as she began to pant, instincts going crazy, firing orders at her brain to *run, run, run.*

There was no weapon made for this creature, no steel that might defend her.

Unfortunately, there was only one thing that would work. In a surge of fear and adrenaline, Hunter opened herself up, releasing years of restraint and control, dropping the walls that kept the world safe. For only a second, she dropped her guard. She prayed nothing lived in the nearby vicinity, as power blew out from her in all directions.

When she lifted her head, the Orobus was gone.

24

Twenty minutes after the explosion, with the smoke still clearing, a cloud of darkness appeared on the horizon, and Thor knew they were in trouble.

Thank the gods Tyr had put him up here as lookout. If it had been, say, Freyr, *that* asshole would have been fucking with his hair or some such shit and completely missed the incoming attack all together. Speaking quickly into the com, he watched Loki, Balder, and the rest jockey into position. Catching a glimpse of Syd's red hair, he scanned the vicinity for Mir, and sure enough, watched as the big guy yanked her behind a chunk of rubble the size of a bus. *Way too close*, he thought, *they're way too close to the dolmen from hell.*

But this was her plan, after all.

Eyeing the incoming storm of evil, he watched the monstrous shadow scatter overhead, while beneath him, darkness wound between the buildings, filling the streets like a black, flowing river.

Something twisted in the pit of Thor's stomach while the Orobus circled, making a lazy turn toward the basin where the stones waited, the whole scene completely still. Except...

From somewhere, behind a half-ruined wall, slithered ghostly, snakelike tendrils. Worming across the gravel-strewn field, they twisted and twined their way toward the largest of the formations, spiraling up the sides like so many rampant vines. In a matter of seconds, Ava had encased the structure with her dark magic, the stone all but obscured by shadowy fingers.

It worked. Curious, the Orobus sucked in on himself, growing smaller and smaller, until he took on an irregular form, a few errant streaks of shadow escaping from it, but for the most part, semi-solid as he pulled himself together.

Thor hadn't realized he was holding his breath. Not until he heard the faint roar of a far-off engine, the deep, churning grind of machinery pushed to its limit, did he release it. When the sound cut off, he knew Hunter had arrived.

Raising the com to his lips, he whispered, "*Go.*"

Tyr focused on his team. Everyone was in position. Thor, Celine, and Fen had given them enough time to get lined up. Syd was in place, Mir at her side. Ava was currently doing her...thing.

Check. Check, and check.

Watching the Orobus condense itself down to a car-sized shape didn't exactly fill him with confidence, but at least so far, Sydney was right on the money. The God of Chaos was acting...predictably. And as he drifted closer to the prison dolmen, seemingly drawn to the writhing root-like tendrils Ava laid over the stones, Tyr was happy to report things were going according to plan.

And the best part? From Thor's one-word message, Hunter had arrived.

The closer the Orobus approached, the more Ava withdrew, inch by miniscule inch. It was a tedious dance, filled with small hesitations, and a slight back-and-forth teasing movements. But as the god drew ever closer to his prison, Tyr allowed the slightest sense of hope to spark.

Twenty feet. The thing was twenty, then fifteen feet away, until finally, he breached the magical line. Ava's shadowy fingers began receding faster, revealing the stones in their entirety, and as they did, the thing hesitated, then shrank back. Along his line of sight, Tyr watched as Sydney raised a hand, and the slightest shimmer of magic sparkled in the air around the dolmen, so faint the distortion wouldn't be noticeable up close.

Another slight, flicker of movement from the redhead and Tyr caught a flash of light, brilliantly bright, a spark against the inky blackness as her fire flamed hot, igniting the oxygen, vaporizing everything within her magical chamber. A high keening rang through the air, the sound of air becoming ionized and turning to plasma. Exactly like Sydney said, the Orobus was sucked toward the cylinder of magic, now glowing red-hot.

And then like some sort of awful movie, everything went wrong.

The cylindrical cone of magic Sydney created began to buckle, the whining sound growing ever louder as the center caved in, and Mir began shouting, dragging Sydney backward, her heels cutting grooves in the dirt as he pulled her farther away.

Instantaneously, the dark god spread himself thin, the barest layer of shadow over the open debris-strewn field, diluting himself. And when the vacuum exploded, the force of it rippled through the Orobus, cut through the circle like some sort of cosmic storm. The wall of debris struck Tyr hard in the face, shoved him backward, and for a second, he couldn't see a thing. Somewhere to his right, a woman began screaming. Ava, it sounded like, and whatever it was—pain or fear or both—made his heart freeze.

Pushing up, he brushed rocks and stone off him and surged for the circle, toward the screaming. White dust was swirling so thickly he might as well be blind, but the sound was a beacon, and he ended up against one of the dolmens, feeling his way along until he found Mir.

"Over here, she's over here."

They found her sobbing against the side of an overturned car, face white beneath the dust, vacant eyes skittering over them, past them as she sobbed uncontrollably, rubbing her arm like it was on fire. A moment later, Morgane skidded to a stop beside her sister, crushing her into her arms.

"I've got you. Jesus Christ, I've got you."

"Where is the fucker?" Mir demanded, covering Syd with his body, a gun in one hand, his eyes scanning the air, debris still falling. Tyr couldn't say. Between the dust, the darkness, and the shadowy presence of the thing, the Orobus was indistinguishable. One thing was for sure, they were sitting ducks if they stayed where they were.

"We have got to get out of here. Right now."

"He's coming, he's coming, he's coming." Ava chanted in a high, sobbing whisper. "Please, please, before he gets here, we have to go. *Oh God. We have to go.*"

While Mir grasped Sydney, Tyr took Ava and Morgane's arms. "I've got my sister, you watch our backs," Morgane told him, flipping out a knife of her own. She pointed through the smoke. "If we head that way, there's better cover." Ava clung to her neck as they clambered up the side of the rocky basin, Tyr feeling the Orobus creep closer with every slow, unsteady step they took.

Shoving Morgane forward, Tyr hissed, "Get to the top and run if you can. Stick with Mir. The others will be waiting, they'll help, once you clear this dust and they see you."

Turning, he headed back down, sliding through the gravel until his boots hit the bottom of the grade and their footsteps faded away. Debris settling was the only sound as he rounded the circle, feeling his way along, one hand on the stones, the other holding the knife.

Ridiculous, but old habits die hard.

Out of the dust, the shadows coalesced into a loose form, then tightened until they resembled something almost human. They were jerky, the thing's movements. And when he opened his mouth, a low, series of sounds came out. A walking, talking parody of a mortal form. Somehow, Tyr found that to be the most obscene thing he'd seen in a long time. And he'd seen some shit.

Let the others clear the area.

That was Tyr's only thought as he took a step forward, knife in hand, head clearing as he searched for a way to kill this unkillable thing.

"I need for you to get down, Tyr." Behind him, out of the slowly settling dust, Hunter's voice was shaking and unsteady. When he made no move, she said it again. And this time, he felt her hand dig into his shoulder. "You *need* to go. I need room...for what I have to do."

Tyr opened his mouth to protest, then caught a good look at her face.

Something was wrong. With her, with her expression, with her eyes. As if she was being eaten alive from the inside. The shaking was her trying to hold in her power. The fear was because...

"Go. Please. Get them out. Now." Her order was barely a whisper.

Tyr ran. Past the circle, up the side of the pit, his legs pumped as he raced across the field, weaving through the debris. Catching up with Mir and Morgane, he caught Ava beneath the legs and shoulder, heaving her up into his arms. "Run." Was all he managed.

Soldier Field was too far, but if they could make the entrance to the underground walkway, it would provide some cover. "Over there," Tyr yelled, changing direction, Ava's arms wrapping around his neck, holding on tight. "We go in there, and we hunker down."

Mir's com went off, and he clicked it on as they rounded the low wall. They breached the entrance, the pounding of their feet a dull echo in the long, cavernous tunnel. "What in the fuck happened?" Fen's voice exploded out of the com unit.

Mir spoke in between breaths. "Things...went to shit. We're down in...the tunnel by the stadium. You have...to get to cover...now."

"We already are. So are the others. But I had eyes on the circle before we did. Hunter's down there..."

Mir threw the com over to Tyr. "She's going to take him out."

Static crackled loudly over Thor's query. "By herself?"

Tyr leaned his head back against the wall, Ava sobbing softly against his shoulder, Morgane beside her, bracing her with a firm hand. "Yeah, by herself."

Because that's how Hunter did things.

Alone.

25

It was all Hunter could do to keep herself leashed long enough for Tyr and the others to clear the basin. Another minute, perhaps, until they cleared the rubble enough, and they'd be safe.

This see-saw feeling of being enticed by the creature, and needing to see it destroyed, was driving her insane. Add to that the power that was clawing at her insides. Chest heaving, she took a good look around and finally got a clear look at her surroundings. She was inside the circle.

The power clawed its way up her throat, practically pushing out of her mouth before she shoved it back down.

Not here, not here, not yet, not now.

Her eyes wild, she scanned the stones, the gravel basin. If she let loose now, she'd wipe out everything within the vicinity.

Which couldn't happen.

The circle *had* to remain standing, the dolmens must stay intact. If they stood any chance of sending this being to his death, or imprisoning him again, they needed this structure. Since their plan had completely failed, she would have to settle for incapacitating him.

But releasing a trickle of her power, a short burst, could do the trick.

She noticed he'd formed himself into some kind of humanoid, a close-but-yet-so-far version of a human. "Looking good, dark god. Definitely an improvement on the whole, spinning orb of evil you had going on before," Hunter taunted breathlessly, estimating the others had almost reached the outer limits of her range. "Needs a bit of work." She panted, circling him, searching the murky exterior for any sign of weakness. "But it's a starting point, I suppose."

Another ten seconds, and she could loosen up her throat hold on the damn thing thrashing around inside of her. And then she'd see. Partly curious, partly terrified, Hunter rounded the creature again, wondering at the form he'd chosen. "Interesting you'd turn into the very thing you wish to destroy. Some might call that projecting."

A series of low, throbbing sounds came out of the thing, sounding almost pleading.

"Yeah, going to have to work on that. A mouth might help."

Her ten seconds was up, and still, here she was, hesitating.

Weakness or fear or simple reluctance, she never figured it out.

In the seconds it took her to doubt, the thing rose up and encased her in shadow and vapor, the ephemeral gloom every bit a physical blow as if the god had reached out and clutched her in an enormous fist. Without thinking, Hunter blew apart, giving in to the horror at being held by something infinitely more powerful than herself.

And like before, he vanished, evading the explosion, leaving her alone in the circle, the stones thankfully untouched. The boom from the explosion ringing across the lake, Hunter climbed on shaking legs up from the pit, cresting the edge and finding nothing but an empty field.

But behind her...

Turning, she saw him reforming, the shadows pulling together quickly this time, growing darker and impenetrable, the stones beginning to shake as his mass grew by the second.

Without another thought, Hunter sprinted for the city, dodging through the debris, leading him away from Tyr and the others, heading straight for the buildings, praying for any sort of cover as her legs pumped hard, dust kicking up beneath her feet.

Deliberately slow, the Orobus followed, his presence a smudge against the night, blocking out the stars in his wake, sliding through the city streets, his progression almost lazy. While Hunter cut through one street, then another, then leapt through a busted out storefront and disappeared.

26

Tyr tossed the com back to Mir.

Nobody knew where Hunter was. She'd disappeared into the city, seconds after the powerful explosion had rattled the teeth in his head. Whatever she'd done might have bought them all time to escape, but the Orobus was gone as well. According to Thor's choppy report, the bastard was right behind her.

Hunter might be a master at evasion, but right now, she had the biggest, hungriest predator on her trail. And Tyr wasn't about to let her go this alone.

He set Ava gently against the wall. "I'm leaving you with your sister, okay? Thor and the others will be here soon. They'll take you back to the Tower. You'll be safe there."

The woman seemed barely capable of speech, rattled as she was, and Morgane pulled her close, her arm going around Ava's shaking shoulders before she met Tyr's eyes. "Go and find Hunter. She can't be out there alone."

Tyr nodded in agreement, taking the knife Morgane offered, sliding it into his belt.

"She didn't let loose. Not really." Ava's voice was trembling so badly he could barely make out the words. "She will though, once she lures him far enough away."

Raising those extraordinary eyes to his, Ava continued, the words hushed and broken. "She couldn't do it, you see, not so close to the circle. Not without destroying the dolmen."

"How in the hell do you know that?" Morgane hissed, meeting Tyr's confused gaze. "There's no possible way you know what she's thinking."

A blare of sound issued from the com, Mir raising it to his ear. "Yeah?"

"She headed up East Thirteenth, then disappeared to the right. She's about four minutes ahead of you." Thor paused. "And something else."

"Yeah?" Mir released the button, his eye meeting Tyr's and holding.

"I've got lots of action coming in from the north end. So you'd better get moving, right the fuck now."

"Got it."

"Ava's right, though," Sydney said as they mobilized, slipping an arm beneath Ava's. "Hunter would have held back so as not to damage the stones, to give us a chance to trap him later." She managed a half smile. "But once she lets loose and hits him with everything she's got, what will that do to her?"

Tyr didn't know, although images of a wrecked, smoldering mountainside stood starkly in his mind. And the wreck of a human being that surge of power had left behind. "Let's not get ahead of ourselves. She'll lead him on a chase, as long as she can manage. Give us time to get everyone home safe. Then she'll circle back once he's lost her scent."

"And if he doesn't?" Morgane pushed. "If her tricks don't work on him?"

"I'm going to make sure her tricks, as you put it, *do* work. She'll lose him in that maze of buildings, and she's never been caught by any creature that's hunted her before. Hell, I can't ever find her, not unless she wants to be found." But fear welled up in his gut, even as he said it.

Clasping hands with Mir, he jogged out of the tunnel, eyes adjusting to the faint light, heading for the silent, jagged silhouettes of the buildings.

The Orobus left a greasy stain on his way into the city, as if he were a slug and his glistening trail was still wet. Tyr followed it as far as he could, to where it disappeared through the open window of a once popular coffee shop. Beneath the stench of brimstone and sulphur, he caught Hunter's effervescent scent and vaulted over the low wall, jagged glass sticking out like so many teeth. Once inside, he skirted overturned chairs and tables, more broken glass, and skittering rats.

Winding his way through, he exited into a boutique, into an alley, then through another series of formerly upscale shops. For an hour he followed, falling ten, then fifteen minutes behind, the foul odor of the primordial creature drowning out Hunter's sweeter, lighter scent. But it was still there, as she led him on a chase, deeper and deeper into the heart of the city, Tyr following every step of the way.

Tyr knew the moment she backtracked for the first time.

So did the Orobus.

Again and again, she evaded, doubled back, circled around. She's spent several lifetimes learning her skill set, and Tyr hadn't exaggerated when he'd said she was the best. Any other predator would have given up hours ago, having lost the scent.

This creature found her. Every time.

And after an hour, Tyr realized she wasn't going to lose the monster, no matter what she tried. By the time they'd circumnavigated the Lower West side, he knew she was exhausted. Hell, he'd had a good night's sleep and was running on fumes. She hadn't slept at all.

If the Orobus cornered her, Tyr shuddered to think of what might happen. It was time he diverted the asshole. The way he saw it, she'd had her chance and hadn't been able to shake the fucker. Now it was his turn.

A running leap had him on the next roof, and he made sure he landed full force, with both boots on the poured asphalt sheathing, the impact echoing across the low-slung buildings in all directions.

"That's right, motherfucker, come and get me."

Hunter was somewhere to the north, the Orobus between them, taking up plenty of psychic space, the feel of him leaving Tyr faintly nauseous. Almost as if he was sucking the life from him, bit by bit, the longer he remained within range.

Another leap had him across the gap of an alleyway, and after a third, he was skimming the ridge of a roofline, boots pounding along the delicate edge, the slithering presence of the dark god hissing in his ears. Tyr ran. Faster than he thought possible, he ran and he leaped and he ran some more, leading the creature out of downtown, west, toward Chicago Midway.

Plenty of room for Hunter to do her thing.

Plenty of space in case things went south.

And if he had to kick some dark god ass, there was plenty of room for that as well.

This part of the city was abandoned, or at least, it felt like it. The neighborhoods burned out and desolate, the streets filled with half-packed, abandoned cars. As if the inhabitants hadn't even bothered to take their meager belongings with them. The terminal loomed large in the distance, and Tyr pushed harder, his muscles burning, the half-healed injuries from days ago already beginning to crack open.

But for Hunter, he'd finish this. His lips twisted slightly. She'd hate him for this, for not trusting her to do the job herself. Which he understood. To a degree. Except right now, her temper was the least of his concern.

Racing across the transit yard, he jumped the fence and rounded the north end of the terminal, skirted the few planes still docked at the jet bridges, and headed out onto the open runway. It was raining, and the concrete turned slick, his boots slipping on the grooved surface. The creature crept around the terminal, a smudge of dark against the dull, gray sky, still formless but compact, the shadows so dense they were black.

"Come on, come out here and get me," Tyr muttered, knives already in hand, crouched into a half squat, his thighs burning from the sheer exertion of these past hours. "That's right, get out here in the open, you motherfucker."

The Orobus's slow, creeping movements were cautious, a sure sign of an apex predator outside of its normal comfort zone. Who knew he was walking into a trap. Not much of a trap, because steel couldn't hurt him, and Tyr was running on fumes, but he prayed Hunter was on her way.

27

H unter could not believe her eyes.

The stupid man was alone, just waiting for the thing to rise up and strike him down.

After the interfering son of a bitch had decided to take matters into his own hands, she'd had no choice but to follow. Tyr made such a racket, even the dark god had become curious. And when he'd left her trail for Tyr's, Hunter had tracked them both, across rooftops and through genteel neighborhoods. At first, she'd been fueled by anger, and now it was sheer will driving her, as she stayed a hundred paces behind them, waiting to see what Tyr might do next.

She certainly didn't expect him to beckon the thing on, sliver of steel in hand.

Then again, she hadn't expected the Orobus to actually fall for it.

Yet there they both were, testaments to raging testosterone and male idiocrasy. Tyr might as well have been waving a red flag and yelling olé.

It was just like him, she groused, to stick his nose in where it didn't belong. She had this situation under control. One more circuit around the city, and she might have lost the creature for good.

Another one and she'd have snuck up behind him and blown him to kingdom come, along with a couple of city blocks.

Bur she couldn't deny, even bleeding *and* exhausted, Tyr made an impression. Especially now, braced for battle. Perfectly honed for conflict, he carried himself with such ferocious certainty, he rattled her to her core. For a second, all she could do was stare.

But with the two of them in such close quarters, her options were nil.

Trying to shake off a feeling of vague, yet familiar déjà vu, she stumbled slightly on the uneven tarmac, sending a stone flying, the sound amplified to unnatural loudness. When Tyr froze, she stepped away from the building, the bulk of the Orobus looming between them. "Tyr," she said clearly, her voice ringing over the concrete, "I need you to back away. Then I need you to run."

"I can't do that. And you have a hell of a lot of nerve asking me."

Stubborn ass.

"Think about the damage I did to the mountain in the Highlands. Then tell me I have a hell of a nerve. Leave. Let me do what needs done."

"I've got this under control." His tight, even voice belied the amount of blood already staining the front of his vest and leathers. Either from fighting or from his old wounds, she didn't know. "You're completely exhausted. I don't want you anywhere near him, Hunter. Trust me, it's not a good plan."

"You don't even know what I'm planning to do."

"You *can't* destroy him. Not if your power *comes* from him. Why do you think he's been tracking you all this time?" Tyr's voice dropped. "*Think*, Hunter. He *wants* what's inside of you. He *wants* his power back. But once he gets it? I can't lose you, if he..." Then Tyr just stopped talking, as if he couldn't get the words out.

Hunter didn't care. She didn't care what the thing wanted.

She only cared about killing it. *Everything* could be killed. And this power inside of her... It killed indiscriminately. It was death incarnate. Of *course* it would kill the Orobus; it killed everything else.

Problem was, she couldn't unleash herself with Tyr this close.

"Go. Away." She hissed, advancing on the shadowy thing between them. "Come back when this is finished." Once she eradicated it, this whole nightmare would be over. All she had to do was penetrate that shifting surface, find his center, and blow him apart.

"Hunter, whatever you're thinking, stop." Tyr's warning didn't so much as slow her down. Nope. She had a plan.

Her next step had the outer wisps of him within reach. And from here, she could barely resist his pull, tugging at her insides. The reek of him was palpable in the air around her, a thrumming, sickening heaviness. Without another thought, she surged forward, plunging her hand, *her entire arm* into that freezing darkness, straight through to the very middle.

Only to find nothing.

The failure flabbergasted her.

She took a step backwards, stumbled more like, her feet clumsy, and in turn, the Orobus lunged for her, oily black tentacles clawing at her face.

Tyr got there first.

Yanking her away, he pushed her to the ground, out of the thing's range, letting out a loud grunt of pain as the ends of the shadowy tendrils raked across the front of him, the sound wet and tearing and awful.

"Damn it, no." She sobbed. "No. *Why didn't you leave?*" Then she was clawing at Tyr, rolling him over, the Orobus advancing with that slow, steady motion, as if the monster had all the time in the world to mow them down. She yanked at Tyr but he was so heavy, and her hands slippery. Blood was already gathering on the concrete below him, a dark, spreading stain, the shredded front of his Kevlar vest wide open and gaping, blood pouring from the fresh wounds.

Hunter knelt beside Tyr's body. There was far too much blood. She ran her hands over him, feeling the *nothingness* beneath his skin. Sightless eyes stared up at a dull gray sky, rain sheeting down his still, empty face. He was as inert as the ground beneath him, as the still, concrete building behind them. Before, he had always pulsed with energy, and she'd sensed him, as if she was somehow plugged into whatever life force kept him going.

"Come on, Tyr. Come on. I know you're in there." *He cannot be dead.* Dimly, she was aware of the creature's approach.

An hour was a blink of an eye. Or the blink of an eye was an hour. Everything, her entire life narrowed down to this unmoving body in front of her. A bare flicker of his chest in the gray morning light. Tyr was breathing. Barely, but he was alive.

If she used her power, *really, really unleashed it*, she'd kill Tyr. She wouldn't sacrifice him, just to kill this *thing*. She couldn't. Throwing herself over Tyr, she covered him as best she could, as the smothering darkness crushed down upon them.

Like before, she felt the thing caress her, an icy cold trail of pain licking down her face.

And then, like a siphon, the Orobus began to draw the power out of her.

28

With each draw of her power, Hunter knew the monster would suck her dry.

Would leave her a husk.

As glad as she was to be rid of it, as long as she'd dreamed of being free of the burden, part of her railed against it. The power, the dark, elemental magic the Orobus was taking from her, had been hers for so long. *Forever.* A foul chill rushed up her spine, sent her heaving to the tarmac, as the thing pulled from her, ravenously, as if the god were starving.

And perhaps he was.

Something dripped from her chin. Copper tainted her mouth. Blood, then. She was bleeding and her insides were being carved out, and her ribs were collapsing as a wave of crushing blackness swamped her. Fighting unconsciousness, she panted, blood running freely down her chin, splattering on the white concrete below her.

Hang on, hang on a little longer. I will live through this, she promised herself.

She barely managed a glance down at Tyr, immobile and gray beneath her.

And still, that depthless hunger feasted.

She should have expended the full force of her magic upon him, when she had the chance. She should have at least *tried*. Now the dark god would kill them both and steal her magic, besides. Soon, he would have *everything*.

A yank, a surge, and more flowed out of her. Eviscerated, that's what this felt like. She was being slowly, methodically gutted, and in its place, she was left with a relentless emptiness as the magic burned its way out of her, to be swallowed greedily.

Hours later, days, maybe, she lay on her side, utterly drained.

Alone.

The Orobus was gone. To where, she did not know. She did not care. Only that he was gone and the relentless siphoning had stopped. Probably because there was nothing left to take. Where there had once been a deep well of power, now there was nothing. The roiling, evil center she'd carried within her was gone.

Her hand was stretched out before her and experimentally, she curled her fingers. They barely twitched. It took time for her to shift, to roll over far enough to lift her head. Every movement brought a fresh wave of pain, and she vomited when she raised herself to her knees. Her seeking hand found Tyr.

Hands skimming over his body, she followed his every line. He was still warm, but...wet. Wet and unmoving and something didn't feel right. Her eyes were unfocused by the drain on her energy, her body barely functioning. She shook him weakly. "Tyr? Wake up."

The words came out as hoarse sounds. In his vest pocket, she found a com unit, the light barely flickering green. Pressing the button, she whispered, "Please...please, help us," before her head dropped to his chest. A slow, steady beat stirred beneath her ear, the sound soothing as her eyes slipped shut.

When hands pulled her away, she struggled before her head cleared, realizing it was only Fenrir and Thor. When they separated her from Tyr, she fought weakly against them, fought to get back to Tyr, who was being dragged, limp and unmoving, to a waiting vehicle.

She'd seen enough death in her life to know.

Know what it looked like, smelled like, felt like. Knew that there'd be no more grumpy silences, no more pissed off stewing, no broody mood swings. No more lovemaking. No more Tyr. All of her life, he'd been there for her.

Would have always been there for her.

He'd spent his life guarding her, watching over her. That much, she'd figured out this past week. They'd never been apart because he'd always known exactly where she was. She'd belonged to him, heart and soul, from the second he'd raised her from the dead.

Thor loaded him into the back, Fen lifting her to her feet as she swayed against him. "Is he dead?"

"No," Fen murmured, slipping his arm beneath her shoulders. "Not yet. We're getting you both back to the Tower. Mir's getting the infirmary ready for Tyr, as we speak. You okay?"

She nodded, grateful he was holding her up. "Just shaken up and worried about him," she lied. "Don't know how long I was out."

"You're white as a ghost." Fen stepped back, then grabbed her when she almost fell. "How much of this blood is yours?" he demanded, his head dipping down while he inspected her face, frowning at what he found. She touched her hand to her chin, finding dried crust there, below her nose.

"Just...a little of it, I think." She was having trouble with her mouth. It didn't want to make words. "Just get Tyr home as fast as possible. Please?" Fen braced her up, led her to the vehicle, and she slid in beside Tyr. Hunter wrapped a hand around his wrist, felt his thready pulse and held on, leaning her head against the seat.

Once they reached the Tower, the flurry of activity swept Tyr away from her.

She trudged behind them, the shouting and panic barely penetrating the descending fog, her feet so heavy she could barely lift them. They took Tyr in the elevator, and she was left waiting for the thing to come back down, slumped against the wall, eyes half closed. Stumbling into it, she punched fifteen, then waited until the doors opened again, stumbled out, and followed the panicked yelling.

Mir had Tyr stretched out on a silver table, stripped down, his chest and stomach looking like they had been flayed wide open. He was writhing, pulling against Fenrir's hands pinning him down to the table. He was hooked up to a variety of machines, their displays colorful and erratic, displaying numbers and graphs she didn't understand, nor want to. All she saw was the face of the man she loved, contorted in pain. The muscles of his neck standing out in long, taut cords.

His howl of pain rocked the room, and she stepped forward, only to be cut off by Fen, moving to get a better grip, securing Tyr down, his feet kicking hard and fast against the stainless table. And then his face relaxed, the muscles going loose. Fen's knuckles went slack, and he stepped away.

Mir was running his hands over the wounds, blueish light dancing from the ends of his fingers, sinking into Tyr's flesh, the gaping cuts closing, sealing shut. Beneath the sheet of healing, blue magic, Tyr's chest rose in a slow steady rhythm. Relief flooded through her, and as the horrors of the past hours were finally unleashed, she retreated into the hall, sank to the floor, tears running down her face, mixing with the dried blood.

TYR'S EYES flickered open while Mir closed the final wound.

"Where is Hunter?" he growled, his throat raw, as if he'd been screaming. The last he'd seen her, she'd shoved her hand, *her whole arm*, for fuck's sake, into the middle of the Orobus. When he'd gone down, the agony of the thing's magic slicing through him, she'd still been on her feet, ready for a fight. After that, things got...fuzzy.

Mir stepped back, his lips thinning out.

"Where the fuck is Hunter?" Tyr demanded. "And trust me, I *will* heave my carcass off this table to go find her, if that's what it takes." He was pretty sure he'd end upon the floor, but he'd crawl to her if he had to.

"She's right outside." Mir's eyes shifted over to the right. "Fen, go tell her he's awake." There was confusion in his voice as he went on,

"I'm actually surprised she's not in here. She rode in with you, and I thought she was right behind us when you were on the gurney..." Mir's gaze lifted, then his voice trailed off. "Oh fuck."

Tyr managed to raise his head as Hunter's unconscious body was laid on the table beside him, her face bone-white, her limbs limp and spilling off the sides of the table. "She was outside... I found her like this... Shit, I didn't know... She said she was only shaken up when we found you both at the airport... Other than the blood on her face... she seemed okay." Fen was babbling, his explanation coming fast between panicked breaths. "Shit. Oh, shit."

"Did the Orobus touch her?"

"No, but I was out." Tyr propped himself upon an elbow, managed to swing his legs over the side of the table. "She touched *him*, though. Shoved her arm right through him, just before he nearly sliced me in two."

He didn't miss the look Mir and Fen traded. Mir quickly stripped off her jacket, gave her arms a quick once-over, then checked the rest of her body. From what Tyr could see, she didn't have a mark on her.

"How long were you out?"

"No telling," Tyr said slowly. "I didn't wake up until a minute ago." He paused, gaze roaming desperately over her, tracking her wan face, the slack expression. "How did you even know where to find us?"

"Hunter called it in on the radio."

Tyr mulled this little tidbit over as Fen muttered. "I don't understand why she didn't just blast him. If she can eradicate the stones, then surely she could blow him away, right?"

"Not when I was so close," Tyr explained. "She was trying to get me to leave. To give her space so she could do exactly that. I refused. And once I went down, she was alone with the Orobus."

"So her options were limited."

Tyr had an awful thought. "She had no options at all." He couldn't take his eyes from her empty, pale face. "And she was too stubborn to leave me."

Mir ran a hand over her, the blue flame sparking, sinking into her body, then fading away. "She isn't injured, not that I can tell. Aside from all of the blood on her face, which is considerable, there doesn't seem to be a mark on her. Unless..." Mir's hands fell to his sides, his gaze growing distant.

"What?" Tyr demanded. "What the hell are you thinking?"

"When Syd went up against the Orobus, when he hit her with his power, it made her nose bleed. His magic, it was toxic, and it made her bleed." His eyes narrowed, the bright blue flame issued from his hand settled in a steady blanket over her body. "There's no trace of him, though, nothing he left behind, anyway." Mir frowned. "Odd."

Tyr's heart nearly stopped. "It's not odd. It's the explanation for what's happened to her," Tyr said softly. "The Orobus took back his power. She couldn't fight him, she was helpless, so he pulled his dark magic out of her. And it's left her too weak to..."

"Shit," Mir bellowed, and instantly, blue flame shot out of both hands, coating Hunter, until she was completely encased in his glowing, healing light. After a few minutes, Mir stepped back, his expression grim. "No wonder she's in such bad shape. No injuries, nothing physical, but her life force... It's gone, Tyr."

29

F reyr checked his weapons, praying Fen was heading his way. No sense in dying a hero with no witnesses. Kind of defeated the purpose.

Thor's warning was correct. Something *was* coming from the north, along with the rain. The skittering of Grim was something they hadn't heard for months, and now there were too many to count.

Everyone else had loaded into the Hummers a few moments ago. Vali and Balder, Thor, Ava, who was a limp, staggering mess, Celine and Syd protesting every step of the way. Fen was lurking somewhere around, and Morgane walked up right beside him with Loki, who was currently filling the airways with his opinion about *that* decision.

"Look. There are plenty of other places you could be right now."

"Yeah?" Morgane said, stepping up next to Freyr, a com in one hand and flipping one of her custom-made knives in the other. "Name one." The look she shot Freyr was pure mischief. "And if it has anything to with the culinary arts, you, my friend, are in deep trouble." Clicking the com off, she leaned in.

"See, he probably was about to make a crack about me baking cookies, or some such shit," she whispered. Freyr was pretty sure this wasn't the best time for a romantic squabble, but he was also glad for the company, so he kept his trap shut.

"*Vantage point.*" Loki's strained voice issued from the com, and damn, he sounded pissed. "I was *going to say* there are plenty of good *vantage points* you could report from."

"News flash, these things can climb. I'm no safer up in one of the buildings than I am down here. Plus, I can't fly." With a wink, she threw Freyr the com. "I seriously don't know why he even bothers. If I wanted to, I could keep him going for days." She squinted down Michigan Avenue. "How many do you think? And do you think *she's* with them?"

Freyr knew who *she* was, and he didn't like the thought of facing off with Hel one bit.

"Probably. We haven't had an actual sighting of her, but it's safe to assume she's skulking around. Enough of her minions are around to know she's holding their leashes. What do you think?"

"I agree." Morgane's voice was tight. "I never thought I'd say this, but I wish Odin was here."

"You and me both."

For a while they waited in silence, the clicking of talons and thousands of claws over stone and concrete the only sound besides their combined breathing. "So...tell me we have a plan," Morgane said calmly. "Or do we just stand here while they overwhelm us?"

"Of course we do. I'm hoping this goes better than Plan A did. See that truck parked over there, the green one against the curb?" Shaking her head, Morgane squinted into the dim. "That's Plan B. When I say move, you follow me, understand?"

The barest nod told him she did, and she continued to wait beside him, tense and taut but didn't flinch, not as five hundred Grim bore down upon them. It was a shiny wall of black, the stench already reaching them, the sickening sweet smell turning his stomach. "Another ten seconds," Freyr cautioned, noting two, small groups breaking rank, scaling the buildings on either side. "And it looks like we'll still have some fighting to contend with after the explosion."

"*Fine.*" Morgane hissed through clenched teeth. "You're sure about this Plan B shit?"

"Pretty sure," Freyr told her, reaching out to grasp her sleeve. He was easing her toward him, intending to draw her into the relative safety of a nearby bank's marble entry, when everything went to shit.

The world exploded in a flash of white, the incendiary flare illuminating the hulking, rounded shapes of Grim before obliterating them completely. Throwing himself over Morgane, he sandwiched her between his body and the street, the sweep of blistering heat obliterating his jacket and his Kevlar instantly, before burning its way down through his flesh. Thanking the gods he'd thought to throw his arm across his face, Freyr kept Morgane pinned, the explosion scattering chunks of demon, concrete, metal, and glass all around them in smoking, stinking piles.

When he was sure the worst of it had passed, Freyr raised his head. Where the truck had been, nothing was left. A handful of demons skittered around, and he drew his knife and a gun, clambering unsteadily to his feet, crouched over Morgane. A few of them attacked, and he made quick work of them, while the rest crept off, disappearing through the smoke.

Moaning, Morgane rolled over onto her stomach, the com squawking frantically on the ground. "Morgane? Fucking hell, Morgane, pick up... Are you there... *Pick up!*"

Freyr reached down and answered. "We're both still here. Not dead, surprisingly enough." He gave her a quick once-over, noted the injuries to her leg. "We're okay, but we're going to need attention down here." The smoke was maddening, filled with the stench of burnt demon, phosphorus, and accelerant. The mixture seared his nostrils. A few feet away, Loki materialized onto the street and dove for Morgane, scooping her from the asphalt, while Freyr continued scanning the clearing fog for any sign of attack.

"I thought we had a fucking plan?" Freyr muttered, his gaze glued to movement in the dim shadows, his ears alert to the sounds of retreating Grim. Fen appeared out of the smoke, Vali right behind him, their faces pale and streaked with soot.

"We did," Loki explained, checking Morgane over, pausing at the leg that was twisted and bleeding. "Faulty initiator on the charges is Mir's first guess." He turned with her in his arms, and stopped, eyes widening. "Shit, Freyr. I think you'd better..."

Freyr figured the end of that sentence out when one of his legs went out from underneath him. Pitching forward onto the street, he barely missed a wet, smoldering pile of barbequed Grim, the gun still clutched in his hand. He managed a hoarse, "Fuck," right before he face-planted. Apparently, the stench of burnt flesh wasn't only coming from the Grim piled around him.

Fen rolled him onto his stomach, and the heavy hand on his shoulder kept him there. "Stay down. Mir's on his way. Let him take a look at you." Fen's voice dropped. "Holy shit. I cannot believe you are still alive."

As the adrenaline rush faded, pain flooded in, scrambling his synapsis. Flashes of agony alternated with the memory of a bright, glaring flash on his retinas, an explosion blowing out his eardrums, a searing heat cutting through his shoulders and back, and the imperative, overwhelming need to protect Morgane at all costs.

Mixed with the knowledge that he felt like he was dying.

30

Freyr woke in his own bed.

Which was amazing, considering the last thing he remembered. A faint glimmer of wry amusement coursed through him. He should be dead. He'd thought he was dead, when he'd fallen face first to the ground, but now he was good as new, thanks to Mir's healing magic and a stroke of luck.

Glancing out the window, he figured he'd also slept for almost an entire day.

Actually, *good as new* may have been an overstatement, Freyr thought, throwing back the covers. With a groan, he heaved his aching body out of bed. While he wasn't dead, his body reminded him he'd come close. He'd avoided the bulk of the blast, but looking in the mirror...

"Damn it all to hell." Half of his hair was burned off, the other half singed black and stank of protein and smoke. His face, thankfully, was mostly untouched, except for a spectacular shiner. Strong hair game was always his benchmark, but it had taken a serious beating in the explosion that had leveled an entire city block. Eyeing his razor, he picked it up, studied the jagged mess that was once his gorgeous, awe-inspiring mane and went to work.

Twenty minutes later, Morgane audibly gasped when he passed her in the hall. "Holy shit, Freyr, I barely recognized you."

"Change of pace. Figured I'd give the rest of these assholes a break from the competition and try to fit in." The quip came out smoothly enough, even though his body rattled like a bucket of bolts as he meandered down the hallway. And yeah, his head was freezing, minus the mop of blond hair.

"Look," she said, moving closer. "What you did..." She glanced down the hall where the War Room door stood wide, the sounds of laughing and raised voices echoing loudly. "Loki's been looking for you," she said, dipping her head. "Now that you're up, he'll want a word with you."

Her eyes were bright when she finally looked up at him, muttering in a teary, hushed voice, "But I want to say thank you. You saved my ass. Mir said if you hadn't thrown yourself on top of me, I would have enjoyed another little trip to the Underworld. Permanently, this time."

"How's the leg?" Freyr asked, every bit as softly, noting she was moving as stiffly as he was.

"Better. Not a hundred percent, but I'll be fine." She waved a hand in the air. "No big deal, really." Freyr knew most of her body was covered in scars, courtesy of her nights spent fighting the Grim in the streets. Morgane was every bit as deadly as the rest of them, even though she was mortal.

"Good," he told her as they neared the room. "At least one thing went right yesterday. Maybe we can salvage something out of the debacle." He swore she mumbled *fat chance* on her way past him down the hall, but he could have been wrong.

Strange thing was, he'd always taken his looks for granted. Kind of like your thumb. Handy, but nothing you really noticed until you tried to pick up a pencil. And then see what the fuck happened. See how much writing you get done *then*. He glanced at his reflection in the mirror he passed in the hallway. Weird. And he realized something in that split second, looking at that unfamiliar, foreign face staring back.

While he had taken his good fortune for granted, he'd also taken everything it had brought him. Which was women, mostly. Lots and lots of women. So many women he couldn't count them, even if he had been moved to try.

But the funny thing was, none of that mattered. None of it had been real. He thought about what Tyr felt for Hunter. Loki for Morgane, Fen for Celine.

Hope. Desperation. Love.

Those feeling were real.

He thought about what he'd seen in Loki's face, when he'd appeared on the street, unsure if Morgane was alive or dead. What Tyr and Hunter had gone through, these past days. He'd never felt anything close to that. Never wanted to. But lately, he'd found himself wondering...

What it might be like to feel, like they did.

He'd never had that. He'd led this glittering, gilded life, full of a few brilliantly colored moments, richly saturated with pleasure and empty promises. None of which made life worth living. Bearable, but not worthwhile.

Hesitating, he paused before he swung into the War Room. They'd be planning. Strategizing. Working to regain some ground, extend their lives another few days. He'd always been perfectly content to sit back, feet up on the table, and wait for orders.

A dutiful, obedient little soldier.

At least now he had the haircut to match.

The low buzz of voice went silent when he walked in. As every eye turned toward him, he said three little words he never thought would come out of his mouth, and figured he'd live, *though not very long*, to regret.

"I have a plan."

Okay, so maybe that was four words.

31

"That's all I can do."

Tyr watched as Mir's blue healing magic faded to a dull glimmer, the color darkening as it settled over Hunter's body, a slight blush blooming her cheeks, her chest rising in a slow, steady rhythm as she slept. This was his third attempt, and Tyr prayed for a miracle.

"This will hold her for a few days," Mir murmured, withdrawing his hand, dark circles beneath his eyes as he met Tyr's gaze. "Any more, and the magic will do more harm than good."

"And after that?" Tyr closed his eyes, praying to whatever the fuck gods were left listening to save his woman.

"She's dying, Tyr. Nothing I can do to change that." Mir's edict stopped him dead in his tracks. Over the past couple of hours, he'd entertained that very possibility, always with a big *hell no* at the end of his wildest imaginings.

"She can't die."

"The Orobus took what's been keeping her alive. There are bills to be paid, Tyr, and Hunter's had more time on this little blue ball than most. Without that power inside, her life force is fading." Mir turned around, just long enough for Tyr to see the utter exhaustion lining his face. "I'm sorry, my brother."

"What can I do?"

"Nothing. You can't cheat Fate. You've done everything, you gave her this life, she's *had* time, and lots of it, Tyr."

But not with me, Tyr wanted to scream. *We haven't had any time.* No fucking time at all. "Bullshit. That is bullshit."

"Maybe so. But it's the truth."

"You've seen it?"

"Nobody sees anything these days." Mir shot him a sideways glance. "You know Odin's the only one who ever *really* saw the future. And trust me, talking to him these days is a total waste of time. I'm giving you my best educated guess, based on all of the evidence I have at hand. The bastard took the one thing that's been keeping her alive."

Standing over the love of his life, Tyr raged. How in the hell had things had gone so far off the rails? This should have been so simple. It *would* have been so simple, if not for their big, fucking, overblown egos. Where this woman ended, he began. But like a perfect circle, it would collapse in upon itself if the sphere wasn't complete. That much he knew.

In all of their history, over all of their years, he'd watched over her. He'd watched her grow, thrive, bloom. He'd watched her roar. Like a fucking lion. No, scratch that. *Like a fucking dragon.* And he wasn't about to let her voice dim out into some kind of whimper just because he'd tried to do the right fucking thing, for once in his life. He was a god, for fuck's sake, maybe it was about time to start acting like one. Besides, who said Asgard was gone? No one ever *confirmed* it. Odin saw the future. But he hadn't been the only one.

There'd been others who could, long before Odin.

Maybe it was time someone looked them up.

Behind him, Mir's voice grew impossibly soft. "I'm so fucking sorry, Tyr. Essentially, Hunter signed her own death warrant by saving you." He turned back to the computer. "And there's nothing you can do about it."

"Bullshit," Tyr said again, this time forcefully. "Try again."

"The Orobus took something vital from her, even though there are no outward signs. Think of my magic as a patch, or at worst, a Band-aid. It will only hold her for a short time. Too much will kill her. Unless we can figure something else out." Mir drew a raspy, tired breath. "I don't suppose you have any ideas?"

Tyr stared down at her, guilt eating away at him. *Would've, should've, could've,* rattling around in his brain until the words were playing in a steady, unhelpful loop. If only he'd managed to lead the Orobus far enough away or completely lose him in the city. If only she hadn't tried to be a hero.

"Blaming yourself won't bring her back. And time isn't something she has a lot of right now," Mir warned him, heading for the door. "I'm wiped out. And trust me, this wasn't the only thing that went wrong in last night's clusterfuck. Freyr and Morgane are lucky to be alive. You are too. So stop feeling sorry for yourself and make these next two days the best she's ever had. I've done what I can.

"Get her out of here, put her in bed, let her sleep. When she wakes up, she'll need to eat." Mir paused in the doorway. "You want to show her how you feel? Then don't squander a moment of it. If this were Syd, you wouldn't be able to pry me away." By the time he finished, his face was hollow. "No chance you could work the spell on her again, is there?"

Tyr shook his head. Maybe he could, *if only he remembered the spell, or had Hunter's cursed stone circle set on hallowed ground, or a million other details lined up perfectly.*

"All I wanted was to keep her forever," Tyr said, his words stopping Mir in his tracks. "And I knew the only way to do that was to make her hate me. Better she hate me and remember me, than make love to me just once and forget me." He shook his head slightly, looking sober. "I wanted to keep her. And that was the only way I thought I could."

"You really are a cold-hearted bastard."

"Yes, I can be." Tyr paused. "But I'd do it again." A ghost of a smile crossed his lips. "Yeah. I'd go through everything again, just for these last few days with her." Not fancy words, but true enough.

"But...?"

"But I'd be a lying bastard if I told you that would be enough." A lifetime wouldn't be enough. Damn it, she was meant to be his. And if she was going to burn down the world, he'd stand next to her while she did it. *And* he'd hold her hand while they watched the flames lick the sky all around them.

"Well shit, you make it sound like it was Fate who brought you two together."

"Maybe it was," Tyr told him, an idea kindling. "You know? Maybe it was."

TYR SCOOPED HER UP, carried her to his room, and laid her down, making sure not to wake her. She was a mess, and he used a cloth to carefully lathe her face, wiping the blood, the dirt away. Frowning at the faint scars he'd never noticed before. He watched her sleep, even slept himself for a few hours. When he opened his eyes, she was watching him, the light in her eyes guttering.

"I'm sorry," she told him, her voice impossibly weak. "I couldn't leave you." When he stroked her cheek, the skin was soft, velvety, the color paper-white. He kissed her gently, grateful her lips were warm. Grateful he still had the chance.

"It's all right. We'll figure this out, Hunter." The words, her name, came out whisper-rough. "I'll fix this." *I'll save you.*

"I don't believe this can be fixed." She managed a slight, hoarse laugh. "When I asked you to kill me, I thought I was ready to die." Tears gleamed in her eyes. "Imagine my surprise when I discovered I'm not."

The words hit Tyr in the gut so hard he couldn't move a muscle. "There are things that need to be said between us, Hunter. Things that *should* be said. Mir said it was Fate that brought us together. Do you believe that?" He licked his lips, Hunter following every movement of his tongue.

"Strangely enough, I do."

"Would you like to know what I told him?"

She nodded, her eyes huge and shining.

"I told him all the things that I should have said in that cave, when everything was about to end."

"Which cave?" she asked softly. "Which time? We seem to be developing a bad habit of ending up in trouble in the same place, you know."

Tyr pressed his lips against her forehead.

"Yes, we do." Somehow, impossibly, she was making jokes when she was slipping further away from him. "I wanted you to hate me, that day I left and rode away." At that, Hunter went still, even her breathing seemed to stop. "It was a stupid plan, in retrospect, now that I think about it, although it did work.

"I needed you to despise me. Because once you did, I knew you'd hate me forever. I figured that was my best chance of keeping you, because then, you'd never forget me." He tucked her beneath his chin. "Had I spent the night with you I'd intended, my one night with the chieftain's beautiful daughter, you would have forgotten me."

"I wouldn't have..."

"You would have and you know it. But the way you looked at me, circling me on your horse that day, with such hatred in your eyes? If you hated me that desperately, I figured you'd never forget me."

A wry smile twisted his mouth. "And that was my master plan to keep you forever."

"That has to be the most boneheaded thing I've ever heard."

"Did you ever forget me? Even once?"

"No," she admitted.

"Then I guess my strategy worked."

"You are an idiot."

Tipping her face up, Tyr kissed her, softly tasting her lips. "You are everything in this world, in this life, that makes me want to see tomorrow. Time with you...becomes irrelevant.

"Because whatever we have, however long we have? Will *never* be enough. So what do you say, love? Will you share this life with me? For however long we have it?"

"I'm afraid it won't be for very long, Tyr," she whispered, her voice rough. She took his face in her hands, her golden eyes brimming with unshed tears. "But yes, I would like that very much."

His eyes burned too, so much he could barely speak past the lump in his throat. "I thought we'd burn the world down together."

Hunter kissed him back. "Yes, we might have done that if only we hadn't been so stubborn." She kissed him once more, slowly and gently and thoroughly. The kind of kiss they might have shared if they had all the time in the world. But it wasn't nearly enough as she tucked herself against him and fell fast asleep.

This time, when they woke, the flush of pink in her cheeks was gone, and she barely could sit, relying on Tyr to prop her upright, her hands worrying the edge of the blanket while her eyes tracking his movements around the room, as if finding every nervous tell.

"How bad were things, when I was out?" she asked, her gaze skimming down the front of him. "And did Mir heal me, like he healed you? There was so much blood, I wasn't sure you were even alive."

Tyr dodged her probing eyes. "He used his magic on you, yes. As for me, it took some doing for Mir to close the wounds back up, but... nothing I haven't been through before."

Hunter wasn't buying it. "Hmm. The truth, please." She said it pleasantly enough, but there'd be no evading the question.

"I'm all right," he said quietly. "But it's not me we need to discuss. Tell me what the Orobus did to you. I might fix it, if I knew where to start."

"There's no fixing this, Tyr. He took his power back. All of it. And now I only feel curiously...empty." She managed a slight smile. "That's what's happening, right? I'm dying?"

Tyr sat on the edge of the bed, pulling her over to him, and kissed the top of her head. "Nope, not today. Right now, you're going to eat a good breakfast and get at least another eight hours of sleep. Once you get that in, then we'll talk."

"Deal."

Tyr stayed true to his word. He watched every move as she shoveled breakfast into her mouth. Then he gently tucked her into bed. She was barely halfway through arguing with him over how she wasn't a bit tired when she passed out and didn't say another word.

If she only knew what she looked like. Curled up in a tight knot like some kind of exotic cat, ivory-skinned with long, dark lashes on her high cheekbones, all that black hair spilling over the pillow. Gods, *what was her ancestry*, Tyr wondered.

Her father had been a fierce, proud man, but Hunter's mother? He'd never met the woman.

Heard rumors. Tales, more like. Nothing he put any stock in, since they all had the ring of superstition and fear.

"Sleep, my princess," he whispered, running his fingers across her beautiful face.

If she was willing to trade her life to an evil god, then he could do the same.

Consequences be damned.

32

"**N**ice hair."

Yeah. Yeah. Yeah.

Freyr expected to take some ribbing, but after a few minutes, the joke got really old. "So, goldilocks, let's hear this proposition of yours?" Loki's lips twitched. These assholes were enjoying his transformation way too much. But Freyr manned up.

"First, we've got to consider the possibility that Hunter won't be able to close the gate. Whatever happened at the airport, she's in no condition to destroy the circle, even if we did manage to lure the thing close enough again."

"Tyr's out of commission as well." Mir's voice rang quietly from the back of the room, and the god looked beat as he cracked his knuckles. "Don't count on either of them, not for a while."

Freyr paused, thinking back on the explosion that almost killed him and Morgane. "We used nearly all of our munitions staging those two smaller explosions yesterday. We'll need more supplies. I'm sending a team down to Valparaiso to the depot. If there are no objections, I need two volunteers." He nodded as Vali and Balder raised their hands.

"Thirdly..." He took a deep breath. "It's something we haven't discussed nearly enough. How is the Orobus accessing those doorways? And what can we do to close them?"

"Do we seriously want to barricade that thing here? On this planet?"

"Not the best option, to be sure." Freyr nodded, in full agreement. "Look, we've been wasting all our time and energy trying to draw him to the circle and lock him away. While we're getting our asses kicked, he's getting stronger."

"He's getting stronger because he's using the doorways to siphon energy from the other worlds." Mir braced his arms on the table as Freyr nodded. They'd discussed this already. And it was time to get everyone else on board. "According to Syd's newest energy readings."

"So we're stopping him," Freyr told them. "We shut those doors down, lock them up tight. Chicago's practically a ghost town. There's nothing left here for him to feed on."

Aaaand...this was where things got complicated.

Freyr looked over at Mir, and he offered a faint nod of encouragement. "My idea is to have Syd use her magic to seal the doorways. Which will force the Orobus to waste time and energy trying to unlock the doors or hunt for another means to access the other realms." As there was no reaction from anyone, Freyr plowed on. "He'll waste his time and his energy to access his resources, which will conserve our own. How close would you need to be, and how long would it take, Syd?"

"A few hours, max," she answered, nodding as she deliberated. "If he hasn't imbued any of his dark magic into the stones. In which case, I'll have to use some fancy spell work to get around it." Sydney met the questioning glances with an explanation. "When the Orobus entered our world through the Bean...the *Cloud Gate*, he left imprints all over the metal. Swirling imprints, like fingerprints burned into the stainless steel. There's reason to believe he's left some sort of imprint on the stones." She mused, tapping her finger on her cheek. "If he has, I'll need time to investigate. Let me take another look at the schematics. Once I'm sure they're clean, just a few minutes per stone, and I should be able to lock them down. I'm just not sure how long my magic would hold out against him." She seemed to do a quick calculation in her head. "Maybe a week at the most?"

A week. It would be something. Longer than they had now.

"How do we draw him out of the city?" Sydney asked.

"I had this crazy idea." He wasn't sure it would work, but with Tyr out of the picture, this was better than nothing. Tamping down the feeling of gut-clenching dread that came with assuming responsibility, Freyr began laying out his plan. When he was finished, to his surprise, the others were actually nodding agreement.

"If this works, it's still only a stopgap solution," Freyr warned them, his nerves relaxing a little as everyone seemed to be on board. "And the whole thing depends on Syd's magic being strong enough to withstand the Orobus's."

"Still," Loki reminded them, "it's an approach we haven't considered before. And it'll buy us time to regroup. Time we need."

"All right." Mir met Freyr's gaze steadily. "Hop to. The faster we get moving on this, the better our chances are."

Freyr watched them all file out of the room, his stomach finally settling down. As he turned to follow them, he heard a sound behind him and found Loki still seated at the table. "I've got something to say to you, goldilocks."

Here we go, Freyr thought.

"It's not often someone surprises me," Loki went on, his drawling voice bored. "But every once in a while, I have to admit, life catches me off-guard." Loki stood, extended his hand to Freyr. "When you saved Morgane, I swear to the gods, you saved the only thing that matters to me."

Freyr lost his breath as Loki yanked him into a tight embrace. "And for that, my brother, I owe you everything."

———————

33

By the time Tyr located the others, there were several surprises waiting for him. He expected chaos. He found order. He expected spirits to be low. They were not. He expected half of them to be drunk, but even there, he was sadly disappointed.

Sober. The lot of them.

There was a new king in town, and he looked...

"Holy hell, what did you do to yourself?"

Freyr looked strangely capable, stripped of his long golden mane and dressed in a plain black Kevlar from head to toe. He looked almost...deadly. He seemed almost...competent. Plans were in the making, plans Tyr had no part of. Even now, he hovered like an outsider over Thor's shoulders, surveying the schematics strewn across the table littered with empty coffee cups and half-eaten sandwiches.

Freyr fanned out the pages and handed him one. "We've got some shit in the planning stages, but I want you to look this over with fresh eyes. Especially after what happened last time. I don't want to get blindsided again."

Surprised, Tyr took a second longer than he normally would have before bellying up to the table. "Nice hair."

"*Whatever.*"

Tyr rubbed the side of his neck absentmindedly, wondering whether Freyr was capable of planning a fucking party, much less a war. "Fill me in."

And Freyr did. Going over each step in painstaking detail, Sydney or Mir interrupting every so often to point out a technical glitch or detail he'd missed. He didn't miss many. "And that's the best we're going to do, since the bastard is so unpredictable. There are variables we can't control. The weather, for one. And how long it'll take the bastard to figure out a way to circumvent Syd's magic. Other than that, we've got the bases covered."

Bases covered indeed. The implications of what the failed mission cost them sunk in. They should have been free of this thing, right now, today. The world could be well on its way to healing, and Hunter wouldn't be on her way to the grave.

Yet here they stood, planning another desperate mission.

But shit... Tyr spun the page covered in Freyr's handwriting and reread it. This was a good, solid plan. Well thought out, most complications anticipated, weaknesses accounted for. Tyr was on the verge of pointing out the one glitch Freyr hadn't anticipated, when Balder and Vali dragged in a couple of heavy, black bags.

"Got 'em." Vali huffed, as Loki let out a foul curse, bursting out of his chair. Beyond the door, Tyr saw another haphazard pile of matching bags out in the hall.

"Tell me you did *not* bring that shit up here." Freyr growled. "The fucking parking garage. Store that shit down in the parking garage."

"I got to show you what we found. Tyr, take a look at these and tell us if we got enough fire power." Vali's face looked like a kid at Christmas.

Zipping open the bag on the table, Balder spread open the canvas, exposing... "Holy fuck." Military grade explosives with optic readers, titanium cases, and hair triggers, all jumbled together in the bag. A tangled mess of deathly weaponry.

"Please tell me you assholes did not transport all of these like this?" Running his hands through his newly shorn crew cut, Freyr was fuming.

"Well, they came in these big, silver cases, packaged up all nice and shit, but they took up too much room." Vali sighed dramatically. "You gotta understand, we've got space issues in the Tahoe. The Hummer's got more storage, but you toasted the extra one last month, so we *had* to take the Chevy. Blame yourself, asshole."

As the bickering picked up, Tyr and Freyr's eyes met over the table, sharing a single thought. *Idiots.*

"You two are seriously going to get us all killed with your bad decisions." Tyr snarled, setting the initiators out on the table gently, one by one. At least twenty and a dozen ignitors. Which meant the other bags were full of charges. Semtex or C-4, most likely.

"So true," Freyr echoed, picking one up and inspecting it. "So will these be enough? I sent these assholes out to the abandoned military base in Valparaiso. Wasn't sure there'd be anything to scavenge, but it looks like we got lucky."

Tyr lined them all up on top of the paperwork and counted. "Yeah, this will make a hell of a crater." He shook his head. "But none of them will work on the God of Chaos or the circle."

"And what is this belief founded on?" Balder asked.

Tyr picked up one of the charges and held it between his fingers. "These won't touch him because he's made of fucking stardust and moonbeams or some such shit. Even a nuclear blast won't touch him because he's made from a different kind of matter, and by that, I mean physical matter."

"He's right," Sydney pointed out. "Nothing touches him. My magic only weakened him, and I hit him with everything I had. But there was no way I could outright destroy him."

Balder spoke, his voice cautiously quiet, "We swung past the museum site on the way back. Just for a minute, you know, to see what was doing. He's growing again. Looks like he might swallow up the marina, maybe the stadium too."

"What happens when he gets too big to control?"

Tyr grabbed a pair of binoculars and headed for the stairs. Taking them three at a time, he reached the small metal door that opened to the roof. The wind was chilling down, as if winter knew it might not get its chance or had never left in the first place. Bracing himself on one of the buttresses, he looked southwest. The whole damn area was engulfed in a maelstrom of black, and Balder was right, the monster was growing.

"We can't fail this time." There was steel in Tyr's voice, steel that he hadn't felt since this whole shit show had started, months and months ago. "We shouldn't have tried to trap him and imprison him, not when we didn't know it was a sure thing. Sealing the doorways shut, cutting him off..." He handed the binocs to Freyr. "We should have tried that first. You've got a plan, and it's a good one, except for one thing."

He clapped a hand on Freyr's shoulder. "I won't be going with you."

34

S triding down to the Trophy Room, Tyr felt the inescapable
pull of Fate. The deep, glacial groove he'd been stuck in for
far too long.

Climbing out was hard.

But staying in was suicide.

He kicked the heavy door wide open and breathed in the scent of
plunder. It only took him a moment to pick out the three items he
needed, slip them in his jacket pocket, and go on his way.

Mir told him he couldn't change Fate.

He was hoping Mir was wrong.

Fate liked shiny, golden things, with sparkly gemstones—preferably diamonds—and a bit of fancy filigree. Tyr strode down the hall
to the weapons room, grabbed a few necessary items and a ham sand-
wich, and sprinted down the stairs. There was one Hummer left in
the garage, and it had his name on it. Heading north, he was about to
take a trip back in time. They'd been stranded on this rock for an
eternity, but that didn't mean Odin hadn't left them a back door. The
bastard always had an exit plan. That's one of the things, well, *the
only thing, really*, that Tyr liked about him.

They'd scouted this outlying portal together, when this world was new and pristine and not quite so...*charred* as it was now. Two hours there, he figured, double-checking the full gas cans in the back, and two hours back. If all went well, this would work.

It had to work.

A couple hours later, he turned into the long, meandering drive. Shit was certainly easier to find these days, marked with fancy stone and stucco signs and Google maps and such. Driving through once-manicured gardens, he passed lines of abandoned cars on his way to the cave entrance. Parking, he snagged the backpack and headed in.

Back in the day, they'd brought tar dipped torches. Today, the extra bright, military grade LED mag light did the job twice as fast with half the trouble. Back in the day, he and Odin had crawled through a hole no bigger than their torsos, wriggling down into the cavern like worms. Now he took the metal stairs two at a time, anxious to get this part, the easy part over with. Swinging the light to the right, he broke through a wooden barrier, two sets of dire warnings about hard hats and falling stalactites, then balanced his way along a narrow ledge that fell away into nothingness. Now came the semi-hard part. Wedging the light into his belt, securing the pack, he crouched down and took four long strides before leaping through thin air, praying he'd find the narrow rock ledge on the other side. His feet slipped on the uneven landing, and he pitched forward, bashing his nose into the stone wall.

But he'd made it. Pulling the light back out, he swung it around. He had about ten inches of ledge to skirt the rounded wall, and then there'd be another cavern to his left. Easy peasy.

Ten minutes later, with all ten fingers raw and bleeding, he rounded the opening into the cavern and looked around. Same musty smell. Same bat cave. Just as dusty as it had been a two hundred years before.

Now came the hard part.

In the back of the shallow cave, Tyr shifted the stone covering from an opening, rolling it across the floor with a loud grinding, the weight of the thing straining even his shoulders. Two hundred years ago there hadn't been a stone. They hadn't needed a stone because nobody knew about this cave, but Odin was paranoid. Now there was this fucking heavy stone, and he'd probably need rotator cuff surgery when he got back to the Tower.

There was also the little problem of not having Odin here.

Odin, who actually knew *how* to open the portal to Asgard.

Or so the bastard claimed. Tyr never really paid much attention to the science-nerdy shit, since he'd always handled the heavy lifting part. Which would make this next part tricky. Mir would have been the ideal person to ask, but he would have talked Tyr out of this. Loki would have tagged along, just to see what happened. And Freyr needed all hands on deck right now.

The stone out of the way, Tyr considered the deep, silent black hole in front of him.

The fact there *was* a hole gave him hope.

Surely, the passage went *somewhere.*

Stepping through, he figured he'd either end up exactly where he needed to be or floating in the middle of nothingness. Maybe, if the Fates were kind, he and Hunter might end up together in the Afterlife.

He thought not.

Those bitches were such assholes.

35

H ome has a certain smell to it.

It's unique to each person, to every place. To some, it's milk and cookies, to others, its wood smoke and pine. Tyr took a deep breath followed by another.

Asgard had always smelled of blood and victory to him. The two somehow irrevocably, obscenely intertwined. But there was no denying it, he was back. Which meant, Asgard had not been eradicated, as they'd long believed. The golden realm had survived, much like they had.

Something else to take up with Odin when he got back.

Settling his mind and firming his intentions, Tyr reached out across this world, or what had once been *his world*, in search of that which he needed. Once he found them, he set off in a north westerly course toward the largest tree on the horizon.

It is told, in the Old World, that destiny is nothing but a groove into which you are placed at birth and out of which you are taken at death. That fate and all of its incarnations are nothing but the universe slotting you into your predetermined future.

Free will be damned.

"Well, fuck *that* shit," became Tyr's mantra as he trudged toward the looming tree. People were created to make choices, bad or good, but choices, nonetheless.

Nothing in this world was set in stone, and everything was up for grabs, *especially* the future. And if there was one thing he knew, it was that nothing, not God, nor Fate, nor fucking destiny itself would ever control Hunter Wallace.

He was about to bet his immortal soul on that.

TYR FOUND them beneath the tree. All his life, he'd given them a wide berth, as it wasn't in his nature to tempt that for which he had no regard. He dealt in death, which meant their prophecies held no interest for him. When there was only one outcome, and it was only a matter of timing, he hadn't really seen the point.

Now things were different.

And now that he was here, he wasn't sure how he should greet them. Somehow, a "Hey, *how're you girls doing*" didn't seem appropriate.

Raising a hand to them, he stopped, evaluating their reaction. Aside from the color of their hair, he couldn't tell them apart, nor could he tell their age. Old, yet young, they were agelessly, unsettlingly beautiful, as if they encompassed all of time itself. No big black cauldron full of bubbling poison, he was glad to see.

A web of ancient magic hung in tatters around them. The old kind, the sort he hadn't seen or felt in a lifetime, licked at his flesh as he stepped closer. This close, the air stank of mold and damp, stirring with fetid, dark things. Circling the trio, they followed him with curious eyes, and still, he was afraid to speak, lest he begin badly. Too much hung on this meeting. Hunter's life, their future. *Everything* was at risk.

Some called them the Norn. Some the Fates. Some simply named them witches. But whatever their names, there had always been three:

Present, Past and Future.

Existing before anything else, they wove the lives of all living things together into a complex tapestry, creating the weft and weave of the universe. Some called them kind and protective. Tyr held no such illusions. They were trying to steal Hunter away from him, and they were the enemy. Like any good soldier, he'd expected tricks. And he'd come prepared.

Reaching into his bag, he laid out three golden relics, beautiful, priceless, all the while riveted on their faces. For any sign of interest glinting in their eyes, for a slight, forward stirring, a hint of quickened breathing. He'd chosen these items carefully, though in haste, and briefly wondered if he'd done right. When the brunette in the middle reached down and picked up the long, tapered dagger, a glittering opal set into the pommel, he smiled inside.

Ah, Past, there you are.

The Glass Knife, capable of carving the shadows of forgetting from a person's past memories. Making them as clear as the day they were made. Similar to the Well of Remembering, the blade had the added benefit of finesse—the wielder could carve out *specific* memories—and leave the rest forgotten.

The wide, golden bracelet sat glittering in the firelight, the black diamonds subtly shifting. The bangle was enchanted, granting the gift of foresight to any who wore it. Tyr knew which sister would be drawn to this particular artifact. *Present.* Being trapped in the *now,* between two sisters who saw everything behind and before her, had to be maddening. She'd be eager to gain an advantage.

And when the blonde reached down, fingering the circlet encrusted with ebony stones, Tyr's eyes flew to the remaining woman, with eyes so dark they resembled the diamonds on the bracelet, lined by kohl.

The Future would not choose any of the tokens.

Because she didn't need them.

Bowing before presenting the neck collar to her, the dull gold set with a diamond the size of a goose egg, Tyr murmured, "I would ask a favor of you, my lady."

"Of course. One favor, and one favor only, warrior."

"Hunter Wallace."

"The human?"

Mir tensed at the note of distaste in her voice. "That she is. I ask you to restore her life."

"Mayhap it is time she moved on." The brunette pointed out, fingering the dull edge of the knife with feigned disinterest. "She has already enjoyed the span of ten humans."

"That she has." Tyr took a deep breath. "But she gave it up for me."

"Which was her choice." There was a hint of malevolent cunning to raven-haired Future's voice, and Tyr knew he must tread carefully. "Free will is beyond our reach, as you well know."

"You have looked to the future then?"

Her dark, deadly stare told him she had. And she had seen everything. A warning, then, might just do it. Tyr shrugged, then turned as if to leave. "The God of Chaos will come for you. Surely *you* know that. When he is finished with the other worlds, and there *will* come a day when he *is* finished, he will find this one. Don't placate yourselves thinking you are hidden here. You're only safe because the Orobus believes Asgard destroyed." A slight, almost imperceptible shiver went through her at the mention of his name.

"Even so," she warned him flatly, "we cannot save your woman. Her time has run out."

"If that is true, then so has yours. I found you, after all," he pointed out grimly as he rounded on them. "It would only take a word to point the creature in your direction."

"You wouldn't dare." The blonde gasped, looking to her sisters.

"Deny me, and I'll do whatever I must. I mean to have my way. You can take your trinkets, grant me my wish, and we can part today as friends. Or you'll discover how I've earned my name." *Ah*, Tyr thought, seeing the furtive look the sisters exchanged. Past neglected to divulge his true nature. And the lengths to which he'd go.

"It would do you all well to turn your sight inward. What I say is true. Look, then tell me if I'm not willing to sacrifice anything or anyone to have my way." He shot a look at the women. Playing them all against one another hadn't been part of his plan, but he'd use whatever advantage he could.

"The Orobus is gaining power on Midgard. What will happen when he discovers the doorway to your world? Even together, can you withstand him?"

Tyr thought not, as the blonde blanched white. These strange creatures were meant for a different sort of magic, not battle, and certainly not with something like the God of Chaos. However...

"Hunter Wallace can help defeat the dark god. She contained a piece of him inside of her for a thousand years. She can do it again."

"*Which* he took back. Who's to say death is not her true Fate?" Present spoke clearly as her sisters nodded. Tyr resisted slapping his hand to his forehead. Stubborn. Why did they have to be so gods-damned stubborn?

"She doesn't have to die," Tyr urged. "You can change her future, it's within your power. You know it and I know it." Fucking fickle Fates. It just figured, he'd come halfway across the galaxy to save the love of his life. And they would make him beg.

"The Orobus will destroy everything and then come for you. All I'm asking for is to give Hunter a chance. One mortal soul against the future of the universe. It's not so large a price, is it?"

"You're asking for everything."

Tyr opened his mouth to deny it, then snapped it shut. *He was, as a matter of fact.* If he lost her, *nothing* would matter. The dark god could destroy the universe, and it wouldn't matter. He'd fight till the end, on principle alone, but his heart wouldn't be in it because there'd be nothing left. "I am. For me, Hunter is my entire world. She always has been."

Future's gaze turned predatory. "As long as you realize that, then it's done." As one, the three of them leaned back, their faces relaxed as if the matter was settled. Tyr blinked. He'd expected hours of bargaining, jockeying for position, taking ground, giving ground. Shit, if negotiations were always this easy...

"Of course"—Future toyed with the heavy necklace at her throat, her fingertips dancing along the diamond—"there will be a price."

Danger, danger. Course correction ahead. "Name it."

Now there was no doubt the dark-eyed witch's smile was dripping venom. "You made a bargain with her in the beginning, no?" Everything inside of Tyr knotted up. Holy shit, how could he have forgotten? How could he have missed this?

"That bargain was made before..."

Past leaned in as well, her eyes narrowing. "You swore an oath, you'd kill her when the God of Chaos was dead. When this is done, you will keep your word." The three nodded.

"That was before..."

"Yes or no." Not a question, actually.

Tyr's brain scrambled around, searching for a loophole in the language, a footnote, an escape clause. Finding none, he did what he did best, he bought more time.

"Yes." No question, he'd never sentence Hunter to death, not right now, certainly not like this. He'd sure as shit not put his woman's life in the hands of this bitch in front of him. And he'd never, ever take Hunter's life.

"We have a deal then, God of War?"

Tyr flinched. He hated that fucking moniker, especially coming out of the mouths of these creatures.

"We do." They hadn't defeated the bastard yet, and he'd put his money on Loki finding a loophole they could slip out of. Feeling pretty damn smug, he picked up his pack and turned to walk away.

"Aren't you forgetting something?" *Not that he knew of.* He'd come here for one thing and one thing only. Deal done, time to go.

"You owe us a tithe, immortal."

"I brought you fucking jewelry. I thought you chicks liked that kind of shit."

"We require something a bit more...organic." When Past licked her lips and looked him over, head to toe, Tyr shuddered. *Aw, hell no.* This was what he fucking hated about the Old Country.

"You ladies want that kind of action, Freyr's your guy. I'll send him your way." The dead-eye stare he got in return said no fucking way. The look he sent them said the same. It appeared they were back to the negotiating table. "Look. This isn't happening. You want something else from me, you got it." As the words came out of his mouth, Tyr cursed himself. "But not that."

"Hunter Wallace and her near-immortal life." The dark eyed beauty mused. "You truly believe her longevity is because of the blood magic you cast on hallowed ground?"

"It was." Tyr told her flatly. "And I'd do it again." If only to keep Hunter out of their reach.

"What if you are wrong?" Future mused. "What if her long life is due to something else entirely? Would you still feel bound to her? Is this guilt pushing you to save her now? Or love?"

"I healed her and made her into what she is. Not escaping that fact." But a kernel of doubt began to grow, if only because of the absolute certainty in those black, impenetrable eyes staring back at him. "And I'm here because I love her. For no other reason. You demand a steep enough price for restoring her life. You'll get nothing more from me."

The three put their heads together, keeping Tyr waiting. The woman in the center spoke, one final time. "Then consider your favor granted. But let us leave you with a warning.

"Destiny cannot be altered. Not by you. Not even by us."

Meeting their cunning, exquisite faces, Tyr reminded himself to never come back this way. Odin had been smart to set up a back door, but shit, he'd forgotten where it led to.

For too long he'd dreamed of coming home, built this place up into some kind of spectacular fantasy, when actually it was a bunch of old, horny women under an ancient tree that probably had Dutch elm disease. This was a dark, ruined world, far from the sun-filled, gilded kingdom he remembered. Hours later, the moment he breached the opening of the cave and burst out into the sunlight, Tyr pulled out the com and called. "How is she?"

After a slight pause, Mir answered. "Just checked on her. Sleeping but she seems stable. Syd's with her, and she seems stronger. I don't know what you did. *I don't even want to know.* But it worked. Now get your ass back here. I don't want to be the one explaining where you are when she wakes up."

Throwing everything into the Hummer and turning toward home, he floored it.

Laid out on his bed, Hunter looked every inch the fairy princess. Black hair fanned out in dark waves over his pillows, those long, sloped eyes closed, long black lashes dark against alabaster cheeks blushed delicate pink. *She was alive.* Future kept her word after all. His hands curled in upon themselves as his breath shallowed out.

I am going to have to kill her.

Hunter sighed and turned on the bed, the sheets wound tightly against her curves. Holy hell, she was alive. Tyr walked over and lowered himself next to her, and instinctively she curled into him, sighed as his arms came around her. "I had the most awful dream."

"So did I, princess. So did I."

"I was in this terrible, black place. Everything was cold and wet, and I couldn't find my way out. Then all of a sudden, this woman appeared, and she gave me her hand and led me home. She was beautiful. Long, black hair."

"That doesn't sound so bad." He was running his hands through her glorious hair, the strands silk between his fingers.

"That wasn't the worst part." Her voice got smaller. "She told me you promised to kill me when this was over." Her breathing turned panicked as her eyes flew open. "Do you remember when I arrived, and I made you promise me that very thing, Tyr?"

He'd gone perfectly still as if somehow, if he didn't move, the words she was about to utter wouldn't reach him.

"I wish I'd never said it. I wish I'd never made you promise me that, Tyr. Even though, at the time... At the time, I was ready to be done with all of this. The world, this life, everything. I was just so— tired. But now..." Hunter turned her face up to his, gently kissing his chin and wrapping her arms tightly around his neck. "I'm not nearly ready to leave. I want to stay with you."

Not your fault. He wanted to say. *I did this.* He wanted to tell her. *I was the one who condemned you to die, not once, but three times now.* But he did none of those things.

Instead, he rolled her underneath of him, feeling her warmth, the lovely sleekness of her skin, his hand following every curve, the way her stomach dipped in, the wetness between her thighs. He nipped and tasted and suckled and bit until he couldn't get any closer to her. Nor any farther apart. Desperate, he wanted them *joined*, damn it. Or more accurately, he wanted them to become one. For all their time apart, he'd felt linked to her in a way that seemed unbreakable. Now, connected in the flesh, he'd never felt further apart.

"Hunter..." His tongue traced a wet path up between her breasts, the salty tang of her something he couldn't get enough of.

"I need to take a shower, Tyr. Like *now*," Hunter murmured, although she made no move to leave, only shifted to give him better access. Which was all good with him, he thought, cupping her breast, his thumb making small, circular motions on her nipple as it hardened.

Though in some small part of his brain, he realized he'd been crawling around in a cave all day, and thinking of the way the Fates had sized him up had him feeling especially dirty. "A shower, huh? We can take a shower."

The shifting, squirming movement halted. "Okay," Hunter said, her fingers winding their way along his face, to his jaw, tipping his face up so they stared at each other. "I think I'd like that."

Rising, Tyr led her to the bathroom, his version of gray marble minimalism. But the walk-in shower had a long, wide bench, and he had plans.

Big plans, as Hunter stripped off the t-shirt, and her breasts popped free.

He turned on the water and thanked Mir for his foresight in installing solar as the steam began fogging up the glass. Grasping Hunter's hands, he led her to the shower. "In here, and we've got plenty of hot water, so take your time." Pulling off his ruined shirt, Tyr paused, searching her eyes before his hand went to his fly. "I can wait, you know. Leave you be. You've been through plenty these last couple days."

Her eyes narrowed, then she slid her panties down her legs and stepped into the shower, the water running in sheets down her back, slicking her hair to the curve of her spine. "There's plenty of room for both of us in here, but if you want to wait your turn, I guess that's up to you." Turning, the wicked smile playing at the edges of her mouth spread.

~

THE HOT WATER felt heavenly coursing down her body.

But not as good as Tyr's hands. Or his mouth. Hunter opened one eye and glared through the fogged-up glass. His murky figure was on the move, and she hoped he was getting naked. Enough with the pussyfooting around. Hadn't they already decided they'd wasted too much time?

And then he came up behind her, pressed the full length of that rock-hard body into hers.

God. Finally.

When his hands came around and cupped her breasts, she fell forward, through the spray, one hand slapping up against the wall. But he had a firm hold of her, pulling her back against him, her body making contact with his once more, friction and heat and water ramping up the hunger coursing through her. His cock was nestled between her ass cheeks, his teeth clamped loosely on her shoulder, his fingers playing with her nipples as they tightened beneath his touch, and she *groaned*. So loudly the sound bounced off the marble. *God, did that sound actually come out of her?*

"You feel good against me, princess." Tyr's breath exploded in her ear, pushing them both under the showerhead. Walking her over to the bench, he spun her around and pressed her down, until she was sitting, staring up at him, watching the water coursing down his pecs, over those toned, cut muscles, across old scars and still-healing ones. Reaching out, Hunter trailed her hand down the narrow line of hair until she grasped the base of his cock and leaned forward, closing her mouth over the velvety head. His gasp was even louder than hers, and she smiled around the girth of him, taking him ever deeper.

A twist of her tongue followed the ridge of his head, and he groaned. Another long, hard lick along the bottom near the vein had him making a sound more like a rough purr. She *liked* those sounds. She wanted to hear *more* of those sounds.

His hands tangled themselves in her hair, guided her, then found a slow, steady rhythm as his hips surged forward, pushing him farther into her mouth, her tongue playing along the edge of his head, then the thick vein along the bottom, before she pressed her teeth in, ever so slightly. He surged forward, filling her mouth.

"Fucking hell." Beneath her hand braced on his thigh, his muscles trembled as if weakening, and she wondered if he was losing control. Tyr's grip on her hair tightened, then he pulled her away, his face flushed, eyes dazed. "Godsdamn it, Hunter, I'm going to cum if you keep that up. And we're not finishing this quickly."

Sinking to his knees before her, he lifted one knee over his shoulder, then the other, until she was spread before him, her shoulders settled against the wall. "My turn," he told her, a devilish smile on his face. And then he lifted her to him and licked straight up through the center of her, sucking her clit into his mouth, rolling his tongue across the nub. Sinking his teeth in, she moaned, the slight pressure causing her to throw her head back with a solid clunk against the wall.

"Shit, sorry. Gods, I'm sorry." He dropped her feet to the floor, slid beside her, and rubbed the back of her head, his clever fingers massaging the knot. "Damn it, I got carried away." As he apologized, all Hunter could do was blink the tears from her eyes as she leaned into his touch.

Perfect. He was absolutely perfect. Somehow, in all of her imaginings, never had she thought they'd end up like this. So...utterly normal.

"Take me to bed, Tyr. Make love to me." For the first time in her life, right in front of her, she had what she wanted. Just the two of them, with the rest of the world locked safely outside. "Right now."

"Your wish is my command, princess." Shutting off the water, he wrapped a towel around her shoulders, gently drying her off before offering his hand. "I've been waiting my whole life to make love to you. It's about time my wish came true."

She didn't know how, or why, but the words settled her. As if they confirmed what she already knew. For both of them, this was the culmination of years and years of wanting. And even though it might not be the first time, this time meant something deeper, something more because now they'd both been to hell and back, seen the other side, and lived to tell about it.

Hunter didn't remember standing up, she didn't remember moving. All she did know was the warm, wet slide of her skin against his as they nipped and suckled and kissed their way over to the bed, the twist of their bodies as they fell against the sheets, Tyr rolling her onto her back, his mouth still attached to hers.

His clever tongue teased hers, and he tasted *good*, spicy almost, a mixture of craving and excitement and passion all mixed into one. Hunter opened wider, savoring more of him, and he clasped her jaw with one hand, angled her head, and dove in deeper. Tongues dueling, he finally pulled back, eyes dark, his breathing every bit as ragged as hers.

"Damn it, Hunter, this isn't going to take very long." Her hands slid over his huge shoulders, down his arms, then back up, finding each curve of muscle before lightly caging themselves behind his neck. His hips were caught between her legs, his hard-on pressed into her thigh. She moved so they were aligned, firmed her hands behind his nape, her gaze never leaving his.

"We have forever, right?" she murmured, "Tonight, tomorrow... forever. And this...is just the beginning. So now, please."

He thrust in quickly, and her hips bucked, as if of their own accord, taking him deeply, the waves of her orgasm already starting to shiver through her, the muscles of her core clenching hard against his cock. Every hard thrust ramping up the pleasure, every move narrowing her focus to the tightening feeling at the middle of her, the narrowing down to a single point.

Slipping an arm beneath her leg, Tyr angled her up, then pounded into her, her hands still clasped behind his head, their bodies slapping together. And then she exploded.

The orgasm ripped through her, Tyr increasing his rhythm, dropping his head to her shoulder, her hands slipping to his shoulders while he rode her, harder and harder until his body froze, clenched, and her name came tearing out of his mouth.

When he'd caught his breath, he reared up over her, his eyes shining with what she could only describe as reverence.

"Forever. I like the sound of that."

36

The explosives worried Freyr.

If the fidiots had left them in the *pretty little silver cases,* he wouldn't be half as concerned. *But no.* They were shoved into flimsy duffel bags, and here he was, wiring the switches to the power sources, then the charges, just waiting for the bright flash of light that told him he miscalculated.

A munitions expert, he was not.

The other thing that worried him was the incessant, malevolent drain from the Orobus, poised about fifty feet to his left. The fucker was seriously a black hole of epic proportions.

Shoving his worry to the side, Freyr reminded himself again, this was all his idea.

If this little display worked, if it gave Sydney her window of opportunity, then they'd seal the doors closed, and the Orobus would spend the next few days attempting to open them. In the meantime, they'd pick the remainder of his army off, one by one.

With a little luck, leaving only the Orobus and Hel to deal with.

He'd take those odds.

They were certainly better than the ones they'd faced these past months. Winding the last set of wires together, Freyr ghosted to the next location and got to work, hunching his shoulders behind the stadium seats so the squad of Dark Elves patrolling a few paces away wouldn't spot him. He'd been dodging elves and Grim all around the site, hundreds of them, forming a wide barrier around the stones. With the wind blowing in hard off the lake, his scent would be negligible, but the creatures had noses like bloodhounds, and one couldn't be too careful.

The plan is solid.

He kept telling himself that.

It is not going to get all of them killed.

He kept telling himself that too.

One site to another, Fen's careful, clipped voice running down the minutes into his ear, Freyr planted device after device, dodging the elves patrolling each area, the Grim dripping from the girders and shadows of the underground roads, as he laid a trail of incendiary breadcrumbs along the path he hoped the creature would follow.

When he arrived at the terminal end, he back-wired both devices before climbing the metal steps to upper street level. Ghosting his way to the lookout position where Fen waited, he surveyed the area, mentally mapping out the sequence of the detonations, and calculating, again, the time it should buy them. If things went right.

Raising the com to his lips, he took a deep breath. "That's it. Once everyone's in position, let me hear you."

One by one, they reported in. Celine and Morgane, Thor and Vali, Mir and Sydney. Balder.

Good to go.

It took him longer than it should have to tell Fen. "Hit the button."

Nothing prepared Freyr for the fear he experienced when the explosions started. As they'd discussed, planned, and hoped for, the Orobus recoiled as the first explosion hit him on his south flank, which took out a handful of Dark Elves and created a divot the size of a house. The next one was close to the water and blew the creature back through the openings of the stone circle, decimating anything alive in that quadrant, reducing Grim and Dark Elves to ash.

Out of the cloud of smoke, elves ran in disarray while Grim scuttled out of hiding places by the hundreds, only to trip smaller landmines planted over the past few hours, wreaking havoc, and scattering the carefully concentric circles of guards the Orobus had positioned around the stones.

One by one, bombs detonated, to the north and west, until the God of Chaos was a small shadowy sphere and pretty much everything else was dead. A final explosion sent a small contingent of elves south, toward the underground walkways.

With an audible *pop*, Fen cracked his neck and rose. "I'm up. See you soon." Vanishing, Freyr raised the binoculars just in time to watch him reform at the mouth of the walkway, his hulking, lupine form filling the entire opening. Freyr swung the glasses over to the circle.

Tentatively, the Orobus began moving toward the tunnel, and Fen roared into the faces of the elves, picked one up and tore him in half, spitting the carcass at the feet of the others before loping into the murky mouth of lower street level. The elves and the Orobus followed him, vanishing into the dark.

"Mir, time to get her in there."

Mir appeared inside the circle, Sydney in his arms. The moment he released her, a shimmer encased the entire site, and Freyr watched the redhead move from stone to stone, Mir right on her heels. Although he couldn't see a thing, he hoped she knew what she was doing.

Swinging the glasses to his right, he checked his Cartier watch, counted down the seconds, and hit the next switch. A hollow, distant boom echoed down the corridor of buildings a heartbeat later. And for the next half hour, that became his world.

Check Sydney's progress, hit the switch.

Hope and pray Fen was staying a few steps ahead of the Orobus.

When Syd was halfway through, Celine's tense voice crackled in his ear. "How many more, Freyr?" She had to be beside herself, worried for Fen.

"Three. We're doing good, Celine."

In fact, he had no idea how they were doing. It was all guesswork from where he stood. Sydney's magic *should* be sealing the doorways shut. Svartlheim was the most crucial because that's where the vast majority of the elvish armies were stashed. But the other doors hid horrors far deadlier, though in fewer numbers. Squinting through the glasses, Freyr watched Mir throw him a thumbs up.

"Three down, three to go," he muttered to himself.

Sydney wasn't planning on touching the biggest one, moved between the remaining three, then detonated the third to last bomb. With any luck, Fen was out of the lower street levels now and ghosting his way back. Leaving the Dark Elves and the Orobus trapped below when Freyr set off the final charge.

None of them were foolish enough to believe the collapsed rubble of the street would hold him, but they could hope for some delays. "Morgane, Celine, it's time to get you home." Thor and Vali would transport them to the Tower, then ghost back here for reinforcements. Mir would get Syd out of the circle, the second she was finished sealing the last portal.

Or the second the Orobus reappeared.

The binoculars pressed to his face, Freyr continued to scan the scene, finger on the trigger, one eye on his watch. Sydney was almost to the next stone when Fen limped out into the rubble field, his huge body smoking, shiny with blood. To the south, the Orobus came barreling out of the tunnel, making a beeline for the stones, dragging a trail of shadow and spume behind him as Fen roared a warning.

"Get out of there. Get the fuck out," Freyr screamed into the com, measuring the distance, the impossible odds as Mir lunged forward, tackled Sydney, and they both vanished just as the Orobus collided with the stones, striking them with such force the impact created a sound wave that threw Freyr backward.

When he raised the glasses again, the creature was moving from stone to stone, a confused, contorted dance of dark smoke, circling, probing, his movements increasingly frenetic. No sign of Fen anywhere.

"He's already looking for a way to open them back up." Mir spoke from behind him, lowering Syd to the floor, her eyes wide and frantic. "Shit, that was close."

"I missed one." Sydney told them, miserable. "I couldn't get the final one closed, damn it."

"But you sealed the ones where his armies are, Syd," Freyr pointed out. "And that's what matters right now. Let's get out of here before things get ugly." Sure enough, below them the dark god was losing his shit. Now he was working on them all at once, his desperation building, the center of his form rising as he rotated, encompassing the circle, obscuring them from sight while a keening noise filled the air. Around them, the wind picked up, and tore at Sydney's hair.

Mir gathered Sydney in his arms and vanished, Freyr following right behind.

37

Waking up, Hunter reached out and found Tyr beside her, felt that familiar spark she always sensed when she was close to him, and a sense of calm swept through her.

There was a newness to this thing between them, a fragility. Yet it was strong, and it was growing. Maybe she could crash against him for a thousand more years, and he would always catch her. She liked to think this was true. Even all those years apart, all those miles apart, time and distance didn't matter. And maybe, they never had. Not when it came to the two of them.

When Tyr opened those eyes of his, she met them with a soft smile and no words, for she had none that seemed right or fitting or compelling enough, so she kept her mouth shut while he stared, watching her face.

Finally, she had to say *something*. "First, I thought I was dying, then I had that crazy dream. But it's fuzzy, now. Something about a woman...and some promise. But I feel good. Better, even."

His brown eyes just...gazed at her adoringly. "Better? Or the same as before?"

It took her a moment to realize what he asked. "Better. *Definitely* better." The absence of the evil within her, and the peace she felt in its wake was...lovely.

A bit more of the almost-reverent consideration as he looked straight at her.

"What did you *do*, Tyr?" Because the last she remembered, she'd barely made it back to the Tower, practically passed out in the hallway. Now she was...fine.

He fixed her with a penetrating stare. "Why would you assume I've done anything at all? Mir used his magic on you, and it worked."

For a moment she considered this, a perfectly reasonable explanation. Except something didn't sit right. For one thing, she couldn't account for some missing hours. Quite a few, in fact. For another, there was an unsettling feeling of wrongness about those dreams she couldn't shake.

"And what about the power the Orobus drew out of me? When he took it back, I felt like I was being sucked dry. I think I was dying. And things are fuzzy." For a second, the room turned blurry, and she realized she was tearing up.

She heard Tyr's gentle plea, "Stop crying, Hunter." Then even softer, "For gods' sake woman, stop with the crying, you'll undo me." She began shaking. *He didn't deny it.* "Am I dying, Tyr? That's what's happening, isn't it? I'm dying."

"No." He told her flatly. "You are *not* dying."

"You sound pretty sure of that fact."

"I am." Tyr folded her against him, his big body comforting, solid. "I am because there is no way I'll allow anyone to take you away from me. Not now." He pressed a kiss to the top of her head, pulling her in tighter. "Not ever."

"*What did you do?*" The words tore out of her, a desperate fear beginning to build. "I didn't go from near death to feeling great in a matter of hours..." She stopped, a horrifying thought occurring to her. "You did it again, didn't you? You used your magic on me?"

"No, I did not." He let her go, and she began pacing the room. "I wouldn't do that again, Hunter. Not with how things ended last time. You know me better than that."

"Do I?" she snapped. "*Do I?*"

"I did not heal you. Mir did. I wouldn't make the same mistake twice." Tyr groaned in frustration. "Look, after the monster took back his power, you were *close* to dying, Hunter. *But not dead.* Mir used his magic to heal you, *it's what he does.* He healed me, Freyr, Morgane..."

"What happened to Morgane and Freyr?"

"Explosion downtown that went wrong," Tyr explained slowly. "It was a bad night. For a lot of us. But you did *not* die. I did *not* use my magic on you. I swear to the gods." His dark brown eyes met hers steadily, no trace of dishonesty in them.

Yet. There was something wrong about this.

Hunter knew it. Her gut tingled, which meant something was off.

But Tyr's face was clear, and in truth, she felt lighter, better than she'd felt in eons. The evil was truly gone, and for once, she felt clean without its suffocating presence eating her from the inside.

"I'm sorry, I just feel...strange. And I don't have an explanation for why." Scowling, she settled back beside him. "Maybe I'm still exhausted."

"You lost a part of yourself." Tyr held out a hand to quell her protest. "Even though you never wanted it, still, a part of yourself was stolen away. I expect it will take some getting used to."

"Perhaps," she murmured, settling against him once more. "But this feels like more than that."

"For once, Hunter, stop thinking." Tyr pulled the covers up around them, cocooning them together. "Just sleep."

And for once in her life, she did just that.

OVER THE NEXT FEW DAYS, Hunter wondered at the change in Tyr. Days were spent sending out scouting parties, intent on eradicating the remaining clusters of Grim and elves roaming the city. Fen spent three miserable days in the infirmary, his pride hurt at being outmaneuvered by the Orobus, his flesh shredded by the thing's dark magic. Celine never once left his side.

Through it all, Tyr seemed disconnected, somehow.

Add to that, her dreams were troubled.

She tried to remember them and came away with vague impressions of bargains badly made. *And the woman.* There was a disturbing familiarity about her, as if she'd once known her but just couldn't quite recall her face.

She carried the dream around with her for days. And the memory of it tugged at her at the most inopportune times. When Mir asked for input on cordoning off the stone circle. When Tyr asked if she was feeling all right. When Celine asked her if she was sleeping. Those occasions, the image of the woman would slip seamlessly into her mind, like a reminder of something she couldn't quite grasp. Or didn't quite want to.

But Tyr.

He was constantly touching her, always right beside her as if he couldn't bear to let her out of his sight. It was wonderful, comforting, and a bit unnerving. And his approach to the Orobus problem? Almost as if he didn't want the problem solved at all. When Freyr proposed his strategy to eradicate the rest of the elves in one fell swoop, using Sydney's magic, Tyr waved his hand, dismissing the idea. When the newly serious Freyr demanded he at least consider the idea, he shut him down quick.

It was almost as if he didn't want to fight anymore.

At night, he rushed through whatever dinner had been cobbled together, then herded her into their bedroom, and kept his hands and his mouth on her until morning. Nights were quickly becoming her favorite part of the day.

Those were the hours of her life that felt right, as if their worlds finally fell into alignment and were rotating in the same orbits. It was everything else that seemed out of place. As if she'd gone to sleep and woken up in a topsy-turvy world.

Pausing at the door of the War Room, she observed yet another meeting going nowhere. Meeting Tyr's eyes, she stopped him from leaving with a shake of her head. He was needed, whether he realized it or not, and he had to stop stalling. Steam was practically coming out of Freyr's ears, with Thor methodically pounding on the table, a sure sign of impending implosion. She got her feet moving and headed toward the kitchen, hoping to find Syd or Celine, any friendly face to help her pass the next few hours.

Ava was sitting alone, as was usual, in front of the huge triple windows that had once fronted the banquet hall. Hunter stopped, debating. Even the woman's demeanor sprouted thorns, a sure sign of *leave me alone* sticking out all over her. But instead of turning tail and leaving, Hunter's usual approach to anything involving humans, she moved forward. Before she knew it, she was alongside the brunette, staring out over the lake. She had to admit, there was a certain symmetry to the flat plane of water, which differed from the chaos churning inside herself.

"I've been waiting a long time to talk to you, Hunter." Ava's voice was soft yet hard, tinged with a bitterness born of terrible things. Hunter wished she'd found out more about her before sidling up next to the woman. "It's difficult, isn't it?"

"I beg your pardon?"

"To be one thing inside, yet another on the outside. To have such a lovely façade, yet never truly show yourself. You've been having a dream. It's bothering you."

Not a question. And something only Tyr knew about. And not even he knew the full truth of it. "Yes."

Ava's midnight-blue gaze slid over, and Hunter stilled her gasp. There was power lurking inside those eyes. The same power that had once brewed so fiercely within herself.

"When the Fates decide, when they weave your fortunes, their magic creates something unique. A place in the universe made just for you. A future from which there is no escape." Something shifted in the navy depths. "You become the gutter ball, and there is no getting out of it."

Hunter didn't believe in the concept of Fate. "I believe in free will."

"You mean you believed in free will?"

"No, I *believe* in it. As in present tense. Nobody determines my future except for me. My life is made up of my own choices."

"That may have been what you believed. That may have even once been true. But your world changed a week ago. Your life ended on a tarmac when your power was stolen from you. You know this. *You feel it.*"

A chill went down Hunter's spine. Now she knew why this woman sat alone. However Ava knew, whatever she knew, prompted Hunter to ask, "First of all, I never wanted that power. But it's true, I feel different. Except I don't know why. Or how."

"But you know who?" A tilt of her head had those extraordinary eyes swimming into crystal clear focus, as if the answers lay somewhere in their depths.

Hunter shuddered. "I glimpsed a woman in my dreams. She seems familiar, but I can't place her. Black hair, blacker than black eyes. She was kind. She led me out of that terrible place. She told me...something about Tyr, but I can't remember."

"There's a reason she's in your dreams. Perhaps, she's come to you for a purpose." Ava smiled, and in that smile, Hunter saw sadness and something like regret. "Perhaps, it's a sign. You know, often we make promises we should never make. Sometimes we're willing to do anything for love. Even if it's for the wrong reasons.

And everyone...*everyone* has something to lose. And there comes a time when they must make a terrible choice. How much are they willing to sacrifice for love?"

"What are you trying to tell me, Ava?"

"You woke a week ago, alive and well. Yet the last thing you remember is dying at the hands of the Orobus. There is no god on this world, nor any other, who can *give* life."

Oh God.

Hunter froze as things began to fall into place. The dreams, the strange woman, this overall feeling of wrongness. "So I *was* dying."

"You were dying," Ava agreed.

"And Tyr did *something* to save me. Something that had a cost attached to it." Which was why he wouldn't let her out of his sight or his bed. Why he seemed determined to keep her within arm's reach at all times.

"That he did."

"If you know... What's the price?" Because there was *always* a price.

"He made a deal with the only creatures who could change your fate. And they asked for something in return. A trade *you* suggested, from the very moment you arrived," Ava reminded her quietly. "A life for a life."

The particulars of the oath she'd forced on Tyr came back to her in stark detail as everything fell into place. "Of course. How could I have been so stupid?" Hunter groaned. "And yes, yes, I know I proposed the idea in the first place. And I well remember the *why* of it. I was exhausted. And I didn't see the point of going on, anymore. Except now..."

"Everything's changed?"

"Everything's changed," Hunter agreed. *Everything* was different. They were finally happy. "Oh God." Hunter exclaimed as another, awful thought struck her. "*That's* why Tyr won't finish this war with the Orobus. Once he does, it means he'll have to..." She couldn't even bear to say it.

"Yes, he will." Ava nodded, an equally sober look pasted on her face. "And that will do things to him that would be worse than death. Think of it, Hunter. You may have orchestrated the perfect murder. Life, in its perfect, profane little circle. Him, sacrificing all to save the world for you. You, giving up that which has kept you alive to save a man you hated for centuries.

And so. Here you both are. Shoe's on the other foot, this time around. If the Fates get their way, he'll be alone for an eternity, knowing all the while you loved him and wanted to live."

Hunter only heard one, single word in that big, long, complicated diatribe. Because there was really only one word that mattered. "What do you mean...*if*?"

"Seriously. That's your take away from everything I just said?" Ava leaned back with a ghost of a smile playing across her face. "Well, let's just say that the Fates have always had a twisted sense of vengeance. Did you know they wanted something from Tyr, something he was unwilling to give them?"

"What would that have been?"

"Something you have been enjoying rather a lot of these days."

Hunter blushed, then felt the heat of something else blow through her as her hands curled into fists. Jealousy.

"Hold up there, girl. Not so fast. He turned them down flat. Loyal to a fault, that one is." Ava leaned back until her spine curved against the glass, cutting a dark profile against the sparkling brightness of the lake. "Since he refused them, this was their way of getting even."

"Who *are* you?" Hunter uncrossed her arms and widened her stance. Whatever this creature was, clothed in human flesh, she was certainly not human. Hunter had walked around like that herself for long enough to know.

"Oh, sorry. I'm Ava Burke, Morgane's sister, I don't believe we've been formally intro—"

Hunter's hand went to her knife, found the holster empty. *Damn it.* "Not what I'm asking and you know it. What are you? You are one of us?"

"If by one of you, you mean one of the unfortunates who the big, bad God of Chaos put his dirty little fingers on and marked for his own personal use, then yes, in that sense, I am one of you." Ava's eyes swirled to black for an instant before cooling down to their dark blue. "But for this conversation, the one you and I are having here, all alone?" Ava stilled for an instant and considered Hunter carefully, as if weighing a million possible choices. "Sure, why not? Between you and me? Let's try the truth, for a change.

"I'm unlike any creature you've ever come across, princess. Not even what was inside of you compares to what's in me, and I'm quite familiar with the measure of power you controlled. And the cost. But enough about me. This war is just beginning. And we'll lose without you on our side. Which means my goal is to keep you in play."

Now Hunter was all ears as excitement wound its wicked, wicked way up through her. She felt like finally, for the first time since she'd watched her city burn, she was being allowed into the inner circle. Someone was about to give her a chance. "I'm listening, Ava."

"You know I was in hell, right? For about two years, they tell me. It's weird, there are things I remember. From before. Family stuff, good memories. The kind of warm and fuzzies you want to hold on to, always remember kind of stuff."

Hunter nodded, encouraging Ave to continue. "But *that's* the shit that doesn't feel real. Those are the memories I have in my head that feel like a dream. Morgane tries to remind me sometimes, tells me stories about Mom and Dad, when we were little... But to me, that's all they are. Stories.

"What does seem real? The screaming, oily, black place I was stuck in for fucking ever. The place that robbed me of every good memory I had, every ray of sunshine. Every single piece of goodness was sucked out of me down there. And you don't even *want* to know what was left in its place."

Oh, Hunter could see it with her own eyes. In the way the woman stood, with a far-off gaze that bore through walls and people and everything in between. She'd already tasted death, and it didn't scare her one bit.

"I'll never be the same. I'll never be whole again. Not the way I was, anyway." A slightly bitter smile twisted her lips. "But you know what? That's okay. Because now I'm something *better*.

"Remember that, princess. Change is good. Embrace it. Fucking *savor* it. Because the ability to change will make you stronger."

Turning her gaze out the window, Hunter considered Ava's words. The world *was* different. Certainly this war had changed them all. Unfortunately, Hunter had just lost what made her special. In truth, she did feel...*human* these past few days. She hadn't thought of it as a necessarily *bad* thing.

But now that she was normal...*mortal*, she wouldn't be any help in the war to come.

Ava's low warning brought her back to reality. "There's a bigger game afoot, princess. Layers upon layers of scheming and betrayals, and like I said, you're an important piece. *If* we mean to win."

"How do you know any of this?"

Ava laughed, the sound lovely, and at the same time, terrifying. "Because of my time in the Underworld. Because of this darkness stuck inside of me. Because I listen and I learn and I keep my mouth shut. And I'm good at piecing things together."

"All right, then. What kind of games?"

"The kind of games that require us to work together as a team. *United,* despite everything that's happened and what *will* happen these next few months. And I'm talking about *you,* especially, princess. For all of us to survive, you'll have to be fucking unbreakable."

Hunter lowered herself onto the window seat across from Ava and met her eyes. "All right. That I can do."

Ava snorted. "The Fates. Those fucking bitches saved you, sure, but like everything they do, it comes at a cost. *Their cost.*" She shook her head. "Although I cannot believe you're the one who came up with such a boneheaded idea in the first place. But fear not, I'm going to help you out. My time in the Underworld taught me a few things."

Hunter's heart raced. "Like how to keep Tyr from fulfilling his promise?"

"Like that, yes. But more importantly, like how to actually win this war."

"But the Orobus..."

"There's a difference between defeating and stopping, between killing and controlling. And that difference means the line between life and death. For you, at least. For now, the monster is contained. The trick will be trapping him permanently."

Hunter considered it. Ava's reasoning was solid. "So you're thinking if we only contain the creature, the goddesses will spare Tyr from having to kill me. What makes you think the Fates will abide by a technicality?" A wave of futility hit Hunter as she settled herself against the window frame, staring at Ava. There was no way it could be this simple.

"The Fates are bound by the language of the agreement. Rules of magic and all that. Besides, there's the chance they're playing another game, entirely. Just ask Hel, that bitch could out-maneuver anyone alive. Just ask Odin." Ava's gaze narrowed as she looked over to Hunter. For a second, she paused, as if she was about to say one thing, before finally muttering, "She's an interesting woman, the Goddess of the Dead. You'd do well to study her tactics."

If Ava was looking at Hel as some kind of role model, Hunter had serious questions about the woman's mental health stability. "What do you *know*, Ava?"

"I might have heard something. When I was down below," Ava hedged.

Hunter rubbed her eyes. The room seemed to be dimming down. "Well spit it out. Syd has no idea how long her patch job on the dolmens will last, and once he opens those doors up, this city will be swamped with Dark Elves and Grim. And I'm not going to be a whole lot of help, being I'm now mortal," Hunter pointed out as the woman's face tightened.

Blue eyes flashing, Ava leaned in, "Don't undersell yourself, princess. We need stronger allies, and even a bit of divine intervention might help. And everyone has a weak spot. *Everyone.* The trick is, learning how to exploit it. But before I tell you any more, we need to have a little chat with a friend of mine." Hunter watched the light fade from Ava's face. "Well, *friend* is probably too strong a statement, but you'd better hear what he has to say."

Ava reached over and squeezed Hunter's hand.

"Remember when I said I've been waiting to talk to you? Well, so has someone else. There's something you have to know, before we go any further. He's the only other person who knows the truth, and after this little discussion, princess, you might find out how far you can bend before you break."

38

F or weeks now, she'd known exactly where he was.

And not just physically, although the old, walnut library on the second floor of the Tower did have a certain turn-of-the-century quaintness she certainly appreciated. No, Ava knew exactly where Odin was in his head.

He was blind, according to the rumors.

Thus, frustrated and feeling vulnerable, according to psychology 101 and Freud. Which meant wallowing in self-pity, keeping to himself, and pouring copious amounts of alcohol down his throat made perfect sense. Except, of course, it didn't.

"Why are we here again?" Hunter whispered in her ear, the narrow corridor swimming in dust and cobwebs. "Please tell me the magical solution to all of our problems is behind that door."

"It is," Ava murmured absently, her thoughts focused on the god who actually *was* behind the door. "*If* he's sober enough, and we can get him to cooperate, this might actually work out. And if this goes smoothly, then maybe..." Her words trailed off as a dull, heavy thud echoed through the oak door. "Goddamn it."

Hand on the knob, Ava pushed in, Hunter right on her heels, and stepped into a scene fresh out of a frat house post-keg Sunday morning. Odin was sprawled out over a dilapidated leather couch, naked to the waist, long, white hair tangled and matted, his eyes unfocused. Empty bottles spun across the room, kicked out of the way by Ava as she strode across the room and got right in his face.

"Damn it," she muttered. "I do not have time for your bullshit right now. You know why I've come, I know you've already *seen* this." She snatched the bottle out of Odin's hand, sloshing liquor all over both of them. "You do not have the luxury of wallowing in self-pity. We have real problems, and..."

A sloppy smile curved Odin's handsome mouth. "How's the view from that ivory tower of yours, Ava? Bet it's pretty nice...when you're sitting up there all alone." It was a miracle he managed to lean forward, without face-planting at her feet. "Lotta nerve you got... coming down here to lecture me... When all you've done is hide your head in the sand for *months*." Satisfied, he flopped backward as the sofa creaked beneath his weight, a shimmer of frosty magic coating everything in the room.

"...sides, what's it matter? While world's gonna be toast in no time." Odin's normally crystal-clear eyes were glassy. "Orob...buss... Orrrr...Orbuss's gonna open up *aaall* the doors, empty out his little realms of doom, and flood ours with his Frankenstein monsters. Not a lot we can do about it." The once-king snatched the bottle back from Ava and took a loud, noisy swallow. "So yeah, no hope there. We're aaaaall doomed, 'cluding you and me."

Ava felt Odin's magic lift her hair, send rivulets of electricity down the back of her neck as she stared down at him. Still impossibly handsome, still impossibly arrogant. Still *impossible*.

"This won't work. He's too wasted. I thought maybe..." Her voice trailed off. She'd hoped for his help, hoped he'd be able to make Hunter *understand*... But now, revealing the truth would have to be done some other way. In this state, Odin was, quite possibly, dangerous. "Come on Hunter, let's not waste any more time here."

"Hunter Wallace?" Odin's voice took on a hint of interest. "The one and only Scottish princess?"

'You're too drunk." Ava warned him, already halfway to the door.

"I thought you could give us answers, but we'll find them somewhere else. Wallow in your expensive liquor, you idiot."

"Still have a death sentence hanging over your head, woman."

"And, yeah, we're out of here," Ava said quickly, pushing Hunter toward the door. "He's too far gone and definitely too unpredictable. No telling what he'll say in this state." Her gaze lingered on him a moment longer than necessary, taking in his disheveled appearance. "*Or do.*"

Even now, his magic suffused the entire room, its terrible strength tugging at her, ice cold and virulent. He followed them out with his silver, baleful gaze, before his words lured them back.

"I showed Tyr the doorway to Asgard, myself. Showed him how to return. So he could talk to the Fates, you see," Odin explained, his tone even. "Knew he'd need to go back one day. To save *you.*" He tried pointing, but his hand flopped like a dead fish. "'Cause, you know, I could see the future. Once."

This time, when Ava tugged on Hunter's arm, the woman didn't budge an inch. "Tyr made a deal with *the Fates* to spare me?"

"Not 'zactly. Tyr *blackmailed* the Fates into saving you. Rather clever, even for him. They had no choice, not with the threats he made. But in the end, they turned the tables on him. In the end, I suppose, they won. Unless of course, you fail and the Orobus wins, in which case Tyr won't have to kill you at all." Odin scrunched his brow, as if re-evaluating his logic.

"Even if it's true," Hunter said, shaking her head, "you're not giving us anything new to defeat the Orobus. We should talk to Sydney or Mir. My guess is they'll know something new by now."

"*Right,*" Ava said, once again steering her toward the door. "Great idea. We explore other options." Even now the icy bite of Odin's magic was freezing her nose; each word came out in puffs of white breath.

"Not so fast," Odin said from behind them. "You and I aren't finished."

"You and I are *totally* finished." Ava's voice became cuttingly sharp. "Have been since the day we met, which, as you remember..."

"I'm not talking to *you*, Ava." All of a sudden, Odin's bleary eyes looked uncomfortably aware. "Although the two of *us* are far from done." Shakily, he stood, one hand still wrapped around the neck of the bottle, the other one pointing directly at Hunter. "You, on the other hand, you chose an interesting sanctuary by coming here. Why not head north with the rest of your New York team?

"You could have gone anywhere on earth, Hunter. What made you choose the Tower?"

That's when Ava knew this was a mistake. Because of how still Hunter went. And the small, almost unnoticeable smile curving the corners of Odin's mouth.

HIS MIND WAS A PLEASANT JUMBLE. Or had been, before Ava barged in here with the exotic stranger on her heels. Now memories were rising to the surface. Things he did not want to remember.

Things he'd been drinking hard to forget.

They'd left him alone for days now, even Balder having given up and abandoning him to his steadfast, endless drunkenness. And he was *almost* there. Oblivion beckoned from the bottom of just *one more* bottle. Another long swallow burned its way down to his stomach as he considered the two women before him.

Ava, the dark-haired beauty, so twisted up into his feelings that every one of his fantasies was filled with her. Except she'd rather gnaw her arm off than be in a room with him.

And Hunter Fucking Wallace.

The fact Hunter was in Chicago meant time was almost gone.

He managed to keep his gaze firmly on Hunter, instead of allowing it to drift over to Ava, where it wanted to be. Another swig burned through him before he remembered he should be speaking. "North would have been the logical choice. Regroup. Mount a counter offensive. Hit their forward flank, especially when it was weak. But you chose to come here. And seek out Tyr. Why?"

Damn, that sounded almost logical.

Maybe the alcohol wasn't working nearly as well as he'd thought.

"Because most of my team was dead, that's why. Which you'd know if you weren't hammered. The ones who survived were injured, barely able to care for the ones who made it through the attack. Our objective was to get them out alive. And for your information, I *did* cover their flank. Long enough for them to get across the river."

He swore she muttered *asshole* beneath her breath, but he couldn't be sure.

"You're right Ava, let's get out of here. This is a colossal waste of time."

For someone who was used to the entire universe falling to their knees before him, Odin wasn't entirely sure how to handle Hunter blowing him off. Especially as Ava turned away as well, without so much as a pithy parting shot.

"Ever wonder *why* the Orobus and Hel were hot on your tail while you hauled ass across the Midwest?" He met those stormy golden eyes with a grin. "Because *I* know." Taking another long, deliberate swig, he didn't miss the way Ava's mouth tightened in anger as he sent a faint caress of his magic over to her. Sure, he was drawing this out, but shit, he was bored and frustrated and more than a little pissed off at the way Ava was behaving.

Like she didn't even give *two shits*.

"Somewhat disturbing, isn't it, when a primordial entity takes a special interest in you? Even more disturbing is when you *don't know why*." Despite himself, the grin widened. He wasn't sure where this reckless, pernicious attitude was coming from, but he was damned if he could control it. The whiskey might have had something to do with it, though.

"I already know why, and the matter has been settled. Which you'd also know if you weren't drunk all the time," Hunter snapped, hands on her hips. "I'm in no mood to play games with you. Especially not right now."

"Odin…" Ava warned him, her angry, husky voice more of a turn on than it should have been, especially with the way darkness was beginning to leach from her eyes. "Not like this. Please."

"Of course, it might not have been him following your scent, at all."

"It could have been someone else entirely."

Ava had gone quiet, the pleading in her eyes only driving him to add, "It might be you don't know who you really are." Ava's hand lay loosely on Hunter's arm, tendrils of smoke and shadow practically enveloping the both of them.

"*Damn it*, Odin."

"Ever take a good, hard look in a mirror, Hunter? From what I understand, your father was nearly as blonde as I am. Ever wonder where you get those high cheekbones, that long, black hair? Those exotic, otherworldly features?" Odin despised the way his voice turned low, the way it hummed with glee. The way Ava's face paled, while Hunter's sharpened, the way the air in the room thrummed with malice.

Hated it. And was completely incapable of stopping himself.

"One would think, after all this time, you'd have figured out who you were, girl."

Please. Ava silently pleaded.

Now, Hunter's voice shook. "I don't understand. What's he talking about?"

Odin took a swig. He'd glimpsed this exact moment, so many times before. And never, in any of his many visions, had Ava been here with him. *He hated that she was.* He hated she saw him like this, weak and powerless and cowardly. And for a second, an apology hung on the end of his tongue.

But when her eyes, her beautiful dreamy eyes met his, and in them he found nothing but contempt and hatred, he ended up spitting out, "I don't think Ava wants you to know the truth, Hunter."

39

Tyr was about out of excuses.

He'd dodged and evaded and pussyfooted his way around the problem for hours now. Pretty difficult for an immortal who's usual *modis operondi* was to lower his head like a bull and charge.

But going to war meant possible victory.

And in this case, victory meant defeat.

Tyr was not about to fucking lose everything. That was not happening. Not to Hunter. Not to him. He'd been stuck in this room, arguing, all night. Watching the battle of wills playing out around the table. To attack or retreat. Use the explosives now or wait. While he hemmed and hawed over every recommendation, he wasn't blind. Tyr saw the suspicion in everyone's eyes, saw the knowing looks Freyr shot him every now and again. *He did not care.*

He'd searched for Hunter a couple times, not finding her in bed, or the kitchen, or the roof.

So here he was, stuck in yet another endless, futile meeting.

"We've been picking off the elves, one at a time. Grim too." Tyr finally cued into Freyr's latest report. "Gotta piss Hel off, all of her minions disappearing. The Orobus still appears intent on opening up the portals, but no luck so far."

"How can you be sure?" Thor actually sounded *bored*.

"Because the city's not flooded with his armies," Freyr replied drily. "So far, so good. Most recent numbers put the elves and Grim at less than a few hundred, each. By the end of the week, we'll only have Hel and the dark god to contend with. Manageable odds." Freyr paused. "*More manageable.*"

Tyr managed a responsive grunt. *Manageable odds.* All of these were merely stopgap actions. None of them, not *one single thing* they were talking about actually stopped the Orobus. Nor saved the planet, or the other realms, or halted the destruction. Which meant they were still miserably failing.

Which was good.

At least, he kept telling himself that.

"Once we've eradicated the last of the elves and Grim, Mir wants to take Sydney back down to the site. See if she can use her magic to create another cylinder."

"Because that went so well last time," Tyr grumbled before he could stop himself as Mir let out a warning growl from across the table, blue eyes flashing.

"At least she's trying to do *something*. We're all trying to do *something*. Unlike you, we're not sitting on our asses, making excuses, and what? Waiting this thing out? Because it's not clear to me, or anyone else, what your course of action is at this point." For the first time ever, Freyr actually sounded pissed off. "Unless your master plan includes piling up so many lame excuses, the Orobus can't climb over them all to kill us."

Freyr snorted in disgust. "So how about it? Explain to me why you're blocking every scenario I suggest. I suppose it's because none of them are fucking good enough for you."

"*Or* you're afraid to go after the bastard," Mir mused with a sideways look at Fenrir.

"I am." The second the words came out of Tyr's mouth, he felt a twinge of guilt. These were his brothers, and he owed them an explanation. They were right, his delaying tactics were going to get them all killed. "But it's not why you think," he added quickly. Opening this door and the layers of complications might only make matters worse, but he had to tell them the truth. "It's because of Hunter."

"I told you we shouldn't have trusted her. Nothing but a fucking walking disaster, just like Mir always said." Fen's lip rose in a toothy snarl.

The hairs on Tyr's nape rose, but he quickly tamped down the anger. Fen had once risked everything for Celine, while he'd been the one standing in their way. Now, he knew exactly how Fen had felt. "I bargained with the Fates to save Hunter's life. In exchange, once the God of Chaos is dead"—his gaze met Fen's steadily—"I have to kill her." Utter shock filled Fen's face.

"Those *bitches*." Fen bit out the words.

"Yeah," Tyr managed, frustration throbbing in his bones.

"I don't get it, why did you agree? There's a thousand other ways around..."

"It wasn't completely their doing, Freyr. It was partially mine, partly Hunter's." His voice was layered with sadness. "When Hunter first arrived, she forced me into an agreement. She'd help us defeat the God of Chaos, if I'd undo the spell from all those years ago." His smile turned bitter. "I didn't have much of a choice, and trust me, I never thought I'd keep my word. Now I'm trying to figure out a way around this."

"It's an impossible choice," Tyr pointed out, his dark gaze skimming across the faces at the table. "Either us or Hunter. Neither are a decision I'm ready to make."

"No shit." Mir's voice was hoarser than usual. "Why didn't you tell us?"

"Because it's too fucked up for explanations." If only Hunter could hear him now.

Now he sounded defeated.

40

While Odin was doubtlessly very, very drunk, he was telling the truth.

Hunter's finger drilled into Ava's chest. "He's right. Why don't you want me to hear this? What about *your* little speech about me being *strong*? Or was that just lies?"

Hunter whirled back to Odin. "So out with it. Tell me what you know. And tell me straight." For a second she didn't think he was going to reveal anything else.

He seemed as surprised as she when he blurted out, "What do you know about your mother?"

"Only what little I gleaned from my father's stories. He loved her very much. And it was hard for him, after she was gone." Hunter paused, remembering how her father's face used to light up at the very mention, the *thought* of his dead wife.

"Father used to make...claims about her, called her a siren, even a goddess. But the villagers had names for her as well. Sorceress. Demon. Witch. Those were the stories I spent most of my childhood hearing." Hunter shook her head. "But they were only stories. Stories told by superstitious, frightened, uneducated people."

"Did you ever wonder why they were scared?" Odin asked, his voice insinuating. "Or did you never bother to ask?"

"What are you trying to tell me? And why can't you just spit it out?"

"Because this is so much more fun," Odin said, taking another swig of whiskey before offering Hunter the bottle. "Have some, you're going to need it." When she refused, he winked. "Suit yourself, but you'll wish you'd taken me up on it, trust me." Ava wrapped her long, pale fingers around his arm, squeezing so tightly his skin turned white.

"Please," she pleaded softly. "Not like this."

"Oh Ava, don't you know?" Odin's smile turned gentle. "*None* of this matters anymore."

Hunter watched him skim a finger up Ava's face, tenderly, slowly, as if they were both lost in the moment, before Ava yanked away. The room was instantly plunged into freezing, bitter cold, Odin's icy magic sweeping in around them.

"Just so you know, your father's term for your mother was apropos. Goddess. However, the villagers, the whole, superstitious lot of them were also correct. Demon or sorceress also worked." He allowed himself an empty chuckle before offering her the bottle again. This time she took it from him with a shaking hand.

"Your mother was not born of this earth. Nor of any other realm. Well, none you'd want to inhabit. Not unless you were dead."

It took a minute for what Odin said to register. And as the ramifications began to sink in, her world turned upside down.

"That...you can't be right."

Hunter took a long draw of whiskey, barely noticing the searing heat as it went down. "No. That's not right at all." She had to be missing something, she had to be misunderstanding. Odin was too drunk to know what he was saying.

She looked to Ava, and the woman was white, the circles dark beneath her eyes. But when they landed on Hunter, when their gaze connected, all she saw in them was regret.

"Legend has it, Hel once had a daughter. With a Pictish chieftain, the only mortal she ever deigned worthy of her divine charms. But in the end, Hel left her child and returned to the Underworld. Someone had to rule, after all."

Hunter barely heard Odin as he went on, musing, "I sometimes wonder if she might have stayed, if she'd had a choice. For what it's worth, your father believed she was happy, for the short time they were together."

When Hunter looked at him, he was too slow to hide the flicker of sadness in his eyes.

"You are the only child of the Goddess of the Dead." He leaned in, smelling like a distillery. "Do you still think it's a coincidence the two of them, armies in tow, followed you all the way back to Chicago?"

"That is *enough*," Ava snapped, pulling Hunter back, away from Odin, away from this awful truth that couldn't possibly be real. "We are done here."

"Oh no, we are most certainly not done," Odin said, taking the bottle back from Hunter. "We are just getting started, and I, for one, am looking forward to putting this *bullshit* to rest, once and for all."

"I...I have to think. Nothing you said...*none* of it can be true. I'd know if that woman was my mother. I'd feel it...I'd feel..." God, Hunter couldn't even say it. *Evil*. That was the word she was searching for. She'd feel *evil* if Hel was her mother, and right now, she didn't feel anything at all except shock and disbelief.

"Did you get to the part where she can help us win?" Odin asked Ava, his tone perfectly, reasonably calm. "Please tell me you already covered that?"

"Fuck you," Ava spat at him.

Dimly, Hunter felt Ava's hands on her. "Come on, Hunter, let's get upstairs. You'll need time to sort this whole thing through. Let me take you back to your room, and I'll find Tyr, and then you two can talk." Ava gently tugged Hunter to her feet and led her to the door. They were almost through when Odin made his parting shot.

"Right. You can tell him his archenemy is about to become his mother-in-law. Not sure if that'll happen before or after she destroys the world, but hey, one big happy family, right?"

THE ARROGANCE TINGED with a hint of meanness was what did it.

Pushed her right over the edge.

Ava knew the truth about Hunter. Knew everything would all come out, sooner or later.

But there were ways of revealing the truth. Kinder ways. Gentler ways. Ava brought Hunter here, hoping Odin might help explain in a way Hunter would actually believe. After all, they were the only two people, *besides Hunter's actual mother*, who knew her true ancestry. But Odin, the cruel, son of a bitch, and the means by which he'd chosen to reveal her parentage, in a whiskey-fueled rampage, just pissed her off.

Letting go of Hunter's arm, Ava turned, with the simple intent of giving Odin a good, verbal slap down. When her whole world went dark. The Orobus's power was growing. And all of this arguing, all of this hostility was adding fuel to an already volatile fire. The simple fact was, she was a mess since the incident a week ago at the circle.

She was a mess because the creature had touched her. A tendril of his black, creeping power had coiled around hers for a mere second, before she'd been able to break free. But not before he'd stroked her, with all the tenderness of a lover's touch.

Nor before she'd shivered in utter delight.

That's when the screaming had started.

For a few minutes, she thought the sound was coming from someone else, before she'd realized it was her shrieking. But then she'd rubbed her numb, freezing arm and discovered the raised ridges on her flesh. As if he'd *marked* her.

As his.

Refocusing, Ava fumed, striding to Odin, hissing low enough so Hunter couldn't hear, "You bastard. How dare you spring every-thing on her like that? Bad enough you drop the nugget about Hel. You want her to fall apart? You want us to fail, is that it? Just because you're ready to curl up and die, doesn't mean the rest of us are."

His voice every bit as low, Odin leaned in until his words were hot against her face. "Aaaw Ava, and here I thought you cared."

"I fucking care as much as you do. Drink until your liver gives out. I do not. Give. A. Shit." It was difficult to breathe, hard to push air in and out. "But I swear to you, this is the only family I have left, and *I will save them*. So get out of my way, asshole."

Armed with that arrogant smirk, he leaned back, and she had to clench her hand to not reach out and slap it off his face.

"With pleasure. This was fun, we should do this more often. And Ava?"

"Hmmmm?" She could barely think through the blood pounding in her ears.

"You're leaking."

That's when everything went to shit. A pulse, a ripple of power went through her, and Hunter took a cautious step back through the doorway. Whatever strength held the power at bay was crumbling. She was nearing a meltdown, and here they were, the three of them locked in a tiny space.

Tossing the bottle, Odin cursed and took a shambling step toward her, reaching out as she fended him off. His magic tangled with hers for a second, the cold of it buffeting her before it faded away.

"Get out of here, both of you," she ordered, her hand already masked by shadow, the flesh turning smoky gray, her vision obscured by swirling darkness. "Get Hunter out of here, she's mortal now, damn it." If this power exploded from her, there might be nothing left of the Tower. Or any of them.

Feeling pressure on her arm, the bite of fingers forced her gaze upward. She met Hunter's steady, golden gaze. "Ava. You need to focus. Take deep, steady breaths."

It was all she could do to catch a single breath. "Listen princess, you don't understand. He touched me, at the circle. The Orobus marked me. And now I'm his. Get out of here...now..." A scream tore from her mouth, the sound tinged with madness, as a burst of power ripped up through her body like the forked spear of a lightning strike, the sensation unlike anything she'd ever experienced.

Ava had the vaguest sensation of Hunter wrapping herself around her, cocooning her with her body, while the whole world went black. Light disappeared as her bones went rigid, another scream ripping from her mouth as power—limitless, endless power—engulfed them both.

41

"What *was* that?" Thor swung his feet down off the table and moved to the door, throwing a hand out to catch the doorjamb while the building rocked. The rest of them pushed chairs out, rose, began checking weapons.

"Felt like the whole damned building moved. Explosion?"

Fenrir sniffed the air, shooting to his feet. "No trace of accelerant in the air. Could this be an earthquake?"

Now they were all on the move, making for the door as a group, even as the floor shifted wildly beneath their feet, throwing them to their knees.

"Fucking earthquake, I'm telling you." Fen growled. "I've got to get Celine out." In the hall, they split up, each heading for their own quarters, only to be met by Celine, Sydney, and Morgane, staggering toward them as debris fell from overhead.

"Where's Hunter?" Tyr yelled, as dust and fragments of plaster fell to the floor. "Has anyone fucking seen Hunter?" Mir, his hand wrapped around Sydney's wrist, shook his head as they barreled past, heading for Odin's Great Hall. Mir threw an arm across Fen's chest as he ran for the stairs, dragging Celine behind him. "No. Not the stairs, if the building goes, you don't want to be caught in the stairwell.

Follow us to the Great Hall, the ceiling and floor are reinforced, it's our best chance."

Fen quested the air, then pointed down the steps. "Well, Hunter went *that* way. Odin's down on the second floor, old library. Start there."

Cursing, Tyr hit the door to the stairwell and descended, yelling her name every ten steps. When he hit the bottom of the second-floor stairs, he swore he heard muted, faint shouting. "I cannot *believe* you came down here. *Stubborn, stubborn woman.*" Hitting the door like a battering ram, he stumbled into the lower corridor, the narrow space filled with plaster, beams, and swirling dust. He ricocheted off the walls, tossed like a ping-pong ball as the building swayed back and forth. Following the screaming, he finally burst through the door and froze, eyes bulging out of their sockets.

Ava, or what he assumed had once been Ava, was wrapped tightly in Hunter's arms, a writhing, monstrous thing, wrapped in shadows, with a dark, contorted face that was the personification of madness. Hunter held on, eyes squeezed firmly shut, as if blocking out everything except the effort it took her to hold on to the bucking woman. Ava's black eyes shifted back and forth through the room, searching for any and all escapes, her mouth gaped open, a cacophony of sound emanating from it. He'd never heard the like of it, not on any of the Nine Worlds.

Odin watched the entire thing, numb, shock written all over his face.

Shuddering, Tyr forced his feet to slide across the floor toward them. Whatever language was coming out of Ava's mouth, the mere sound of it was tearing him apart. And Hunter was right beside it. As if she heard his thoughts, Hunter's pinched, white face turned to him, and she managed a small shake of her head, warning him off.

Odin stumbled over, gripped Tyr's shoulder, hanging on for dear life. "I didn't... I didn't mean it," he said, his eyes wild, face pale as he watched Ava and Hunter writhe on the ground. He shook his head wildly from side to side. "I was... I never wanted this. Never."

"We have to get them apart. Ava will kill her if we don't separate them. And the building's about to come down," Tyr told the former king, scanning the rapidly disintegrating room.

Tearing himself away from Odin's grasp, Tyr stretched his fingers to grab Hunter, but they hit something. A field, a force, an invisible surface repelling him. He couldn't reach her. He bellowed for her to take his damn hand, but at the sound, the Ava-monster's head snapped around and a gaping, saw-toothed grin came over her face.

With a grunt, Hunter flipped Ava over and away from him, and that was when he finally noticed the light. A faint, white glow emanated from Hunter. It had a gentle, silvery tint, like the dawn. Amazed, he watched it intensify, long moments passing until the luminosity overtook them both, eating away at the black shadows, revealing nothing but a limp, still woman in Hunter's arms.

With one, last, final lurch, the building rocked back into place, Hunter rolled off Ava, who slumped onto her side, unconscious. In two strides, Tyr was on his knees beside Hunter, grasped her shoulder, finding her warm and breathing, before reaching over and rolling Ava onto her back. The gentle rise and fall of her chest was all he needed to see. At least she was still alive.

Odin stumbled his way over to the couch, fell back into it, dropping his head into his hands.

Tyr cradled Hunter's face in his hands. "C'mon, wake up, open your eyes." When her eyes fluttered open, Tyr could have praised the gods. "That's it, that's my angel. How do you feel, anything hurt?" He ran gentle, cautious hands over her, feeling for broken bones, anything out of place.

Hunter shook her head as if in a daze. "No. I don't think so. I just feel really, really...warm. Like I was on fire."

Pushing to her elbows, she stared around. "What happened? Where's Ava?" she mumbled, clumsy and dazed as she tried to sit. He put a firm hand against her shoulder and held her steady.

"Not so fast there, baby. Let me see your eyes first. Look at me. Hunter, right here." As her eyes shifted and met his, he let out a long breath he hadn't realized he'd been holding. They were Hunter's golden-amber eyes. Not black, no hint of whatever possessed Ava.

"There you are." He leaned in and kissed her, their chaste kiss turning into something else as he realized how close he'd been to losing her. Again.

The soft cough had them scrambling apart.

"Do you two need to get a room or something?" Ava's voice was rough, as if she'd been screaming for hours.

Tyr shuddered, remembering the sounds she'd uttered only moments ago.

"Shit." Ava brushed dust and debris off of herself. "Shit." Now her voice held a note of panic, and her eyes darted all over the place, taking in the scene, the wrecked room, the long cracks spanning the windows, and Hunter's disheveled appearance. "What the hell happened?"

Tyr opened his mouth to explain, but Odin beat him to it. "It was *me*, Ava. I pushed you too hard. My head's all messed up, and I was an asshole."

Her face paled, but she didn't add anything while Odin explained to Tyr, "They came to confirm the truth about Hunter. But I couldn't leave it at that. *I should have.* But I couldn't." He still hadn't budged from the couch, hair hanging in front of his face like a curtain.

"What do you mean...*the truth* about Hunter?"

But before he got an answer out of his king, Hunter's hand closed around his arm. "Suffice it to say, you and I will have a lot of ground to cover tonight, but for now, let's get Ava upstairs. That's the best solution. For now." Hunter shot a long, meaningful look at Odin.

Tyr nodded and watched Hunter's other hand close over Ava's as she explained in a calming voice, "You lost control. You tried to fight it, but it took you over. The power inside you was so strong, it took both of us to contain it. But we did."

Confusion knit Ava's brow. "What do you mean, *both of us*? How the hell can you help me with what's inside of me?"

Hunter glanced over to Tyr. "I'm not sure, but somehow I was helping hold all of that power inside of you. It wanted to escape, but couldn't get past me."

"You were glowing." Both pairs of eyes turned to him, and Tyr cleared his throat. "You were glowing all over, and then it was like the radiance of your light burned away all of the shadows encasing Ava." He shook his head vehemently. "Don't know any other way to describe it."

"That's what if felt like, even though I had my eyes closed most of the time." Hunter rolled her neck, then her shoulder. "God, I ache all over."

"Me too." Ava's voice seemed small, vulnerable.

Tyr's heart softened a little, just looking at her. Not seeing the monster she'd been moments ago, but the lost, vulnerable girl she was right now. Someone who was fighting every day to remain as human as she could, trying to keep what was left of her sanity while the world burned around her.

Surveying the scene, Odin, and his fucked-up appearance, Tyr made an executive decision.

"Enough of this brooding, martyr shit. Ava, you're coming to live on the community floor. We'll set you up in a room, a *proper* room, not the damned attic, and you're going to start eating with us." He decided to temper his edict down a bit, seeing the look of horror on her face.

"Not *every* meal," he amended, looking to Hunter for reinforcement. "But you have to start eating with us, working with us, socializing. You can't keep to yourself all the time, it's not healthy." He paused. "Fair enough?"

"I'll try," Ava said in a small voice.

"That's all I ask. We haven't been trying hard enough, none of us have. We can do better." Tyr offered a hand to Hunter, pulled her to her feet, and then his other hand to Ava, lifting her up as if she weighed nothing. "Let's get you out of here."

It turned out Ava's attic room was an even bigger disaster. As she folded up her few, meager belongings, the sound of breaking glass tinkled through the room followed by a blast of chill air. Tyr shook his head. "This floor isn't even habitable anymore. Don't worry, we'll find you something better. We've got to have some extra rooms in this place, right?"

"Take mine," Odin offered.

Tyr eyed Ava as she muttered, "Don't be ridiculous. I can't take your room. That would be..." Ava tapered off, unsure of what that would be, apparently. And the way she was kneading that arm of hers, Tyr thought she might rub right through the sweater.

"Why not? I've been crashing on the closest couch for months. Sometimes in the stairwell. And chances are, you'll appreciate the luxury more than me at this point." Odin shrugged. "Unless you come up with a compelling reason, then it's yours. No sense in a perfectly good room going to waste."

Tyr pushed, "He's actually right about this, Ava. At least until we figure something else out. Mir will have to give the building a once-over to determine structural integrity. In the meantime, take the damn room."

Hunter cut in. "Let's get your stuff downstairs. If you grab that pile, I'll get this one."

An hour later, Tyr and Hunter walked in on an argument. One would think facing the end of the world would leave the gods nothing to fight over, but apparently, who sat on Odin's golden throne was worth trading punches over. Thor skidded across the floor and hit a marble column with an echoing boom just as Tyr swung the tall doors open. The silence was deafening as they entered, and Tyr cleared his throat, feeling an announcement of sorts was in order.

"Ava's moving down to the main floor with the rest of us, and Hunter's moving in with me. Anyone's got any objections to either, I'll kick their fucking ass. Starting tomorrow, we go after the God of Chaos with everything we've got. Any questions?"

Freyr lifted his hands and his slow, rhythmic clapping echoed against the marble. "It's about fucking time."

"Yup. Now let's go assess the damage to the building, see what we can salvage, and get some fucking sleep. It's been a hell of a day."

42

"So yeah, that's pretty much all of it."

Hunter huddled into a ball, gazing out the cracked window, trying to ignore the steady breeze that blew through the openings. Clad only in Tyr's t-shirt, the wind chilled her to the bone. Somehow, they'd have to patch these up or they'd all freeze. And all of a sudden, this once-delightful view only served to remind her how tenuous their current situation was. Big hands slid over her shoulders, and she resisted the urge to relax into them.

"I can't believe I'm the child of a monster," she whispered.

She stiffened as Tyr chuckled. "*You*, my love, are the daughter of a Highland chieftain. A rather arrogant one, if I remember rightly." He stroked gentle fingers through her hair. "And that is the only thing that matters."

"You don't understand."

"Oh, I don't? After all this time, if there's anyone on earth who understands you, it's me, woman. So don't be telling me what I do and don't understand. Because *I* understand just fine." He tweaked her nose as he sat next to her. "I always knew there was something a bit devilish about you. Just wasn't sure until now what it was."

How could he possibly joke about such a thing? Words failed her as she stared helplessly over at him. She was different from who she thought she was. She was mortal, or near-mortal. Half death-goddess, or something like it. Chewing her lip, Hunter realized, in fact, she had no idea what she was anymore.

"And don't be sitting there looking at me like I've sprouted two heads. Sulking around, staring out windows, feeling sorry for your-self won't solve a thing. I've given you twelve hours to mope around, angel. Which is about ten more than I should have."

When he went to brush her hair back again, she snatched his hand in horror. "What happened to your arm? My god, Tyr, your skin, it's..." As realization hit, the words failed her.

Turning his hand over so his palm lay on her leg, she inspected his hand and forearm. Burns, red and raw, already healing, covered his skin and the back of his hand. Hunter grabbed his other hand, pushed back his sleeve, and found the same thing. "I burned you. *I did this*?"

Tyr merely shrugged. "When you saved Ava and the Tower and the rest of us. When I tried to grab you, your glow shielded the two of you. Not so bad, and I'm already healing up. See?" He rotated his wrist, showed her the new, pink skin near his elbow. "Besides," he added, tipping her face up so she looked him in the eyes, "there's not going to be any regretting any of this. I won't allow it. We move forward. Together. We promised, remember?"

When she didn't say a word, he gripped her chin firmly. "We will *not* waste time on regrets. We will not waste time, period. You and I have done enough of that. What do you say, angel?"

Hunter wanted to scream. She settled for, "You might have to find a better nickname for me, considering."

Tyr grinned. "Well, I think it's *perfect*." He nudged her. "Do you happen to remember the discussion we had the day you arrived? About whose blood is bluer?"

Hunter groaned. "Oh please, don't bring that up now. This is not the time, Tyr."

Leaning in, he tasted her lips, taking his damn time. "Oh, I think this is the perfect time. Half death goddess and half Scottish..." His eyes began to gleam. "By the gods, you really *are* a princess. All you need is a crown."

Hunter felt burning as her throat closed up. None of this, not *one bit of it* could be true.

"Don't... Aw, please don't... I was kidding, please don't cry, angel." Tyr cradled her head in his big hands and laid her back on the bed. "I'm sorry. I was only trying to make you feel better. Please angel..." He skimmed his lips along her jaw, resting on the place just below her ear.

"I love you. Exactly how you are. No matter where you came from, I've been consumed with you ever since the day I first set eyes on you. *Nothing* will ever change that." He nibbled his way up to her earlobe, trapped it between his teeth. "And now I'll just shut up before I screw things up even worse."

"Not possible," she muttered, even as she leaned farther into his touch. "I don't want anyone else to know, not until I'm ready to tell them myself. How am I supposed to just sit back and accept this, Tyr?"

"Shutting up, remember?" he murmured, his hands already lifting the shirt over her head, revealing her creamy flesh, goose pimpled in the cold room. Dipping his head, Hunter felt his warm lips skim over her breasts, her abdomen, lower.

"Yeah," she said, sensations already rocketing through her, "shutting up is good."

"Hmm." Was all she heard as Tyr hooked one of her knees behind his shoulder, then the other. A swipe of his tongue up through her center brought a moan to her lips, another had her arching back, and her hands tangled in the sheets. A flick, a twist of his tongue, and a ragged sigh escaped her while she pushed herself against his mouth, thoughts of parentage and bloodlines completely forgotten as Tyr teased her until she shuddered, the climax tearing through her like fire.

Tyr flipped her over, and she raised herself onto her elbows, Tyr positioning himself behind her, his teeth closing on the nape of her neck ever so slightly before tracing a path down her spine. Her head dropped down and Tyr pushed in, stretching her wide, the sensation of him sliding inside making her feel deliciously full. She drove her hips back, and he sank in even deeper, one hand closing around her hip, the other braced on the headboard.

"This all right?" Tyr asked, lowering his head until his lips pressed close, the words bursts of breath in her ear. "Tell me what you want, angel."

"Harder."

He thrust, found a fast, pounding rhythm, dropped his head until all she heard was his rough breath in her ear. With the glide of him inside her, the sureness of each stroke, she plummeted, further and further down, the tightening muscles bearing down on him until everything released, the cry echoing from her before she was even aware she made a sound.

Tyr pounded into her, stilled, and then shuddered, the tremors rocking through his body until he fell atop her, the haze of her orgasm a blissful stupor as he trailed his fingers down along her arm.

$\sim$

AVA STARED up at the cantilevered ceiling. "Why in the hell did I ever agree to this?" she huffed, beyond resentful for where she was right now.

She felt exposed. She felt vulnerable.

But damn it, she felt relieved.

The worst had happened, and she'd survived. They'd all survived. Mostly due to Hunter, but still, things *had* all worked out. The disaster she'd feared, from the moment she'd been rescued from that hellhole nine months ago, had come true. And yet here she was, in a cushy, comfortable Sun King bed, living to tell about it. And as an added bonus, it was *Odin's* bed. She snuggled deeper into the thousand count sheets under cashmere comforters and sighed.

The man sure knew how to live.

"So what am I doing *here*?"

Because it was confusing, how she'd gone from walking down a city street with her mother and sister, carefree under the city lights, to being cast into the Underworld condemned to unending misery, to being rescued by her sister, to sitting alone in solitude, endlessly rehashing said events until they played like a catch-twenty-two loop in her brain. Light. Dark. Light. Dark. Light.

The whiplash alone made her neck hurt.

Ava shifted her legs under the sheets until they were in a cool place. The bed still smelled like Odin. Not that she knew what he smelled like or anything. But the sheets, this entire room smelled of wintertime and frost. Idly, she surveyed the space, the way her little piles of clothing disappeared amongst the grandness of the tall, gilded mirrors, the elegance of the hand-carved furniture. And a flash of anger went through her. How dare he give up? How dare he walk away, when they needed him the most?

When *she* needed him.

He was an asshole, sure, but he was the asshole who held this place together.

She threw back the covers and walked to the windows, tracing her fingers across the duct tape holding together the spiderwebbed cracks that she'd caused earlier with her little...outburst.

"Jesus. Thank God, Hunter was there."

Because even though Odin took the blame, Ava knew she'd been on the verge of an explosion for a while. *Weeks*, since the Orobus touched her, she realized, rubbing her arm absently.

Odin *had* to stop drinking. She didn't care if he couldn't see the future. He was strong in other ways. She needed him around, head clear, like old times. In some weird way, he grounded her, and without him poking and needling at her all the time, she felt untethered.

And for her, untethered meant dangerous.

Because when the limitless energy first spiraled out of her, she'd welcomed it. For a second. Just for one, traitorous, weak blink, she'd caved, and that had been the opening the shadowy power had needed. But then?

Ava shuddered, staring out at the bleak city. The sheer force of that power had taken all of a second to consume her, and then she'd been helpless against its deadly might. Helpless against *him*. Rubbing her arm, she stared at the raised ridges there.

The marks the Orobus had left on her flesh.

The idea of these marks frightened her more than anything else. The knowledge he'd marked her. Perhaps even claimed her, somehow. And that his power and her power had, for a second, danced together. Still, she'd have to tell the others. They needed to know.

Because when he'd touched her, she'd seen things.

But there was something else, something she could not tell *anyone*. Something that filled her with such intense shame she could hardly bear to face it.

She had not fought him.

Not one bit.

She hadn't even tried.

43

Tyr liked things simple. And simple, for him, meant war.

"Listen up. It's time to get back to doing what we do best."

The band was all here. Everyone, the gods, the girls, everyone who had a stake in their survival. Everyone except Odin, who was still on his never-ending bender.

"Everyone's going to have a job, and everyone will do their job. Freyr—you, Mir, and me will work on strategy. Thor and Fen, you're defense. Loki, Balder, counter strategy, see what weaknesses the God of Chaos might find when he does come after us. Consider every single contingency, hear me? I want to be prepared when that bastard hits us.

Hunter, scout the streets, look for any sign Hel has slithered into the city. I suspect she'll be looking for opportunities, now that this fight has escalated."

They'd agreed on this strategy the night before. No one would know the truth about Hunter's parentage, not until Hunter tracked the goddess herself, or, gods forbid, saw Hel with her own eyes. Tyr hoped it never came to that.

"Morgane's going with you." Tyr's gaze met Loki's in perfect understanding while he gave his next order, praying it would be followed to the letter. "You two will stick together. Tight. Do not take *any* chances."

"Ava and Celine. I want you to figure out ways to leverage the Otherworld and the Dreaming to our advantage. The way I see it, they're just two more potential battlefields we've got to cover. So figure out how to best utilize them when the time comes."

"Syd, Mir. You two are on advance planning. I want an overall contingency plan. Any way to use magic against them, ways to amplify your power." He sucked in a breath. "And I want an escape plan. For all of us. Some place we can go if this world goes to shit." He raised a hand to stave off the rising dissent. "I have no intention of abandoning this world. I have no intention of losing this one, either. But shit happens. Better to retreat and fight another day, right?" He sent an especially pointed look at Fen. "Some of us have more at risk here than others. I'm doing whatever I can do to keep everyone safe. Let's get this done."

"I notice you gave me two jobs." Mir held out both hands to stop Tyr when he started to give an explanation. "No problem, it was just an observation. I've got it handled, no worries." Mir left, the other filing out behind him, their voices subdued.

"Hell of a halftime speech." Loki's voice was dripping with amusement. "And glad to see you back in the game. Not worried about what'll happen once we kill the bastard?"

Tyr lowered his voice to a whisper. "Of course I am. That's why I'm giving you another job too. Something I expect you'll fucking excel at. Spectacularly."

"Lay it on me."

"I want you to find a loophole. Any godsdamnned loophole to get me out of this bargain I made with the Fates."

Loki looked uncomfortable. "That's a hell of a big favor."

"Tell me how that's different from anything else you've ever done in your long and colorful history of manipulating everything and everyone to your own ends?"

"But we're talking about *the Fates*, my brother."

"Yes, it is the Fates," Tyr agreed. "And they used Hunter's words against her, boxed me into a corner and screwed us both over. So tell me again how this is unethical. I'm using their tactics against them. Love and war, man, love and war." Tyr knew he had a satisfied smile on his face when he'd finished. "I never fucking lose. And I won't this time, either."

"All right," Loki agreed. "I'll do it. But they're slippery fish, Tyr. Just remember that."

Tyr thought about Hunter and everything else that was on the line here. "I've met them, remember? Between you and me, I'm counting on finding a work around." His smile turned pure evil. "But if I fail, then I have you. You're my backup plan."

Ice glinted in Loki's blue eyes. "Thanks for picking me to do your dirty work."

"Yeah, well, I *do* have a tendency to play by the rules," Tyr admitted, once he was sure everyone else was out of earshot. "But right now, I don't much care about rules. If this is our final stand, I'm willing to do what it takes to keep everyone alive." He met Loki's gaze steadily. "*Whatever* it takes," he reiterated.

"That's an awfully big promise," Loki told him in return, his eyes burning. "This time... Things feel different to me, as well. As if we've run out of options, finally. We're certainly running out of soldiers," Loki warned.

"Tell me about it. If the Orobus destroys this world, even if we manage to escape another one, our chances of survival go down dramatically. You know it as well as I do. We make a stand here," Tyr told him. "Worst-case scenario, we get the women somewhere safe, then we come back and finish this."

Loki nodded. "Most likely scenario, I agree. So what's our timeline? I'm thinking weeks, but it might be less." Idly, Loki spun his knife on the table. "And what about Ava? The way I see it, she's the wild card in all of this."

Tyr had to agree. He didn't want to admit it, but something about the explosion, *something* didn't add up. There was more to her recent instability than Odin pissing her off. "Someone could talk to her. You saw her in the meeting..."

"At least she's *coming* to the meetings," Loki pointed out.

"True. But not one wisecrack. And I expected to see her hanging with her sister. But not so much as a word passed between them today, and I was watching. What's your take on the whole situation?"

Loki took a moment before he answered. "Morgane's worried about her. She's tried to get her to open up, but Ava's shut down tight. Keeps saying she needs more time, but if you ask me..." His voice trailed off, and he looked uncomfortable.

"Don't stop there. You might as well get it all out there."

"If you ask me, Ava's hiding something. If Ava lets her get too close, Morgane might figure it out. And Ava doesn't want anyone to know what's in her head right about now."

"You think it's more than Odin pissing her off."

Loki nodded.

"Good, we're agreed. We figure out what she's hiding, then. And where the fuck *is* Odin? I haven't seen him in days."

"Last I heard, he'd been drinking on the roof."

"You have got to be shitting me."

"Wish I was. Look, I don't know what's coming, but wasting time on Odin is just that, a waste. Forget him. He's completely checked out." Tyr wished it wasn't true. But after months of heavy drinking, it looked like the bastard wasn't coming up for air. And Tyr was tired of waiting.

"All right, enough with the personnel problems. On to the elephant in the room.

"Somehow, we've got to force the Orobus away from the site. What if we spread him out thinner, over a larger area?" Tyr met Loki's gaze. "Freyr got me thinking. Basic Art of War stuff. If we attacked on multiple fronts, he'd be forced to change shape," Tyr mused. "His Dark Elves are gone, almost all the Grim too. This is as good a time as any. He's practically defenseless at the moment."

"Until he brings his armies through. And you know that's only a matter of time."

"Yup, so we work fast while we have this narrow window of opportunity." Tyr ran a hand through his hair.

"And what about Hunter?"

Tyr hesitated. "She's not going anywhere near that thing. Almost lost her once already. Besides, he already took what he wanted from her. No other reason for him to be interested in her, at this point. She has other leads to pursue at the moment."

Loki's blue gaze narrowed. "So you have an ace up your sleeve, and you're not telling me what it is."

"I'm telling you what I can."

"Fine. But if you keep secrets, expect them to come back and bite you in the ass. Ask me how I know." Loki hesitated. "I'm trusting Ava less and less these days."

Tyr clapped a hand on Loki's shoulder. "We all deserve a second chance. We at least owe her that. She's holding something back, but she might have her reasons. And if she's part of this whole mess, then where does she fit?"

Loki's eyes blazed as he considered it. "Well *that's* something we've never asked ourselves before."

"Right. We need to lay *everything* out on the table, see where *everyone* fits. All this time, we've been busy putting out fires, focusing on pieces of the problem. When have we ever taken the time to see the big picture?"

"Maybe it's about time we did."

44

———

Hunter was trying to figure out why they were all packed into a bathroom.

It was a really nice bathroom, but a bathroom none-theless.

Ava was curled into a ball in a corner, Sydney and Morgane were together, whispering, and she was stuck over here by herself. Wondering what in the hell was going on.

"Sorry I'm late. I had to figure out how to slip away without Fen noticing," Celine said, closing the door behind her. Chewing her lip nervously, she looked to Ava. "All right, we're all here. Where do you want to start?"

Hunter's gaze swung to the brunette in the corner, who apparently was in charge of this little meeting.

"You know what I'm asking you to do, right?" Ava inquired in that sultry voice of hers, eyes so dark and deadly they looked black.

"Are you absolutely sure you're up for this, Celine?" Morgane sounded worried, pulling the same chewing-on-her-lip move and added the twirling-of-the-hair thing, besides.

"I'm sure."

But Hunter noted she was a wreck, even while Sydney settled in beside her, taking her hand. "Okay," Sydney coaxed, "the first thing Ava wants to know... Is there anything you've glimpsed in your dreams. Anything weird?" Trading glances, they all burst out in nervous laughter. "Okay, right. Anything *weirder* than what's already happening. Anything out of the ordinary."

Ava spoke softly from her corner perch. "It will be a vision that leaves you with a feeling of déjà vu, Celine." Her voice held a quiet certainty. "You'll get this terrible, awful feeling inside of you, and that's when you know you're close."

Celine's hand tightened until her knuckles turned white. "Yeah, I know what you're talking about." Her eyes seemed to grow larger in the dim light of the bathroom. "There's this...place that keeps coming to me in my dreams. Over and over again. I don't know where it is. But it's big and cavernous...and echoing, and we're all inside. I'm never sure *why* we're all there, if the God of Chaos brought us together or if we came to fight him..." She squeezed her eyes shut, while she added, "But we're all together."

"Keep going, Celine, you're doing great," Sydney urged her. "Did you see anything else?"

"Ask her about smells," Morgane added, circling the room, seemingly unable to land anywhere.

"It's cool, like a cave, or maybe it's winter. And yeah, the place smells. Kind of like dirt, earthy, you know and..." Celine thought for a moment, then tacked on, "There's the sound of water. Running or falling and the sound is loud, almost deafening."

Morgane stopped her there. "Take a break, Celine. Syd, give her a sip of that water. So it's a cave, or it's cold, but you're not in the city, you're pretty sure?"

Celine's voice was shaky. "Y-yeah." She firmed her mouth. "Yes. The place feels closed in, and I can smell woods, or leaves, definitely not city smells. And my feet are on rock. Rough rock, I think. And now that I'm remembering, yes, the sound of the water is constant, it's roaring, like a rhythm." These final sentences came out in bursts of breath, Celine struggling over each of them.

"So a cave?" Syd prompted. "And the roar of the water, would you say it sounded like waves?"

Celine nodded, as if she were past speech.

"Were the rocks a certain shape or color, or were any markings on them, Celine? Anything at all, something that might set them apart or distinguish them?"

"Not color... Only.... Oh, they looked like *my* rock."

As Hunter watched, Celine drew something out of her pocket. The object was palm-sized, dark, like a goose egg. Flipping it over, the surface caught the faint light, and Hunter saw it was covered in lines, markings of some sort. "The inside of the cave was covered with *these* marks, ceiling, walls, *everything*. Round and whirling, like fingerprints. Dug into the rock." Celine slipped the stone back inside her hoodie.

Over in the corner, Ava drew a harsh breath before folding herself into a ball.

"All right, that's enough." Sydney's voice grew shaky, too. "I think you've given me enough I can establish some possible locations. There are only a few underground dolmens near an ocean or sea. Here, take a sip of water, Celine."

Hunter's gaze, and everyone else's, turned to Ava, still balled up in the corner while Morgane paced closer, setting her hands on her hips, and facing her sister. "All right, Ava, spill. Celine's seen *something*. Now tell us, why did you ask us here, and what does all this mean?"

"I wanted to talk to you...because I know something no one else does." Ava's voice turned reedy. "When we were at the circle, the day everything went wrong, the Orobus touched me. A bit of his magic, it touched me."

"But he's touched me before, almost killed me and Mir, the day we fought..." With a wave of her hand, Ava cut Sydney off.

"Not like this," Ava insisted. "Not the way he did with me. Our magic intertwined. It danced, it sang, it... I don't fucking know... We *communicated*. And in that moment, he knew me."

Her eyes grew depthless. "And I *knew* him." Imperceptibly,

Hunter felt Ava's peculiar energy pulse through the air, the tingle as it passed over her, and she shifted until she stood beside Ava as her voice dropped lower. "This place Celine described, I've been there too, in *my* dreams. The stone circle may be the hub of his operation, his way of moving armies, multitudes of beings between realms.

"But that circle isn't the *heart* of his operation. Nor the true source of his power. *That's* coming from somewhere else."

Trembling, Ava raised her sleeve, revealing her arm, one inch at a time. Hunter froze as she glimpsed the markings, the narrow, white ridges shining in the light. Celine drew the stone from her pocket and held it out, its shiny black surface covered with the same markings.

Raised, circular ridges.

Like fingerprints, burned into the surface.

"Every one of us in this room has been touched by the Orobus. There's no doubt the circle should be destroyed. But this other place, if that's where his true power stems from, that should be our real target." Ava hesitated. "He was so *focused* on me when I glimpsed his thoughts, that he might not realize we're aware of this secondary site."

Sydney hopped off the bench. "There's only a handful of places matching that description. Let me see if I can narrow it down to one."

"I don't want anyone else to know," Ava said, her voice hushed, trailing her fingers over the ridges on her arm. "Not until I figure out what these marks signify. And until I'm convinced I'm not a threat, I'll be keeping my distance from the rest of you. No offense."

A low murmuring of assent passed between them all.

"All right, Ava, your secret is safe with us," Morgane pronounced, her gaze never leaving her sister. "Sydney's magical lockdown is keeping the Orobus busy. And you're right. We should capitalize on this information while he's focused on the stones."

"Except we have to do the jobs Tyr tasked us with," Hunter reminded them all, her gaze straying to the door. "And Morgane and I are already behind schedule."

"Right," Morgane agreed, "which means we'd better leave. Right now."

"And we're heading for the dolmen site?" Hunter responded, already pushing to her feet.

"Nope, the portals were a secondary site. Let's poke around Millennium Park. That's where the Orobus came through first. My gut tells me there's something there we missed. I want to take another look."

Hunter paused, weighing the ramifications of this new information. "All right. If I'd known the Dark God came through anywhere but the stone circle, I would have checked it out myself."

Sydney caught Celine's arm when she went to stand up. "I'm good," Celine said, even though her face was pale, and she was wobbling on her feet. "You know what? On second thought, I do think I'll take a nap," she told them, swaying as she held onto Sydney. "Just a short one."

"C'mon let's get you settled." Sydney threw them a worried look before helping Celine out into the bedroom. "To bed with you, missy, and then I'll cook you something really special." They watched Sydney help Celine into bed. "Get some sleep, and I'll check on you in an hour."

Filing out of Celine and Fen's room, it occurred to Hunter that they probably could have picked a better place for a clandestine meeting. Especially when Fen's giant body was blocking the hall they needed to get through.

"Going somewhere, ladies?" His greeting was velvety soft. "And please do not let me find out you were talking to Celine." Dangerous, like a predator's warning snarl.

"We're heading to the War Room." Hunter stepped in front of the others, blocking them, placing a casual hand on her knives. "And you're impeding progress." The wolf didn't budge. "Tyr's going to have a shit fit if we don't get busy. You want to be the one to tell him why?"

"Nice try, sweetheart. But just in case you were wondering, I wasn't born yesterday." His eyes drifted over them as if deciding to kill them or let them pass. "So I'll ask you again, what the hell were you doing in there with *my mate*?" This time, there was a hint of fang with the question.

When Hunter hesitated, Ava chimed in. "We had a girl's meeting. You know, *girl* stuff. Which is code for *none of your damn business.*"

Fenrir got right down in her face. "Everything about her business is my business. *Everything*, do you hear me? You weren't going behind my back, were you? Using her talents to find something out, the kind of information you couldn't get anywhere else, perchance?"

Ava's hands went to her hips, her stance straightened. Fenrir leaned forward until they were almost nose to nose. Morgane stepped up beside her, shoulder to shoulder, and pushed against his chest, with a low warning, "Fenrir..."

"You did, didn't you?" Nostrils flaring, the air in the hallway seemed to change, charged with his rage. "You went behind my back, and you..."

"Fen. Stop it." Celine's sharp order had the desired effect. He froze in his tracks and then backed off a few steps when she ordered, "Come here." Her tired voice was edged with resignation. "They didn't do anything. They needed answers to a question. So I told them about the dreams." Without a backward glance, Fenrir shouldered his way through and slammed the door in their faces.

"Should we go in there?" Hunter wondered out loud. "He's awfully big."

"Oh, don't worry, she can handle him," Morgane assured them. "She's got him wrapped around her little finger, and he *doesn't* bite, actually. She'll be fine. Now we've all got work to do, so let's get to it. Hunter and I will start at Millennium Park."

45

"How long ago did he arrive?"

Hunter could still smell him. The Orobus stank of sulphur with a touch of decay, a sickly sweet combination that curdled the stomach and tormented her nose.

Morgane straightened up, her body unfurling in one smooth movement. "Close to nine months ago. But the pieces were already in place. Syd was setting up the dolmen circle in the museum, Celine had written out most of the spell, my sister was in purgatory waiting to be freed. You were in New York, that last, little piece of himself ready to be called back home. Everyone just waiting to do their part." Her voice dripped with bitterness.

"But we're seeing the bigger picture," Hunter's observed, taking in their ruined surroundings. "After all these months, finally, the pieces are coming together."

And she was beginning to see what Ava and Odin already knew.

"You sister. What was Ava like, before?"

"Ava?" Morgane huffed out a laugh. "You know, it's funny, all these months and no one's ever really asked me. Probably because they're scared to death of her. Gram used to call her a princess." Hunter jolted a little at that, before Morgane went on, "But she never really lived up to that nickname. No, Ava's always been a bit sharper, a bit edgier than everyone else. My mother always said she was the beautiful one, and with those cheekbones and those eyes, you can see why."

Morgane paused, absently kicking a chunk of metal. "But Ava's always burned too bright. And now, with this power inside of her, there are times I'm afraid for her."

"Afraid of her?"

Morgane shook her head. "No, not *of* her. I love my sister, always have, always will. But she was born to be *more*. Now she has the power to do so." Her head whipped to Hunter. "These marks on her arms. If the Orobus *has* claimed her... Was she saying what I think she was?"

Hunter paused, thinking through her answer. "She's scared it's true. Perhaps you should talk to her, ask her what happened."

"Don't you think I've *tried*?" Morgane brushed back her hair, frustrated. "I *have*. Many times. She blows me off or shuts me down."

"And you don't want to push too hard?"

Morgane's eyes widened. *"Would you?"*

"No," Hunter admitted, remembering the writhing body she'd held so tight, the madness, the sense the woman would not come back from what was happening to her and might not have wanted to. "If your sister is correct, then he's marked her for a purpose. And she has every reason to be frightened. But we won't allow her to become another of his pawns."

"Agreed."

"Tyr gave us a target." Hunter tested the air, the wrongness of this place, before looking to the west. "We have a few hours left, what do you say we pursue leads?"

Morgane warned, "Hel isn't your normal predator. All Tyr wants is her location, which means we gather leads and that's it." Morgane stared off into the wreckage. "Which also means we don't confront or get close."

"Ah. So that's why he sent you along?"

"To be the voice of reason, such that I am."

"I may have been *born* human, but Tyr made me into something else." Hunter traced the markings on the shiny stainless steel. The ragged edges caught against her fingers. "I've hunted on this world for a thousand years. But you are correct. I promise to exercise caution."

She purposely kept her eyes averted from Morgane's as she added, "We should head in the direction of the river, I caught the scent of Grim, a lot of them."

"Loki said the Grim are gone."

"Are they?" Hunter asked, tucking her knife back into her belt. "I suppose we'll find out. If there are Grim in the city, then Hel may be close by." Hunter rounded the jagged section of debris, marking the way the light seemed to bend in around the entire area. As if time itself had been warped.

"You know," she continued, "your sister and I are very much alike. Closer, perhaps than I care to admit."

Morgane scoffed as Hunter added, "I'm serious. When the God of Chaos shoved a piece of himself into me that day, it was like containing a thousand entities. For a time, *too long* a time, mind you, they ruled me. I did..." Ducking her head, Hunter pretended to examine one of the long claw marks. "Terrible things. To my family, to anyone I came across. I killed hundreds, perhaps thousands. I don't know."

"How can you not know?" Now there was a trace of horror in Morgane's voice, as perhaps there should be, Hunter thought, wryly.

"Because Tyr never told me how many. Because he felt responsible and he shielded me from the truth as best he could." Hunter told herself the tears were from the wind. That she was absolutely not crying. "But with his help, I wrestled control from the darkness. It took years of work to gain the upper hand, a hundred before I slept at night."

"And a thousand years before I knew the truth."

"What truth?" Morgane asked, her face rapt.

"That whatever birthed that dark power, however that darkness began, after all those years, it was a part of me, it *belonged* to me. And when the God of Chaos stole it away?" A cold, cunning smile curved

Hunter's lips as blood pounded in her ears. "He took what was *mine*. I bent that power to my will, and once I call it back? It will come."

"What about my sister?"

Hunter met Morgane's eyes, even though she knew Morgane wasn't ready to hear this. "Whatever your sister has inside her is ten times as powerful. You felt a touch of that power yesterday when she rocked the building. I tasted it. It surpassed *anything* that I've ever felt before." Hunter paused, unsure how much more to reveal. "Including what was in me."

"Hers is more powerful?"

"It was more...*everything*."

"And now you command this power. Surely Ava could do the same?"

"It took me many lifetimes to accomplish this." Hunter shook her head. "A single mortal life might be too short. What I do know is, your sister—in truth, Ave is *not* your sister anymore. She is something else." As Morgane tried to deny it, Hunter grasped her arm. "I'm only saying she is different. The point is, it doesn't *matter* what she is now. But she has to stay strong. Strong enough to control the power, if not master it. She must, if she wants to survive."

Hunter released Morgane, but she didn't move. "We're all different now, Morgane. Me, you, Celine. Sydney. All of us. Adapt or die. Your sister's adapting, learning to live with this strange power trapped inside of her. And when we face off with the Orobus, I have a suspicion Ava will play a huge part." Though Hunter wondered if any of them would survive it.

"To stand a chance in this war, we need allies. *Strong* allies," Hunter said, repeating Ava's earlier words. She looked out, following the faint, sweet scent that trailed off into the city. "I know what I have to do."

The smell led them past the burned-out hulks of cars and the picked over corpses of the forgotten and unlucky. Winding further west, Hunter and Morgane headed for the river, climbing over the pile of cars at the Orleans Bridge across from the Merchandise Mart. Hunter held out a hand to stop Morgane. Something seemed...*off* about this place. As every instinct lit up, the hollow cawing of crows echoed down the waterway from the east. Crouching down, she pulled Morgan down alongside.

"This is where the scent turns fouler, and it's coming from over there, between the Mart and the construction zone." Hunter didn't like it. Not the way her instincts prickled, nor the way the approach would expose them. Glancing to her right, there were a thousand windows overlooking their position. "You could head back. Report to Tyr, tell him we found something."

Morgane shook her head, whispering back, "I don't think so. I'm sticking with you, if you don't mind. Which means either we both go home or we both go on."

Hunter deliberated, then checked her weapons while Morgane did the same. "If we keep going, we'll need an exit strategy. How well do you know this area?"

"Pretty well. I hunted here every seven months or so. This was quadrant fifteen."

"Best way back to the Tower?"

Morgane calculated. "East on Wacker, south on LaSalle, then straight down Washington to home. Might still know a shortcut or two, depending on the terrain." She shrugged with a grin. "But you know how that goes."

Hunter grinned back. She was really starting to like this one. "We're being watched. Multiple enemies, multiple vantage points, there." Hunter pointed up at the Merchandise Mart. "Up on those floors, and over there as well." Hunter indicated the building to the left. "More than the two of us can handle, and that's why I hesitate to cross."

Morgane motioned downriver. "A half mile east of here, North Wells Bridge is a double-decker, the steel and asphalt would offer some cover."

"Lead the way."

"My pleasure." Morgane moved with efficiency and calm, Hunter thought, a capable machine, trained for this kind of thing. The bridge offered enough cover that they arrived intact and climbed the stairs to the corner entrance of what had once been the largest building in the world. It certainly felt like this place held all the evil in the world, Hunter thought, reaching for the handle.

"Wait a second," Morgane whispered. "I feel—something—this is bad."

"Yes, I'm aware. But we're here. You don't have to go in, but I do. You can scout the exterior thoroughly and report back. Decide how to proceed." For a second, her eyes flickered. "You know, just in case."

Morgane put a staying arm across Hunter's chest. "No freaking way. You are *not* leaving me out here. I'm *not* explaining to Tyr how I let you go inside alone. Lead the way."

"Morgane..." Hunter waffled. Now would be the opportune time to lay everything out. But now was too late as Morgane pulled the door open and the full force of the stench hit them.

Somewhere between toxic waste and rancid, rotting flesh, the smell ate through her senses until tears flowed from her eyes. "Holy shit," Morgane muttered, gagging softly.

The low, skittering of claws echoed along the hall, becoming a kind of continuous white noise that masked their footsteps. This cavernous warehouse of Marshall Fields, built to hold all the whole-sale goods of an entire country, held something else these days. Hunter put her back to the wall and crept silently onward, heading for what looked like a brightly lit opening ahead. The place had been compartmentalized over the years, but there was still one mind boggling, meant-to-impress foyer. Impress it did, as Hunter and Morgane stepped into it, dripping with the bodies of Grim hanging from every surface like flies.

"Holy shit," Morgane said again.

"So *this* is where she's been keeping all of you." Hunter did a quick sweep, calculating numbers, before backing Morgane into the relative safety of darkness. "If only one of us gets out, make sure you make it back to the Tower, do you hear me? No playing hero. They've got to know about this."

"Know about what? Exactly?"

The click clicking of heels, *expensive heels*, on the marble floor drew closer, and Hunter slid a knife out of her belt before Morgane put a hand out and stopped her. "That won't do you any good, I'm afraid," she whispered, fear written all over her face. "We're pretty much screwed."

"She's right, you know. You are. Screwed." Hel's voice was lilting. The low, husky tone echoed from the marble all around, off the glossy floor beneath their feet.

Hunter didn't want to look, not really, but she had to. This was a train wreck of epic proportions, yet she couldn't help herself. *Hel was beautiful.* In a slippery-fish sort of way, with her iridescent, porcelain skin, and her too-black eyes, and a mouth that was juicy-supermodel-plump perfection. The Goddess of Death was pure evil, poured into the ideal, fleshy vessel which had been tailored for it. Hunter stared, mouth agape, utterly fascinated.

"I know, I know, not quite what you expected, am I?"

Hunter just shook her head, stunned beyond words.

The heels clicked and clicked in an obscene rhythm as Hel circled, each sound a bite out of the time they had left. "I've been dying to meet you, you know. Forever. Actually, I've put it off for far too long." Her voice grew deceptively softer. "And yet you waltzed right in, like you didn't have a care in the world." Hel stopped until they were face to face.

Hunter didn't have words. She couldn't actually think. She just stood there and took her in. The woman's cool demeanor, the shape of her face, the curve of her jaw, the mass of black, glossy hair. Except for the color of her eyes, the visage was all too familiar. "You are a brave girl. But you never should have come."

Hunter agreed. They never should have come here. She should have stayed in the Tower. Hell, she should have stayed in New York and let the city burn down around her. A little hysterical laugh burst out of her. She should have left the dark inside of her and never met Tyr and never let him save her. She should have died that day she broke her neck.

That's how things should have gone.

That's what was supposed to happen.

Hunter saw her life pass by in the blink of an eye, with crystal clarity now, how things were supposed to have gone, and yet, she had to ask. She had to know. "All this time, you knew? You knew right where I was. Who I was?" Hunter whispered, her throat raw and aching.

"Yes. All this time," Hel agreed with a wry smile. "But you can't blame me for all of it, child, since everyone seems to have had a hand in where you ended up. Which, I'd like to point out, is right here. *With your mother.*" And as Hel wrapped her arms around her, Hunter heard Morgane's stunned voice behind her.

"Hol-y shit," Morgane said.

For the third, and final time.

46

T he wind tearing at his hair, Odin stared out over the city.
To his right, the Orobus covered the old museum campus like a plague, the reach of his shadows encompassing even the old football stadium, stretching out across the water. To his left, a sudden disturbance pulled his attention north. Events were shifting in the world, but with this infernal blindness, he couldn't tell what it might be.

Atop a broken wall, his ravens awaited orders, the wind picking up their feathers, their eyes bright as they tilted their heads one way and then the other, while Odin...stalled.

He'd been sober for a few days now.

Not that it made a bit of difference. He was still blind, damn it. Part of him hoped the good drunk might shake things loose, but all he'd been left with was a crippling hangover and some memories he wished he could erase.

Primarily Ava's disgust with him.

So he'd decided to see the monster for himself. View firsthand the destruction he'd allowed to happen on his watch. And even seeing it, he still had no idea of what to do next.

Zipping up his coat, he was about to ghost back to the Tower when he heard light footsteps and the scent of her hit him. Months ago, if someone would have told him the smell of a mortal would make his knees weak, he'd have sent them to the darklands to die. Now, he only steadied himself against a girder and prayed he didn't make a complete fool out of himself.

"Odin. They said you were here."

The way Ava's hair was whipping around made him want to tangle his hands in it, pull that silken mass away from her lovely face, but he stayed exactly where he was. No sense in turning this into more of a debacle than it already was.

"I wanted a chance to talk to you, away from the others...to...to..." Those unusual eyes caught the light and his breath caught, noting how incredibly expressive they were. "Thank you for the room. And apologize for what happened the other day. I lost control. It won't happen again."

"What happened was hardly your fault."

"What happened was completely my fault."

He opened his mouth, but when she pressed her hand against his chest, the breath went out of him. "It was me. I've been losing control for weeks, now. And besides, when *haven't* you pissed me off? It wasn't you, trust me." She lowered her hand, rubbed at her arm before turning away and looking at the roiling shadow below them.

Reaching out, he caught her wrist, rolled her sleeve back, even as she fought him. Both of them stared wordlessly at the pattern covering her flesh. "So it's already happened," he murmured, a sick feeling churning in his stomach.

"You... How could you know? I told them not to say a word." Ava angrily yanked out of Odin's grasp. Shoved the sleeve down, her hand shaking as she covered the hideous marks. "They *promised*."

"No one said a word to me, Ava. They kept their promise to you," he said, reaching out for her again, if only to quell her trembling. "I saw this, the marks on your arm, a long time ago. I saw what would happen."

Misery coursed through him at the expression on her face. Betrayal, dread, it was all written there so clearly, and he'd do anything to wipe them away. Hopelessness at their situation kept him drinking. Futility brought him here tonight. If only for this one, brief moment they'd share. "I *saw* what happens, Ava. I know how everything ends. And I can't do anything to stop it."

He couldn't tell Ava he'd seen her future. That it was those visions, *those terrible memories* burned into his brain, he'd tried to wash away with bottle after bottle. He hadn't succeeded. Not even once.

"Why didn't you tell me?"

It was the note of desperation in her voice that had him crossing to her, settling an arm around her, pulling her in. Surprisingly, she came.

"Because it would only have made things worse for you. And I hoped... My visions are sometimes wrong. I prayed this was one of those times."

"So all this drinking, this crazy behavior?"

"Because I can't do a fucking thing about any of this. Because I'm helpless against this dark god, who decided to wage war against us. Because I'm not going to be able to...." He stopped himself, hating he'd revealed as much as he did.

Against him, she cried softly.

"Oh, Ava..." But he didn't know what else to say. Nor how to say it. Alive for millennia, and he couldn't come up with a single word to ease a frightened woman's fears. Off to his left, he felt the slight, unsettling disturbance again.

"Did you feel that?" Ava asked, shifting out from his embrace. "I thought I sensed something before, but I wasn't sure." She peered through the haze of smoke toward the river. "Probably nothing. I'm jumpy these days."

Odin joined her at the edge of the burned-out floor. "It's *never* nothing," he muttered, sending the ravens off in flight with a flick of his wrist. "I sensed it too. *Damn it.*" Scanning the streets, he quickly set her behind him.

Beneath them, the Orobus had vanished.

"Oh God, where did he go?" Ava was scrubbing her arm furiously, as if she might erase him, while searching the emptiness below. "I don't understand it. *He was just there.*"

"Get further inside and find some cover. I'll go and check it out."

What was he saying? He never checked *anything* out. He sent the others to check things out. And yet here he was, going to get himself killed just to make himself look good.

"I'm going with you."

"Nope. Not happening."

"Let me come with you. I don't *want* to be up here by myself. What if something happens to you?"

"Then you'll be up here and alive. That's kind of the point of us not going down there together. If anything happens to me, the others will come for you. Besides, I can ghost myself down there and back up in a heartbeat. You can't."

"*Such* an asshole," she said, but the insult lacked conviction.

It was the way her eyes went dark. The way the blue leached out of them which clued him into the fact the Orobus was up here with them. As Ava's mouth formed a perfect 'O' and shadows snaked around her body, lifting it from the ground, Odin lunged forward, arms sweeping through air where she'd once stood.

Rushing to the edge of the building, he watched as the creature reformed below, Ava's small form stumbling away from him.

Without another thought, Odin pushed himself through the air toward them and reformed, his feet hitting the gravel floor of the basin right in front of Ava, intercepting her as she ran, gathering her up, pulling her behind one of the dolmens as her heart thundered wildly against his.

47

Tyr stalked around what was left of the Cloud Gate, Loki right on his heels, and glared at Sydney. "You're sure they started out here?" She nodded, looking a little guilty.

"And how long ago was that?" Loki bellowed, worry thrumming beneath every word.

"Hours, now. Hunter wanted to check it out. Start at the beginning. You know, maybe find something new?"

"Fat fucking chance of that. We've been over this area with a fine-tooth comb." Loki raked his hands through his hair, surveying the city skyline before turning to Tyr. "Which way? I'm thinking down toward the river."

"Shit. Seems likely. When Hunter didn't report in, I thought maybe her com wasn't working."

"Morgane checks in every half an hour. Like clockwork, I can set my watch by her. Plus, there's no way both coms went down at the same time." Loki stalked away, cursing.

Tyr ground his teeth and followed. He never should have agreed to this. Never. "There's something you should know. When I sent them after Hel, it was only to look for signs of her in the city. But there's a chance, a *slim* chance, they might have actually found her."

The way the muscle in Loki's jaw was working, Tyr knew he'd better fess up. Anything less would make him an asshole. "Hunter is Hel's daughter."

Loki's eyes almost bulged out of his head, so Tyr hurried up and tacked on the rest, "She just found out and sorta has a habit of rushing into things. So yeah, there's a good chance Hunter might have gone after her mother."

48

Odin crushed Ava's struggling body against his. In any other circumstance, he'd have looked at this as a win-win, but since the black shadowy tendrils of the Orobus were already creeping across their feet, he kept his eyes on the prize.

Focusing, he tried to ghost them out.

Nothing happened.

Tried again. Nothing.

Ava shoved her palms against his chest. "You have to leave, by yourself. Your magic won't work with me this close. I have a little of him stuck inside me, remember, so you can't break free of his hold. So for once, just listen, damn it, and get out."

Only part of her order penetrated his thick skull. "No, not leaving you." As things began to go dark, he lowered his head and whispered into Ava's ear, "Not much time. You need to fight him, Ava. You don't belong to him, and you never will. So fight him with everything you have. Never give up. Never. *Promise me.*"

By now the inky cloud was cloaking his face, and Ava's was completely obscured. "*Promise me.*" But she couldn't answer, and when he tried to move, he was rooted to the ground. Ava made a strangled sound, and then he lost sight of her completely, only the feel of her in his arms made him sure he still held onto her.

"You came a long way to kill me." His voice was muffled by the creature's murky presence, but he knew the dark god heard him just fine. "And you've waited a long time. It's funny. I thought you'd make revenge more of a production. Savor it a bit. It's what I would have done, after all." The shadows sucked away, leaving Ava gasping for breath. He gently set her down, balancing her shoulders on the stone behind them. Cradling her head, he pressed his mouth to her ear.

"As soon as you are able, climb to the top of the basin, then run for the Tower. Tell them what happened. *And remember what I said.*" Understanding sparked in her eyes the second he turned away, faced the dark, cresting form poised to crush him.

"Now. Let's see what you've got." Odin invited him, arms spread wide, and when the Orobus sent a wave of black hurtling toward him, Odin stopped it with a white, icy one of his own.

The crash as their magic collided rang across the lake, echoed against the dead city. And masked the sound of Ava as she began climbing.

49

Tyr looked down river, to the looming, massive complex. The place looked empty. But his gut was telling him otherwise.

There's something wrong.

Hunter's in danger, not mortally, but something far, far worse.

"Morgane's in *there*," Loki muttered. "Whatever's going on, they're inside *that building*." Which was all the confirmation Tyr needed.

Ten minutes later, they were hoofing it across the lower level of the Wells Street Bridge, unknowingly taking the exact same route the women had taken. Guns in hand, Loki led the way, going high while Tyr went low, the stench assailing them with the same mouth-gagging intensity, and they paused, then followed the voices.

Of all the things Tyr expected to find when he entered the demons' den, it was not his woman and the deity of evil sharing a bonding experience. But there they were. *Hugging.*

"Get the *fuck* away from her."

"Ah, the God of War." Hel's taunting voice echoed across the cavernous space as she released Hunter from her embrace. "Here she is, love, why don't you come and get her?"

Tyr took a cautious step into the light as Loki stepped back and vanished into darkness. "Hunter, get away from her."

Hunter blinked, shock written all over her face. "Tyr? What are you *doing* here?"

Reaching out, he beckoned, "Come here, Hunter, take my hand." But she shook her head, as if warning him off. Hel crossed her arms over her chest and smiled.

"That's right," she mocked, "go ahead, Tyr. Just try to tell my *daughter* what to do."

Hel continued in a high, mocking tone. "*Surprise.* She is mine. Not yours, *mine.*" Gloating, she continued, "My blooded daughter. Don't look so shocked, Tyr, darling. Who do you think started this whole process? You think the Orobus did this alone? No, he needed *my* help. And like any good game, he has his pieces, and I have mine." Her spiteful gaze drifted over to Hunter. "And then there are the ones we share. Like my daughter. No mere mortal could ever hold all that power inside her. She needed to be immortal." Hel shrugged. "So I created the perfect vessel for our final showdown."

Tyr kept his eyes pegged on Hunter, watching her grow paler with every word. Watching, too, as Loki snatched Morgane out of thin air and disappeared her somewhere safe. One down, one to go.

"The rest of it, as you know, has *always* been up to the Fates. Those meddlesome bitches insist on having their sticky little fingers in everything. Well, so be it. I bent the rules a little."

Games within games, pawns of pawns, winners, and losers. Well, he could play too. And he was about to show his fucking hand for all to see.

"So you're saying I never saved Hunter's life that day? It wasn't me who imprisoned the Orobus's power within her? So what happened, exactly?" Tyr drawled, drawing out every bit of vanity he knew strutted around inside of Hel. "Oh wait, let me guess. You're taking credit for that too?"

"You bet your fucking ass I'm going to. *I made her.* She's my progeny. She's every bit as immortal as you or me. I just left a back door open for the God of Chaos to sneak a bit of himself inside, for safekeeping. For that one moment, she was technically dead, before you decided to swoop in and play white knight to her fairy princess. And the rest, as we say, was history.

"Sure, she burned a bit of the world down with her, but who doesn't in the beginning? True power is hard to get used to. So the village was pretty much toast. But you saved the rest of the Highlands, didn't you Tyr? Always trying to be the good guy. I would have sat back on my heels and watched the world turn to dust, but no, you had to save it."

"You are one crazy bitch," Tyr told her, his voice thrumming with anger.

"Perhaps. But know this. Hunter belongs to me. Not you, not even the Orobus.

"She. Is. Mine. *And I will do as I please with her.*"

THE MOMENT HEL'S arms encircled her, Hunter perceived the change. The firestorm of power which suffused her, the tide of immortality flowing back in. But this time, she didn't fear it, she welcomed it. And now, as Hel and Tyr fought, Hunter looked between the two.

Her beginning. And her end.

She'd come here for only one reason. To beg her mother to join them.

To ask her to unite with them, to become their strongest ally in this bid to save the world. Believing, mistakenly, a death goddess offered their best chance at survival.

But watching Hel, listening to the vile, awful things coming out of her mouth, Hunter knew in her heart that would never happen. Hel was truly the most corrupt, vicious creature she'd ever come across. Perhaps she and the Orobus deserved each other. But still, something in Hunter had to try.

"Hel."

Hunter stepped forward, hands spread, beseeching the woman. "*Mother.* Please. I came here to talk to *you.* I never knew you, never had the chance. But I'd like to, once this is over. I want to know what it's like to have a mother." She measured the shifting emotions in the goddess's eyes before continuing, "But first, we have to survive this war. And for that, we need your help.

"Please. Join us. Help us defeat the Orobus, send him back to where he belongs. After that, we could be a...family, if that would suit. Or you can go on being...you. It doesn't matter, but stop this madness. Please."

"You seriously expect me to join the losing side?" Hel's voice was dripping with mockery. "He's promised me *everything*. I'll be his queen, rule over all worlds. All creatures. I will have no boundaries, *no rules*. What can you offer me?" She scoffed.

"Please." Hunter tried again. "What he's doing... There won't be anything left. He's lying to you, he has no intention of making you a queen."

"Little girl, don't you think I know the difference between a lie and a promise by now? My offer *is this*. You join me. Come over to our side and fight with us and win. Or die with them. But choose."

Feeling the steady weight of Tyr's gaze, Hunter measured her mother up. Beautiful, no doubt about it. Vain, as well. And blind to a fault. For all of her strengths, there were just as many weaknesses. Meeting Tyr's eyes, Hunter saw what was shining in them. The look was pride, pure and simple. Of everything she had ever been.

But I am not what I thought I was.

But what shone from his eyes...only blazed brighter.

I'm more than what I thought I was.

How could she have been so blind for so long? Why had she been content to simply listen to her father's stories all those years? Why had she never dug deeper, never asked more about her mother? *Wait,* she thought, *where she came from was not the most important thing.*

I am the same as I always was.

Which meant nothing had been taken from her, after all. Not even the limitless power, which had been hers all along. Which *belonged* to her. And perhaps the strong allies they needed were not enemies to be cultivated.

Maybe she'd been looking in the wrong place this whole time.

Tilting her head, she contemplated her mother, and for the first time, not as a god. But as an equal.

"*Hunter*," Tyr rumbled, "why don't you show your mother who you *really* are? She seems to be operating under the mistaken assumption you *belong* to her."

Awareness crackled in the air between them, a living, palpable thing as Hunter spun slowly on her heels and faced her mother. Too late, Hel became aware of the things she'd said, how she'd said them, and the ramifications of her hubris-laden tirade. "Hunter, darling, I was just trying to get a rise out of Tyr. It's so easy, really, it is..."

But it was already too late. Hunter drank greedily from the fountain of immortality. Giving herself over to the sensation, Hunter glowed, then exploded in a flash of light, radiance spreading out from her in clear, white rays, cutting like blades through everything in its path. She vaguely heard her mother's screams ring through the cavernous lobby.

When Tyr's hands caught around her middle, they hit the floor, the impact sending them both skidding across the marble. All of a sudden, the stench was ten times worse, a sweet cooked- protein smell that fouled the smoke-filled air.

"Hunter, by the gods, that was sensational."

With a bit of dazed amazement, Hunter saw she was still brilliantly lit, her clothes hanging from her in scraps, all around them the glopping sounds of dead Grim hitting the floor as the monsters fell from their perches.

"We'd better get out of here. Your light killed them. They're dying off, and we'll be buried in dead and dying demons if we don't get a move on."

She agreed, though silently, as he pulled her to her feet amid the growing demon piles and ghosted her straight outside.

The stench still clogging her nostrils, she gagged, then found herself on all fours, hair hanging down, puking her guts up beside the river. Tyr gathered her hair back out of her face, his other hand resting on the small of her back for a moment before rubbing circles against the base of her spine. "Get it out of your system. We've got a minute before we have to move." From somewhere far off, an echoing boom rang through the city.

Tyr's head shot up. "What in the fuck was that?"

"We don't know," Loki said, running up, Morgane right behind him. "Third time we heard it. If I didn't know any better, I'd say it's coming from the circle."

"I'm good," Hunter told Tyr, climbing to her feet and wiping her mouth on the back of her sleeve. "Sorry. God, I'm sorry." Scanning the outside of the building, her gaze was on the demons skittering down along the chamfered corners, almost reaching the ground. As the impact of another deep boom hit them, the creatures skittered back up.

"If that's coming from the circle, we have to head there. In case this is like before. In case the others are in trouble. What if..." Hunter didn't get to finish that thought as the sound crashed against them one more time. "At least Hel and most of her demons are out of commission for the time being," Hunter muttered, her eyes turned south, a feeling of dread growing in her stomach.

His eyes glued in the same direction, Tyr pulled her against him, and then everything went dark. Wind howled around them, and she thought she might be sick again before her feet hit the ground, hard.

50

Tyr couldn't believe they were back here *again*.

One of these days, this gods-forsaken place would be wiped from the face of the earth and good riddance. But when Loki and Morgane materialized directly behind them, he hung tightly onto Hunter and sprinted for cover as another impact passed right over their heads, the ground heaving up beneath their feet.

Inside the circle, a crest of black power rose, then fell, a white spear of magic lancing through it. Tyr was tugging Hunter behind a pile of rubble when the small form burst toward them, feet churning up dust. *Ava.* Somehow, Ava was running full tilt away from the circle, her face tearstained and ghostly white. Morgane dashed out, tackled her sister, and dragged her to shelter.

In a matter of seconds, she'd spit out a somewhat garbled story, backed up by the roar of Odin's magic clashing with the black magic of the dark god's. A hurried order into the com had Mir and Sydney materializing a moment later. Tyr motioned them over to the bank of rubble, and the duo ducked behind bits of carved marble, Doric columns, cornices, and statuary. Safely protected by what remained of the museum, Tyr nodded for Ava to continue her story.

"Odin's picked today to be a hero," Ava said, her gaze fixed on the circle. "Pretty sure it has something to do with me, and I already told him he was an asshole."

Tyr pretended he didn't see the shimmer of tears in her eyes. "That won't stop him, trust me. Even though he's holding his own, he's about to get his ass kicked. The issue is getting him out of there alive. And frankly, I'm not sure how to do that without getting the rest of us killed."

"Except he won't allow himself to be rescued. He's willing to give himself over to that thing. To stop this war." The wave of smothering gloom was growing taller by the second, a behemoth overflowing the stones.

"Ava... I don't think I heard you right." Tyr took a good, hard look at Ava, thinking she might be falling apart. But she seemed solid, given the circumstances.

"Odin doesn't have any intention of surviving this. He's already seen what happens. To us, to the world. *This* is his end game." The way Ava spoke, so calmly, Tyr knew it was true. Aside from her tear-streaked face, she wasn't hysterical at all. Just...resigned.

"It may be his end game, but it could also be ours." Hunter spoke slowly, as the rest of them turned to listen. "So...some interesting developments. Hel is my mother, which means I'm immortal. Or, at least, partly immortal. If that's even a thing. And the darkness I gave back to the Orobus? Well, there were some strings attached."

"Like what?"

"That power *belongs* to me. And now that I know I'm immortal, and can handle it, I'm willing to reclaim it."

Tyr considered her. Then turned to Ava. "You're *sure* about Odin and this mission of his?"

"As sure as I've ever been about anything," she said, gazing at the stones where the booming sounds came less frequently. The black, cresting wave loomed higher, and the whips of white seemed to have disappeared.

Tyr counted heads. "There's only five of us. But it will take too long to get the others down here, pull anything together." He looked to the circle. "Too long to save Odin."

"What if Sydney opened one of the doors? We could possibly push him through, like we talked about at first. Get him off the planet?" Hunter asked, peering over the barrier they hid behind while she surveyed the scene.

Mir nodded in agreement, adding, "Let's choose Niflheim. It's cold and empty, and the lack of life force in that realm might weaken him."

"This is crazy," Loki mumbled. "What makes you think this will work? It's just us, and we have no plan, we're just winging it."

"Because this time, I'm going in there after him. And this time, the Orobus *will* heel," Ava muttered doggedly, her eyes still fixed on the stones. Without another word, she stalked toward the circle, dodging the gauntlet of debris and chunks of marble.

"I'm going, too," Hunter told Tyr, offering him a hand. "And taking back what he stole from me." She grinned. "You always promised to save the world for me. Care to watch me burn it down?"

In answer, Tyr kissed her, fast and hard, then together they jogged after Ava, with Mir and the rest right behind. "If Ava can distract him long enough, will you be able to..." Hunter turned to Sydney, right on her heels.

"I'll open the right door. If there's the slightest opportunity, I'll use my magic to shove him through." Sydney's hair lifted, as a faint shimmer of her power thrummed through the air around them.

They'd almost reached the edge of the basin, tendrils of the Orobus's dark, creeping power slithering toward them, as Ava disappeared down over the edge.

HUNTER FOLLOWED HER DOWN, Tyr right behind her, his hand over her shoulder, a steadying presence. Hitting the bottom, they ran for cover, already feeling the pull of the Orobus's energy. His presence fouled the air, but the shadows also hid her, while Hunter began to draw from his power, recalling the tiny kernel of herself back.

And devouring darkness came.

Nestled inside of her, she savored the raw energy of it, the million horsepower surge she got as the dark magic roared its way through her. From behind her, Tyr yelled, "Ava. What are you doing?"

For Ava was walking straight into the storm. As if two immortal beings were not waging a holy war, right overhead. One hand outstretched, hair blown back, she leaned into the wind, eyes squeezed shut, and disappeared.

"Damn it." Clasping Tyr's hand, Hunter went in after her. The mixture of energy tore at her face, the small pebbles cut her cheeks, dust got in her eyes, and soon she couldn't see a thing, only movement, while her hand reached out and found nothing at all. But finally, they reached the center. Ava and Odin stood together, bloodied and dirty, arms wrapped around each other, Ava sobbing as she struggled to support the pale, silver god. As Odin went to his knees, Tyr lunged forward and caught him around the waist.

Above them, the peak of the Orobus's magic loomed. An apex of power, shimmering with dark rippling energy, poised to crush them all. Then Ava stepped forward and raised a pale hand.

Unbelievably, the thing *obeyed*.

Like some sort of otherworldly, mystical cobra, the creature swayed back and forth in front of Ava's thin form, transfixed. And in that moment, Hunter saw it. The absolute recognition, the connection. The bond.

While Hunter reclaimed a piece of his power...

The creature had chosen Ava for himself.

Beside them, Odin moaned, "No, no, get her away from him. Don't let him have her." With a grunt, Odin slid out of Tyr's grasp and crawled toward Ava, hands and knees scuttling in the dirt.

Threatened, the Orobus struck, a dark lash of power that cut straight across Odin. Deep stripes formed across his back, crimson blood welled before spilling down. At Tyr's angered curse, the thing turned to Hunter and Tyr, and when the creature struck for them, his dark whip snapping down, she instinctively threw up a hand in defense. Brilliance bloomed before them, while the creature's strike rebounded harmlessly off the barrier she erected.

On the other side of the shimmering wall of magic, Hunter and Tyr watched Odin collapse as Ava ran to him, her thin, white arms encircling him.

"We have to get in there, pull Odin out. Get Ava away." Tyr growled.

"I agree, but how?" Hunter gasped, the task of keeping the internal power controlled, and the protective barrier intact, was stretching her to the limit.

"Lower it and I'll go in. It'll only take me a few seconds." Hunter hesitated. She'd already lost him once, and she was loath to give the creature another shot. Behind them gravel crunched, and Mir and Sydney appeared. "Hunter, lower the shield, *do it now*," Tyr ordered.

This time, when the force of the Orobus's power struck her shield, it trembled. As the ripple of power went through her, she gritted her teeth. "If I lower this, he'll kill us all. Sydney, any chance your magic works through mine?"

"Is that a theory you seriously want to test right now?"

Hunter shook her head, the next strike of the creature's power sending her to her knees.

"We either figure something out quick, or ghost out." Tyr snarled. "No way can she withstand another hit like that."

He looked to Mir. "Hunter, give me your hand, right now. We take them both out of here and then you and me return. I'll draw the Orobus's attention, while you rescue Odin and Ava. It's our only chance." Tyr's face held that rigid, tenacious look Hunter knew so well. He'd save them both. Or die trying. "*Everybody's* going home today."

Hunter couldn't breathe. There was no way she'd allow it. No way she'd let Tyr do this; it was suicide. She was ready to argue, ready to fight him over this when everything happened so quickly.

Another sweep of power from overhead crushed the breath out of her, sent Mir and Sydney scattering. Tyr threw himself on top of her, and momentarily she couldn't see a thing.

And then she could.

As the last of her magic faded away, Mir and Sydney rolled from beneath the next crushing wave of power, and she heard Tyr's grunt of pain. Vaguely, she heard Mir's shouting, telling Sydney to open a door. *Any door, to anywhere.* Pushing to her knees, Hunter watched helplessly as Odin lurched up from the ground, crossed the space, hitting the Orobus full force, sending them both away from Ava, through the newly expanding doorway, the light-filled portal swirling like a mirage after their passage, swallowing them up.

With a shout, Mir screamed for Sydney to *seal it, seal it up.*

Her face bloody, with a wave of her hand, she did.

And then the lot of them stood silent, listening to Ava sob.

51

Hunter wasn't sure what to feel.

She wasn't sure she *could* feel, she was so numb.

Dimly, she heard Ava crying. Dimly, she felt Tyr checking her over, his hands tracing her body, her arms, before cradling her face. Inside her, the darkness crawled, eel-like and oily, a foreign feeling after being absent for days. Forcing it down, she made the power heel, made it submit, *forced* it to obey.

Much like Ava had done to the Orobus.

Ava, who was half-hysterical in Morgane's arms.

She felt herself grow curiously light, as if her bones were made of air and her skin transparent. If the wind were to whip through the stones, Hunter thought, it would take her and carry her far, far away. And then, her feet felt the earth underneath, her face the sun, and the wind blew against her cheeks while reality slammed into her.

"Oh Tyr," Hunter said softly, gazing into Tyr's face. "I'm so sorry about Odin."

From the way he dipped his face into her neck, she knew he was emotional and pulled him into the embrace, feeling him shudder against her. Only for a moment though. One quick squeeze and he ordered harshly, "Everyone back. *Now.*"

And then they were inside the Tower, dirty, bloody, pale, and definitely having seen better days. For some reason, she couldn't let go of Tyr, keeping his hand clasped tightly in hers, until everyone else had peeled off and it was only the two of them alone in their room.

"I'm sorry," Hunter told him again. "I couldn't lower the barrier. I just *couldn't*. I didn't want to lose you," she explained, sinking to the bed, her legs feeling rubbery and weak.

"None of it's your fault, Hunter." Tyr stared down at her, still bloody from where he'd held onto Odin. *It could so easily have been any of them.* Only the barest shimmer of magic, standing between them and that...monster. Between them and death. Tyr slipped his hand beneath her chin, tilted up her face so she met his steady, sober gaze. "You can't blame yourself over this. Odin made his choice. From the very beginning, that was on him."

"I can't," she whispered, trembling. "I could have done things differently, I might have..." *What?* Saved Odin and doomed the rest of them? Lowered the shield and allowed the Orobus to swoop in and wipe them all away? Scrubbing her face, her hands came away wet while Tyr knelt at her feet.

"Ah love, it's not like you've never lost people before."

"But not like this. This was different. Today, all I thought about was losing *you*. You, who've always been there for me. I thought you always would be." The shaking grew stronger. "And today, I realized that I've never been alone." Now she *was* sobbing. "For the first time, I was afraid. And I froze."

For once, even Tyr didn't argue. "I know, angel." He leaned into her, his breath a weighty sigh. "And I wanted to bring everyone home today. But I didn't. Trust me, we'll be living with these regrets for a long time. But while neither of us are perfect..." He slipped his arms around her, tucked her into his chest "We *are* alive. So after a shitty day, let's take that as a win, shall we?"

They barely managed to slip out of the bloody clothes and beneath the sheets before Hunter passed out.

52

A week later, and life still seemed surreal.

Yet here Hunter was, curled in bed with the man...*god* of her dreams, and the world was still spinning. The Orobus hadn't made an appearance. The city was clear of Grim and Dark Elves. Made one almost believe in luck.

Tyr's gentle snoring caused Hunter to smile. All those nights in the mountain cave and he'd never snored, not once. But get him into a nice, comfy bed, and it was like sleeping with a chainsaw.

Which was fine.

Except her mind was going a hundred miles a minute. Elbowing him, she whispered, "Roll over on your side." A grunt and he complied, leaving her to ponder the dark city waiting outside the enormous, cracked windows.

Her mother was somewhere out there, gathering forces, demons, and God knows what else, while mentally, Hunter kicked her own ass for believing she could ever convince the Goddess of Death to switch sides. *Still, it had been worth a try.* At least, that's what Tyr told her, time and time again.

He was probably just being nice.

But it did chafe her that Hel turned out to be such a shallow, conniving monster. For Hunter's entire existence, the concept of her mother had been a hallowed ideal. Maybe because she'd put her on a pedestal and there'd been nothing to knock her off. Except, of course, reality.

Now Odin was probably dead, the Orobus was momentarily out of play, Hel was injured but most likely regrouping. Readying for her next strike, which would be brutal. Fast and decisive and big and flashy.

Reaching over, she stroked Tyr's ropy arm, savoring the fact they'd had five days, *five whole days* of relative quiet. When she glanced over, he was watching her with guarded eyes.

"What's the matter?" he murmured. "You're supposed to be sleeping."

"I want to. But there's just too much rattling around in my brain."

He rolled over so they faced each other. "I know what you mean. I keep replaying everything that happened, thinking I could change the outcome, somehow."

"And?"

"Odin... I can't get the sight of him going through that doorway out of my head. Nor him crawling after Ava like he did. But in the end..." Tyr blew out a tired breath. "In the end, what happened with Odin was predetermined. In truth, he'd already glimpsed his death, and his actions were only his way of making that come about."

"Even so, this hurts, him being gone."

"Yeah," Tyr said, pain evident in every word. "It does. And I never expected it to."

His eyes grew shadowed and not just because of the darkness in the room. Reaching out, Hunter stroked his face, her thumb tracing over the faint scar. "I expect you'll feel like this for some time. And I can't tell you how to process what's happened, but I can promise you this. I'll be here, whenever, for whatever you need."

Hunter pulled him to her, his huge body almost more than she could wrap her arms around. And for a few long moments, she just held onto him. Feeling some semblance of peace flow between them as he settled, his racing heart slowing, his body relaxing into hers.

"Oh, Tyr. I waited my entire life for you," she breathed. "And now that I actually have you, I'm never letting you go."

"Thank the gods," he whispered, and she felt that fragile, unfurling of hope again. "Don't know how long this peace and quiet's going to last, but welcome to my life."

"Glad to be here."

For a second his eyes crinkled, just before he began to laugh. Grabbing her, he rolled them both over, nipping her chin. "I'm glad you're here, too, angel. Glad for all of it. And while I'm not anxious to repeat some of it, if everything we've gone through allowed us to end up here, then I'd do it all over again."

Leaning down, his lips closed over hers, running his tongue along the seam until she opened with a sigh. His lips were velvet, the tangling contact of his tongue causing a spiraling ache to burn deep inside of her. She could kiss him for hours. Seriously, the man had a magic tongue.

"Sorry it took me forever to get here, Tyr." Hunter kissed him again, a long, deep kiss they both savored.

"But now that I've found you? I'm here to stay."

EPILOGUE

Contrary to popular belief, it takes a while for rotting demon carcasses to cease stinking.

Hel was currently ensconced in a swanky mahogany and crystal meeting room on the thirteenth floor of the Merchandise Mart, and she could still smell them. Most of her hair had grown back, and her skin glowed with the pink blush of fresh growth, and she was wearing kick-ass Prada with some new Tom Ford heels, and yet... She just couldn't escape the stench.

Plus, she was lonely.

And a little bored.

Her main man was gone, sucked into another dimension by that asshole Odin, and now she was stuck in a holding pattern, hoping he'd find his way back. Soon. They had a war to get on with, revenge to be had, and time was a'wasting.

A glint of light caught her eye, and turning her attention out the window, she watched as a long line of Tahoes slid past, black paint brilliant in the noonday sun. Interesting. Among the ruthless human scavengers and burned-out buildings, she'd missed the part where shiny SUV's were *de rigueur*. Striding along the line of glass, she watched them round the corner, then disappear down Orleans, never breaking formation.

Ten perfectly waxed, detailed, brand-spanking new SUV's.

In a city ravaged by war and chaos.

Hel smiled.

Anyone who profited in times like these was someone she was dying to know.

Another day of healing, perhaps, and she'd be ready to find out who they were.

And what uses she'd have for them.